The Case of the Sun Bather's Diary

Also by Erle Stanley Gardner in Large Print:

The Adventures of Paul Pry
The Case of the Beautiful Beggar
The Case of the Caretaker's Cat
The Case of the Counterfeit Eye
The Case of the Howling Dog
The Case of the Lazy Lover
The Case of the Lucky Legs
The D.A. Takes a Chance
The Case of the Calendar Girl
The Case of the Deadly Toy
The Case of the Hesitant Hostess
The Case of the Sleepwalking Niece
The Case of the Sulky Girl

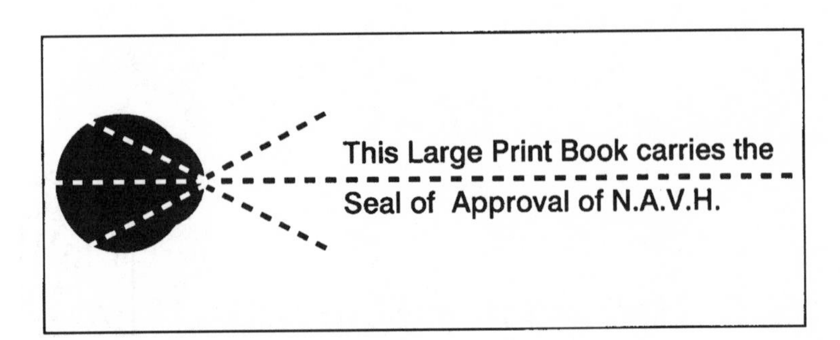

The Case of the Sun Bather's Diary

Erle Stanley
Gardner

G.K. Hall & Co. • Thorndike, Maine

Published in 2001 by arrangement with Thayer Hobson & Company

G.K. Hall Large Print Paperback Series.

The text of this Large Print edition is unabridged.
Other aspects of the book may vary from the original edition.

Set in 16 pt. Plantin by Minnie B. Raven.

Printed in the United States on permanent paper.

Library of Congress Cataloging-in-Publication Data

Gardner, Erle Stanley, 1889–1970.
The case of the sun bather's diary / Erle Stanley Gardner.
p. cm.
ISBN 0-7838-9338-8 (lg. print : sc : alk. paper)
1. Mason, Perry (Fictitious character) — Fiction. 2. Large type books. I. Title.
PS3513.A6322 S85 2001
813′.52—dc21 00-053838

The Case of the Sun Bather's Diary

FOREWORD

Quite frequently I am asked whether there is any such thing as "the perfect crime."

The answer, of course, is that there have been literally hundreds of so-called "perfect crimes." Every veteran medical examiner can tell about cases in which only the painstaking competence of a skilled autopsy surgeon disclosed the fact that a seemingly natural death was actually a murder.

And there are cases which baffle even the most competent medical examiners. In such cases no one can determine with certainty whether the man died a "natural" death or whether he was murdered by means which left no trace.

Is there such a thing as a murder by witchcraft?

I have talked with voodoo priests in Haiti and with *kahunas* in Hawaii. I have investigated some cases of "black magic" and I have been told many strange stories of people who have been "kahunaed" to death in the South Sea Islands. I have seen some things I can't explain; and from people in whose integrity I have absolute confidence, I have learned of many other things. I have spent many hours with Dr. Alvin V. Majoska in Honolulu, discussing the strange "Nightmare Deaths" of Honolulu.

I first heard of these deaths when I was attending one of Captain Frances G. Lee's seminars on homicide investigation at the Harvard Medical School in Boston. Dr. Milton Helpern, the famous forensic pathologist of New York, was lecturing there and remarked that it was not always possible to determine the cause of death. He cited as an example that he had recently been called upon to examine vital organs from bodies sent him from the Hawaiian Islands, and that in each case it had been impossible to discover a cause of death. There was no sign of poison; the heart, lungs, brain, kidneys, and all of the vital organs were in perfect working order.

These men simply had ceased to live, and medical science was powerless to find out why they had ceased to live.

After the seminar, Dr. Alan R. Moritz, then the head of the Department of Legal Medicine at Harvard and now at Western Reserve in Cleveland, a brilliant investigator and pathologist, said to Dr. Helpern, "I didn't know *you* were getting those bodies. They've been sending them to us, and *we* can't find any cause of death."

Driven by intense interest, I finally went to Honolulu and tried to find out about these strange deaths. What I found amazed me. The deaths occurred only in young Filipino men who were in the prime of life and the best of health. These men invariably died at night, under circumstances indicating a nightmare. They would go to bed apparently in the best of spirits. During the night they might be heard to moan. Before help could reach them, they would be dead.

Dr. Alvin V. Majoska is a remarkably competent man. He is on the young side of middle age, an alert, intelligent, observing, highly trained physician and pathologist. He lives in Honolulu because he loves the tropical sea, the warm surf swimming. He loves sailing his boat over the sparkling waters. He is a skin-diving enthusiast. Physically, he is an athlete. Mentally, he has all of the shrewdness and caution of a well-trained medical man.

He devoted months of his time to studying these "Nightmare Deaths," and he has written an article which was published in the *Hawaii Medical Journal*, reprints of which are available. That article was entitled, "Sudden Death in Filipino Men: An Unexplained Syndrome."

Stripped of its technical nomenclature, this article admits, in effect, that medical science is completely baffled, or, as Dr. Majoska expresses it, we are dealing with a "brand new mechanics of death."

It is interesting to note that Dr. Majoska's extensive investigation disclosed that this form of death also occurs in the Philippines, where it is known as *Bangugut* and comes from the two Tagalog words, "Bangun," meaning a person trying to arise, and "Ugul," meaning to groan.

The fact that prior to 1945 no less than fifty-one of these "Nightmare Death" cases had occurred in the Hawaiian Islands (and heaven knows how many more there were that had not been correctly diagnosed) shows the seriousness of the situation.

There is a feeling among some of the Filipinos that these deaths occur in connection with a reflex sex mechanism, and I have in my possession a photograph, which unfortunately cannot be published, showing the elaborate mechanical precautions taken by one of these victims to safeguard himself against this form of death.

In addition to the weird mechanical contrivance which he invented, he arranged to have someone sleeping beside his bed who could arouse him the instant he started to moan.

These elaborate precautions did no good. The photographs of the device which I have were taken when the man's body was in the morgue. The most thorough postmortem investigation, the most complete autopsy that could be performed failed to disclose the cause of death.

At about the time I went to Honolulu to study these cases, they came to an abrupt end. Now, I understand, they have again started, a peculiar sequence of stark terror which strikes in the tropical night.

I was able to find only one instance of a man who had made a recovery, and it is, of course, impossible to determine whether his experience was the same as that of the men who had died.

This man was sleeping in a room that he shared with a young, alert and very muscular Japanese. In the middle of the night the Japanese heard this Filipino emitting the peculiar moans associated with this dreaded type of death.

Acting with rare presence of mind, the Japanese hurled himself physically upon the Filipino, as though coming to grips with an unknown force, and he succeeded either in awakening the Filipino from a nightmare while he was still alive or in fighting off the invisible forces of witchcraft, whichever you wish to believe.

I managed to locate this Japanese. I interviewed him, photographed him, and secured not only his story but the story that had been given him by the Filipino after he had awakened from his all-but-fatal "nightmare."

These nightmare deaths are tremendously interesting, and the fact that they exist at all is a challenge. It shows the need of giving more and more attention to legal medicine and of educating a greater number of forensic pathologists.

I love the Hawaiian Islands. I was, and am, fascinated by the "Nightmare Deaths" of Honolulu. Through the investigation of these deaths I formed a valued friendship with a man whom I consider exceptionally competent, an outstanding example of the highest type of medical examiner; and so, I dedicate this book to my friend:

ALVIN V. MAJOSKA, M.D.

— Erle Stanley Gardner

CAST OF CHARACTERS

PERRY MASON — When the famous criminal lawyer played the fall guy in a hot "numbers" game, he almost became a defendant himself 15

DELLA STREET — She was the perfect jewel of a secretary to Mason — and lots more besides 15

ARLENE DUVALL — A blond nature girl, with a mysterious source of support, who adored sun-bathing in the altogether but would rather die than reveal her secret diary . . . 15

COLTON P. DUVALL — Arlene's father, he was the convicted "It" in a hide-and-seek game involving $396,751.36 26

PAUL DRAKE — A tall, thin, deceptively slow-moving private detective with a knack for getting the facts fast. 40

DR. HOLMAN B. CANDLER — A physician, one-time boxer and a trusted friend of Arlene. To him a murder was good news 46

JORDAN L. BALLARD — An ex-bank employee, he was rooting home a hot tip on a horse while the bank was being robbed 88

BILL EMORY — He'd been the driver of the Mercantile Security Bank's armored Car 45 the day of the robbery 105

HORACE MUNDY — A sleuth who lost one trail, then picked up another he didn't want 121

ROSE TRAVIS — Dr. Candler's head nurse. Attractive, magnetic, she knew how to make waiting for the doctor a pleasure 161

HAMILTON BURGER — The D.A., a man grimly determined to see justice done — to Perry Mason. 166

HELEN RUCKER — Sackett's curvaceous, redheaded girl friend, whose bathing suit revealed more than it was supposed to . . . 210

THOMAS SACKETT — A muscle man with a jeep, a shady past and a document that became too hot to handle. 211

• 1 •

Della Street, Perry Mason's Confidential Secretary, placed her palm over the mouthpiece of the telephone and said to the lawyer, "Do you want to talk with a girl who has been robbed?"

"Of what?" Mason asked.

"She says of everything."

"Why is she calling me instead of the police?"

"She says that's something she'll have to explain."

"So it would seem," Mason observed.

"She sounds like a nice girl, Chief. She's in quite a predicament."

"All right. Tell her to come in and I'll see her, Della."

"I asked her about coming in. She says she can't. She has nothing to wear."

Mason threw back his head and laughed. "Now," he said, "I've heard everything. I'll talk with her, Della. What's her name?"

"Arlene Duvall."

Mason said, "Throw the communicating switch so we can both listen, Della. This I have to hear."

Mason picked up his phone and, when Della Street had thrown the switch, said, "Yes. Hello. . . . Perry Mason speaking."

"Mr. Mason, this is Miss Arlene Duvall."

"Yes."

"I want to see you on a matter of the greatest importance, I . . . I have money to pay for your services."

"Yes."

"I've been robbed."

"Well," Mason said, winking at Della Street, "come in and see me, Miss Duvall."

"I can't."

"Why?"

"I've nothing to wear."

Mason said, "We're not particularly formal here. I would suggest you come just as you are."

"If you could see me you'd cancel that suggestion."

"Why?" Mason asked.

"What I have on wouldn't hide a postage stamp."

"Well," Mason said impatiently, "put something on. Put on anything. You —"

"I can't."

"Why?"

"I tell you I've been robbed."

"Wait a minute," Mason said, "what is this?"

"I'm trying to tell you, Mr. Mason, that I've been robbed. Everything I have in the world has been taken — my clothes, my personal effects, my car, my home."

"Where are you now?"

"At the fourteenth hole at the Remuda Golf Club. The members have installed a telephone out here. The golf club seems to be deserted just now. I lied to the operator at the clubhouse by telling her I was a member, so she put the call through. I need clothes. I need help."

Mason, suddenly interested and curious, said, "Why not call the police, Miss Duvall?"

"I *can't* call the police. They mustn't know anything about this. I'll explain when I see you. If you can arrange to get some clothes to me I'll pay —"

"Just a minute," Mason said. "I'll put my secretary on the line."

He nodded to Della Street.

Della Street said, "Yes. Miss Duvall, this is Miss Street. Mr. Mason's secretary, again."

"Miss Street, if you could get some clothes to me, just anything I could wear. I'm five feet two. I weigh a hundred and twelve and I take size ten or twelve."

"Just how am I supposed to get the clothes to you?" Della Street asked.

"If you could . . . if you could bring them, Miss Street, I would be glad to pay whatever it's worth. Oh, I know you don't *do* this sort of thing. This is all out of the ordinary and everything, but I simply *can't* explain over the telephone, and . . . well, you're the only hope I have in the world. I can't appeal to the police and I most certainly can't go around like this."

Della Street glanced across at Mason and raised her eyebrows. Mason nodded.

"Where will you be?" she asked.

"I don't suppose you're a member of the

Remuda Golf Club."

"Mr. Mason is," Della Street said.

There was relief in the voice. "Well, if he could give you a guest card and you could put some clothes down in the bottom of a golf bag and start out . . . you could come directly to the fourteenth hole. Back about fifty yards beyond that hole there's a patch of rather thick brush that runs down to a service road, and if you'll just yoo-hoo — heavens, here come some golfers! Good-by!"

The phone was slammed up.

Della Street waited a moment then gently hung up the telephone and looked across at Mason.

Mason dropped his own telephone into the cradle and said, "Now we've heard everything."

"The poor kid," Della Street said. "Imagine being out there at eleven-thirty in the morning in broad daylight without . . . Chief, how in the world *could* she have been robbed? How could she have lost everything and — ?"

"There," Mason said, "is the part that intrigues me. Do you want to go out, Della?"

"Try holding me back."

"I think I'll go with you," Mason announced.

"You would," Della Street said, smiling.

"No, no," Mason went on, "I won't go out on the course. I'll just drive you out to the golf club, give you a guest card and be waiting there when you come back. You can get her some clothes?"

"She can wear my size," Della Street said. "I have an old dress I was going to give away. It's nothing particularly fancy — a sport outfit with shorts and a skirt. It will at least enable her to get across the golf course without having a wolf pack howling in hot pursuit."

Mason glanced at his watch. "My next appointment is at two o'clock. We can just about make it, Della. This thing has *really* aroused my curiosity. Let's go."

• 2 •

From the veranda of the clubhouse Mason saw the two girls appear against the skyline as they came over a hill on the fairway.

They were almost of a size. Arlene Duvall was perhaps half an inch shorter than Della. She walked with a springy, athletic gait. Mason could see their heads turn from time to time as they exchanged comments on their way to the clubhouse.

The lawyer walked down to the foot of the terrace to meet them.

Della Street presented Arlene Duvall as though she had been an old friend.

Mason's hand was gripped with firm, strong fingers. Slate-colored eyes looked steadily into his.

"Thank you, Mr. Mason," she said, "for everything."

She was, Mason noted, a creamy-skinned blonde, with hair that had the color of honey and a sheen which made it seem smooth and silky.

"Miss Street is the one to thank," he said.

"I've already thanked her."

"You two could swap clothes very nicely," Mason said, making conversation.

"Except that *I've* nothing to swap," Arlene Duvall said.

"Your clothes were stolen?"
"Everything was stolen."
Mason said, "Your phone call certainly furnished a welcome change in the humdrum of a routine day."
"Are your days ever routine?"
"Too many of them."
She laughed. "I'm pretty well satisfied Miss Street thought I had worked out a novel method of arousing your interest, that —"
"Was it?" Mason asked.
She shook her head.
"If it had been," Mason told her, "it would still have worked. Anyone who had ingenuity and daring enough to plan a scheme of that sort would have aroused both interest and curiosity."
"Unfortunately I can't claim any credit for what was probably an original approach."
"What happened?" Mason asked.
"It's a long story."
Mason led the way up to the veranda, ordered drinks, then settled back in the chair. "Let's hear the story."
"I was living in a trailer."
"All by yourself?"
She nodded.
"In a trailer camp?"
"Only part of the time. There's a service road that runs to the back of the golf course. Very few people know of it. I think perhaps I was the only one who traveled that road regularly. When they bought the course it was part of a

large tract of land. There's a long wooded stretch down below the fourteenth hole, and a stretch of sloping, grassy meadow. Then there are more woods and then the highway.

"I found that I could drive in on this service road, park my trailer and have complete privacy. No one seemed to object. In fact I don't think anyone ever went down to that part of the club. It must be two hundred yards in an air line from the meadow to the nearest fairway, and it's probably another two hundred yards in an air line to the road. It is, of course, longer the way the service road winds in through the woods."

"Go on," Mason said.

She met his eyes. "I'm a nature girl. I like to get out and prowl around through the woods. I like to go barefooted. I like to take all my clothes off and brown in the sun."

"What," Mason asked, "do you do for a living?"

"At the moment, nothing."

"All right, what about losing your things?"

"This morning I followed my usual routine. I had stayed down in the meadow all night — in fact, I'd been down there about three nights, parked with my house trailer."

"Weren't you afraid?"

"No. After all, a house trailer is about the safest place one can be. When you lock the door from the inside there's no way anyone can get in. Even if they smash the windows it wouldn't help. The windows are too small for a person to climb in from the outside."

"So this morning you went sun-bathing?"

"I followed my usual custom. I slipped out of my clothes, took a robe, crossed the open meadow into the woods, then took the light robe off and just walked around in the sunlight for a while, feeling the air on my skin, the grass on my bare feet. You'll probably think I'm crazy. If you haven't been a sun bather you'll never understand the freedom, the caress of the air, the warmth of the sunlight, the touch of a passing breeze. Oh, what's the use?"

"Go on," Mason said, "tell me about what happened."

"Well," she said, "when I went back to where my car and trailer should have been, there wasn't any car and there wasn't any trailer."

"You're sure?"

She nodded.

"You couldn't have mistaken the place?"

"Heavens, no. I never lose my way in the open and I've been out here for . . . well, ever since it began to get warm."

"Your ignition keys?" Mason asked.

"I have the ignition key to the automobile and the key to the door of the trailer in this little key container that was in the pocket of the light robe, but anyone who really wants to take an automobile doesn't need to bother with an ignition key. Isn't there some way they can short-circuit the wires behind the dash?"

"You called me instead of the police?" The way Mason made the statement it was more of a question than an assertion.

"Naturally. Can you imagine a girl attired in a diaphanous wisp of sunlight, having two police officers from a radio call car determining what had been stolen by taking an inventory of what was left. And, of course, that would make a beautiful story for the newspapers. I can just see the headlines: SUN-BATHING BLONDE LOSES EVERYTHING EXCEPT SMILE AND SUN TAN. And then, of course, newspaper photographers would want pictures with the proper back lighting."

"Was there," Mason asked, "some other reason?"

"For not calling the police?"

Mason nodded.

She toyed with her glass for a moment, then met his eyes. "Yes."

"What?"

"I think . . . well, the police may have been the ones who were behind the whole thing."

"You mean that the police stole your car and trailer?"

She nodded.

"Because they wanted to search it carefully, thoroughly and at their leisure."

"Looking for what?"

"My diary probably."

"And why were the police interested in your diary?"

She said, "Mr. Mason, you're going to have to take me on trust."

"You haven't put up much collateral so far."

"I don't mean as far as money is concerned. I'll see that you get a reasonable retainer by ten o'clock tomorrow morning. But for the rest of it — I mean the personal evaluation — well, you're going to have to take me on trust, that's all."

Mason said, "You're having a hard time telling your story. Suppose you just blurt out the part that you're trying to avoid and then we can get down to brass tacks."

"Do you know who I am?"

"I know that you're an attractive young woman, probably in your early twenties; that you, according to your own story, exist without visible means of support; that you were living a highly unorthodox life in the house trailer, and that for some reason you have been afraid to make friends."

"What makes you say that?"

Mason said, "The answer is quite obvious. Nine hundred and ninety-nine women out of a thousand who found themselves attired in next to nothing on a golf course would have one or more close friends to whom they could appeal. To call a lawyer whom you have never met indicates there are parts of this story that you haven't told and apparently are trying to keep from telling."

"Do you know my father?" she asked.

"Who is your father?"

"Colton P. Duvall."

Mason shook his head, then said, "Wait a minute. There's something vaguely familiar about the name. I — What does he do?"

"He makes license plates."

"A manufacturer?"

"No. He is a laborer," she said, and then added, "in the state prison."

"Oh," Mason said.

"He is," she went on, "supposed to have stolen three hundred and ninety-six thousand, seven hundred and fifty-one dollars and thirty-six cents."

"It seems to me I remember it now," Mason said. "It was a deal in connection with some bank, wasn't it?"

"A bank and an armored truck, a shipment of currency."

Mason nodded, watching her narrowly.

"He's been in prison for five years. He's supposed to have the money secreted somewhere. He's being subjected to the sort of pressure that is indescribable in its refined cruelty."

Mason studied her and she met his gaze candidly. "Officially," she said, "I am the daughter of a thief."

"Go on," Mason told her, "tell me the story."

"I've told it."

"Not to me."

"I just did."

"You've just outlined it. Let's hear the rest of it."

"My father worked in the Mercantile Security Bank. They have half a dozen branches. There's one branch in Santa Ana. In order to keep balances straight, cash is shipped by special armored truck to the various branches. On this day there was a shipment of three hundred and ninety-six thousand, seven hundred and fifty-one dollars and thirty-six cents. Dad personally wrapped it up. An inspector was supposed to have been watching, but Dad was a trusted employee and the inspector had made one big wager on a horse race. He had a small portable radio and . . . well, when it was time for the race to be run he tuned in on the radio. He said afterward that he was listening but that he kept his eye on Dad, that Dad sealed the package, then wrapped it and stamped it with sealing wax. Dad put his own seal on the sealing wax and the inspector put his own seal on it."

"And then?" Mason asked.

"Then, about ten minutes later, the man who drove the armored truck came up and gave a receipt for the package."

"When was it delivered in Santa Ana?"

"About an hour and thirty minutes later."

"What happened there?"

"Apparently the package was in order, the seals seemed to be intact, the Santa Ana cashier gave a receipt but asked the driver of the armored car to wait as he had a shipment of vouchers going back."

"And then what?"

"A few minutes later the man came running out and said there'd been a mistake somewhere. He had received the wrong package."

"What was in the package he had received?"

"A great big bundle of canceled checks."

"Any clue as to the — ?"

"They all came from one file in the main Los Angeles bank — the file marked 'AA' to 'CZ.' "

"And where was that file located?"

"Right near the shipping room. Someone had evidently lifted out the cash from the box, scooped up stacks of canceled checks and dumped them into the box, then the box was wrapped and sealed."

"And they think your dad was the guilty one?"

She nodded.

"Just what was the evidence against him?" Mason said. "It would seem to be largely circumstantial."

"Well, Dad was the one who had charge of the cash. The inspector, who lost his job over it, couldn't have made the substitution without Dad's knowing it. Ordinarily Dad couldn't have made the substitution without the inspector knowing it. But there was, of course, that matter of the radio report on the horse race."

"The man who drove the armored car?" Mason asked.

She shook her head.

"Why not?"

"The package was delivered unopened. It had the seals of the inspector and my dad on it. The address of the bank to which it was to be delivered was in Dad's writing and the amount of the money inside was listed in Dad's handwriting."

"How many persons in the armored truck?"

"Only one. The armored truck is really quite a gadget. It's designed especially for use in branch banking transactions. The driver notifies the bank when he is ready to pick up a shipment. The bank has two armed guards on duty. The car parks at a reserved loading zone back of the bank. The armed guards look out and make sure everything is all clear; that there are no suspicious persons or cars about. Then they open the door and step out."

"Then what?"

"The banker takes the package out and puts it in the locked cash compartment in the truck."

"The driver doesn't put it in?"

"No. He never gets near the money. He drives the truck. Someone from the bank always handles the money."

"In this particular instance, who handled the actual cash?"

"Dad."

"Then what?"

"Then the money compartment was locked. The driver got in the truck and the doors were locked from the inside. There's armor and bulletproof glass. The driver started for his destination and the branch bank which was to receive the shipment was told the approximate time of arrival over the phone."

"How about receiving the shipment at the other end? How are those shipments customarily handled?"

"When the armored truck pulls up at the reserved parking zone at the branch bank, the driver sits inside and waits until the bank door is opened and two armed guards come out to stand on the sidewalk. *Then* the driver unlocks the truck door and *then* the representative of the bank comes out and unlocks the cash compartment of the car with his own key and picks up the package and takes it into the bank."

"The driver of the car doesn't have a key to the cash compartment?" Mason asked.

She shook her head. "And, believe me, it's a very complicated lock. You don't open it *without* a key."

Mason said, "It would seem that the person at the branch bank had as much of an opportunity to substitute as your father did. The seals certainly were broken by the time he had looked into the contents of the package and —"

"But the seals were unbroken when he received it. Furthermore, there were . . . other things."

"What?"

"All right," she said. "Now I'm coming to the really hard part."

"I thought so," Mason told her. "Go ahead."

"Dad had some of the stolen bills in his possession."

"How did they know?"

"It was due to a coincidence. It just happened that one of the bank's clients had been propositioned in a blackmailing scheme. He communicated with the police. The payoff was set at five thousand dollars. He was instructed to pay off in cash. The police had the bank make up a package of currency and the numbers of all the bills were listed.

"Well, something happened to upset the blackmailer. Apparently he learned that the victim had called in the police. So he didn't show up for the money. The man who was to have been the victim of the blackmail held the money for a week and then, not wanting to leave that amount of cash in his possession, brought it back to the bank for a deposit.

"It happened that this large shipment of cash was going out to the bank at Santa Ana. So when that five thousand dollars was brought in for deposit, the cashier simply counted it and passed it over to the accountant who was making up the shipment. So that five thousand dollars in bills was in the package.

"No one knew about it apparently except the accountant and the cashier. After it turned out the shipment had been juggled, the cashier reported to the police and the police were smart enough to keep quiet about it.

"The police put researchers in all of the banks. They said there had been a kidnaping with a ransom payment; that there hadn't been any publicity as yet but the police had the numbers of the bills and they had men listing the numbers of every twenty-dollar bill that was brought in for deposit. It was a terrific task, but they did it — and they kept the master list of the numbers in the hands of one man in the FBI. Only that man knew the numbers of the stolen bills.

"Well, a service station man brought in one of the numbered bills for deposit. The police were sent out to ask him where he had got it and if he remembered who gave it to him. He told them that as it happened he remembered the whole thing because it was a bill Dad had given him in payment for a new tube. Just the tip of one corner had been torn off the bill and the service station man happened to remember it."

"And then?" Mason asked.

She said, "Then the police went to Dad. He told them of course he bought the tube. The police then told him that the bill was one of those taken in the shipment that had been stolen. Dad told them that as nearly as he remembered, the bill was part of money he'd been carrying in his wallet for more than a week. He brought out his wallet to show to the officers and there were two more of the numbered bills in the wallet. That cooked Dad's goose."

Mason narrowed his eyes. He searched her face. "That," he said, "makes a pretty open-and-shut case."

"That's what the jury thought."

"You still believe in your dad's innocence?"

"I *know* he's innocent."

"What else?" Mason said.

"Well, naturally everyone thinks he has a fortune in money buried somewhere. They played a very ingenious game. They threw the book at him. They charged him on a lot of different counts, and gave consecutive sentences.

"Now the parole authorities smile at Dad and say, 'Look, Mr. Duvall, if you want to make it easy on yourself you can tell the authorities where that money is hidden. They'll dig it up and you'll go free on parole. You might even be able to get a commutation of sentence to time served. But don't think you're ever going to enjoy that money. Unless you tell us where it is, you're going to stay in here until you're too old to enjoy anything.' "

"Yes," Mason said, "one can appreciate that attitude."

"And," she went on, "they have hounded me. They think perhaps Dad buried the money and told me where it was."

"Go on."

"I tried to keep my job but they were shadowing me all the time. They were checking me every time I turned around, and . . . well, I decided to put in my entire time trying to prove

Dad was innocent."

"In other words you retired."

"I changed my activities."

"As far as work is concerned you retired."

"All right, I retired."

"On what?"

She said, "There — as I told you — is where you have to take me on faith. A . . . a friend is financing me."

"How did you happen to call me when your trailer was stolen?"

"Because I'd been intending to ask you for an appointment for several days."

"Why me?"

"Because you have the reputation of being one of the outstanding lawyers in this part of the country."

"Did it ever occur to you that lawyers have business expenses, that I have to pay my clerical and secretarial help, that I have to pay rent, that I have to pay telephones, that I have to — ?"

"Of course," she interrupted impatiently.

"And what did you intend to do about that?"

"Mr. Mason, before ten o'clock tomorrow morning I will be in your office. I will pay you fifteen hundred dollars. That will be a retainer."

Mason stroked his chin. "What do you want me to do?"

"I want you to start right now and try to find my trailer before it's too late."

"When will it be too late?"

"When they find certain things — my diary for one."

"Where is your diary?"

"Concealed in the trailer."

"Is there anything else concealed in the trailer?"

"Yes."

"Some cash perhaps?"

"Don't be silly."

"And where do you expect to get the money you have promised to pay me tomorrow morning?"

She shook her head.

Mason said, "Look, Miss Duvall, I wasn't born yesterday. Anyone who took that trailer is literally going to tear it to pieces."

"I'm not so certain."

"Why not?"

"I took steps to see that perhaps they wouldn't."

"Such as what?"

"I kept a double set of books, and one is easier to find than the other — the wrong one."

"Go on," Mason told her. "You keep leading with your chin."

"I keep a secret diary in which I keep a record of all of the things I have discovered so that in case anything should happen to me Dad wouldn't lose the benefit of the work I had been doing."

"Have you accomplished anything?"

"I think so."

"Want to tell me about it?"

"Not now."

"Why?"

"Because you're suspicious of me and you're going to have to accept *me* wholeheartedly before I take *you* into my confidence."

"Look," Mason said, "let's be reasonable about this thing. You're an attractive young woman. Your dad was working in a bank on a salary. Almost four hundred thousand dollars disappeared from that bank. Your dad goes to prison and you quit work. You buy yourself a trailer and an automobile. Fully paid for?"

"Yes."

"And you become a nature girl. You trip around in the sunlight. You run barefooted through the dewy grass. And then you tell me you're going to call at my office tomorrow morning and give me fifteen hundred dollars. Those are the simple facts of the case as I see them at this time."

"All right," she said. "I know what you're thinking. You think that Dad buried the money. You think that I dug it up. I can't help what you think. You won't work for me unless I give you money. Yet when I promise to give you money you become suspicious. Will you take me on trust for twenty hours? Will you undertake the job of finding my trailer, and will you start work on it right now?"

Mason drummed with his fingers on the table top. Her slate-colored eyes regarded him with unwinking intensity.

"What do you want me to do?"

"Find that trailer and find it fast. It can't have gone too far. A car and a trailer are noticeable."

"Anything particularly peculiar about this trailer?"

"It's a last year's Heliar. There aren't too many of them. You can ring up the factory and get specifications."

"What was your car?"

"A Cadillac."

"You're rather good to yourself, aren't you?"

"There's no use fighting your way over roads with a trailer and a light car. You want a car that's heavy enough to hold the road and pull the trailer along behind."

"You see lots of big trailers pulled by light cars."

"Sure, they pull them, but it's not the most comfortable means of locomotion. You have to keep driving all the time. When you hook the Heliar on behind this Cadillac you can just forget you have a trailer. All you do is sit at the wheel and watch the miles dissolve beneath the wheels."

"And do you mean to say the police and the income-tax people and everyone haven't had you on the carpet asking you where you get this money?"

Her smile was a one-sided twisting of the right corner of her mouth. "They did for a while. Now they've quit."

"You only *think* they've quit."

"No, they really have — as far as getting me on the carpet is concerned. But I don't think for a minute they've given up. They're following me around. If I go into a store and buy groceries, within thirty seconds someone is apt to slip a note to the cashier telling him to save the bill that I turned in. That bill will be checked to see if the numbers on it are those of the stolen money."

"And yet you hop around and sun-bathe."

"Up to now," she said, "I didn't think anyone knew about this place."

"Don't kid yourself," Mason said. "They've been watching you. They've had you trailed with cars, with motorcycles. They've probably been watching you from helicopters."

"I thought that I'd worn them out."

"You want to bet?" Mason asked her.

She thought for a moment, then shook her head.

Mason said, "While you've been traipsing around in your bare feet, feeling the caress of wind on your skin, a couple of detectives have been sizing you up with binoculars."

"That's their privilege."

Abruptly Mason said, "All right, you're going to be at my office with fifteen hundred dollars."

"At ten o'clock tomorrow morning. Make it nine-thirty."

Mason said, "I'm going to take steps to find

your trailer because I want to find out what the answer is. Now then, let's have a complete understanding?"

"What is it?"

"If you're on the up-and-up," Mason said, "I'll try and protect you. If your dad got away with that three hundred and ninety-six thousand dollars and you have all of it or part of it concealed and are drawing on it from time to time, I'm not going to be an accessory after the fact. Do you understand that?"

"What do you mean by that?"

"I'll turn you in to the police. I'll find where the money is hidden. I'll turn it over to the authorities, and I'll get my fee by collecting a reward."

Her smile was enigmatical. "Fair enough," she told him and stretched a muscular hand across the table.

Mason took the hand, said to Della Street, "Got Paul Drake of the Drake Detective Agency on the telephone, Della. We're going to work."

• 3 •

Paul Drake, carrying a sheaf of reports, entered Mason's office shortly before five o'clock, said, "Hi, Perry. How are you, Della? Got something on that trailer case for you, Perry."

Mason glanced at his watch. "Anything really hot?"

"Uh-huh."

"You must have been working fast."

"That's what you said you wanted."

Paul Drake dropped into the client's big, leather chair, riffled through some of the reports, then, awkwardly ill at ease in the conventional position, slid around so that his legs were hanging over one rounded arm, the other supporting the small of his back.

Tall, thin and casual, there was about him an air of lazy indolence. His face seemed disinterested. His eyes, which seldom missed any significant detail, belied their efficiency by appearing completely bored.

Drake said, "One of the men who was in on the theft is a man named Thomas Sackett. He's living at 3921 Mitner Avenue — that's an apartment house. No one seems to know too much about him. He's supposed to be a prospector and spends quite a bit of time out in the desert — an outdoorsman — drives a jeep, throws a sleeping bag in the back end, a few boxes of provisions, pick, shovel, gold pan and a tent. Takes off on trips and they don't see him for a week or ten days, then he'll be back and hang around for a while."

"And he was in on stealing the trailer?"

"That's right."

"Perhaps," Mason said, glancing at Della Street, "he just wanted to steal a trailer and take it out in the desert so he could park it and live in it."

Drake shook his head. "The trailer itself," he said, "is up for sale on a consignment basis at the Ideal Trade-In Trailer Mart. Sackett left it there for sale. He put a price tag of twenty-eight hundred and ninety-five dollars on it. The man who runs the place doesn't think it's worth over twenty-five hundred. Sackett arranged to put it up for sale on consignment. Sackett didn't use his right name, by the way, but used the name of Howard Prim when he brought the trailer in."

"And it's up for sale?"

Paul Drake nodded.

"I wonder what's in it?" Mason said. "He could hardly have had time to have cleaned it out."

"One of my men checked it and made as if he'd like to make an offer," Drake said. "The thing hasn't been cleaned up but it's sure been stripped of everything in the line of personal belongings — bedding, dishes, cooking utensils, provisions, everything. It's just stripped right down to the bare trailer, just as it came from the manufacturer."

Mason said, "They must have worked fast."

Drake nodded.

"How in the world did you get all that information in this time?" Mason asked.

"Just a lot of routine work, Perry. You wouldn't be interested."

"But I am interested. My client is going to be very much interested."

Drake held up the sheets of flimsy. "Well," he said, "you told me not to spare any expense, to put as many operatives on it as I needed. These are their reports. They tell the story."

"Never mind the reports," Mason said. "How did you go about it?"

"Well, it's not too difficult," Drake said. "You told me where the trailer had been stolen. I went down there and looked around. Someone drove off the car and trailer. The question was, did he walk into the place and pick up the car and trailer, or did someone drive him in? That, of course, is the first question a detective would want to have answered.

"So we looked around and found some automobile tracks turning in on the old road. They were tracks that had been made by a jeep. That, of course, gave us a break. Those tracks came in and they went out. When they went out they were superimposed over the tracks made by a car and house trailer. We know that because they were the last tracks going out, the freshest tracks on the road.

"Well, it was a job of tracking. We could see where the jeep had gone in, and then the car and house trailer had been driven out over those jeep tracks and then the jeep was driven out.

"Well, of course, we had the license number on the trailer. Ordinarily you'd have expected they'd juggle license numbers. However, a Heliar is a rather distinctive house trailer. It has some features you don't find on the others, and there aren't too many of them sold. It's a relatively high-priced unit."

"I still don't see how you found it," Mason said.

"That's what I'm trying to tell you. There's nothing romantic or glamorous about this business. When you come right down to brass tacks it's just a matter of routine. For instance, the tracks indicated there had to be at least two persons in on the deal. Well, just figure it out for yourself, Perry. They only had four things they could have done."

"What were they?"

"They could have driven the Heliar along the road, headed for some distant city or some place out of the state; they could have parked the trailer in some trailer parking place; they could have run the trailer into a back yard or private garage; or they could have put the trailer up for sale.

"Now the one thing that could have stymied

us was if they'd put it in a back yard or a garage. That would have licked us. So we didn't bother about that. We turned to the highways. We'd got on the job pretty fast, within a couple of hours of the time the trailer was stolen. You can't take a car and a house trailer through city traffic and get *too* far in two hours.

"I have an arrangement with various all-night service stations along the different highways — one on the coast highway, one on the inland highway, one on the desert highway — well, anyway, I cover all of the main highways. Of course, a person has lots of different routes to use getting out of town, but once you start really traveling you only have a choice of about seven main highways. I have service stations that are under a working arrangement with me. I called up each one of those service stations. They all started looking out for a Heliar trailer.

"Then I started a girl telephoning all of the trailer camps to see if a Heliar trailer had checked in during the afternoon, and another operative telephoned all of the various trailer sales places to see if they had a Heliar trailer for sale, a secondhand trailer, one that hadn't been on the lot too long.

"Reports began to come pouring in. A Heliar trailer had passed Yermo on the Las Vegas road. A Heliar trailer had gone through Holtville on the road to Yuma. There was a Heliar trailer between Ventura and Santa Barbara.

"A check showed that one of them was an eighteen-foot Heliar, the other was the big thirty-two foot job. The one out of Yermo was the only twenty-five foot Heliar which matched the one we want. I did some checking on time and it would have been pretty difficult for that trailer we wanted to have made it to Yermo in the time that was available.

"There were two Heliar twenty-five foot trailers that had checked into trailer camps around the city. I had men go out to look those over. Then we struck pay dirt in this Ideal Trade-In Trailer Mart. They had a Heliar that had been brought in just a few minutes before we telephoned. A man by the name of Prim had it on consignment. Well, we dashed out to take a look at it, and, shucks, there was nothing to it, Perry. It still had the same license number on it.

"Well, we got a description of Prim, and his address which, of course, didn't mean anything because it was a phony address, but when he'd driven the trailer in he'd been driving a jeep, and the man who runs the place is pretty smart. He's had a lot of experience and when he sells a trailer he has to guarantee title, so he just jotted down the license number of the jeep to be on the safe side.

"Well, we ran down the jeep license number, found it was registered in the name of Thomas Sackett, 3921 Mitner Avenue. We had an operative check out there to find out what was known about Sackett and picked up the information I just gave you."

"Any chance that it's not the same man?" Mason asked.

"None whatever. We have his description. Five feet seven, weighs a hundred and seventy-five, blond, about thirty years of age, walks with a very slight limp."

"How about the Cadillac?" Mason asked.

"The Cadillac we haven't located," Drake said, "and we're not going to be able to locate it unless we can notify the police. That's a dragnet operation. There are too many Cadillacs, too many places where you can leave them. The house trailer was different."

"That's darn fine work, Paul."

Paul Drake dismissed the compliment with a gesture. "Just routine," he said. "You have to figure all of the different things a man can do with a house trailer, then you have to figure how to check on them, and you have to be organized so you *can* check on them."

"Well, it's darn fine work just the same," Mason said, "and it may give us a valuable lead."

He turned to Della Street. "What about our client, Della? How can we reach her?"

"She left us a number," Della Street said. "Care of Dr. Holman B. Candler, at Santa Ana.

"She said he was a trusted friend and we could give him any information we might want relayed to her in case we learned anything before she called in at nine-thirty in the morning."

Mason glanced across at Paul Drake. "Do you have someone keeping an eye on that trailer, Paul?"

"Sure. I have two operatives on the job. That's one thing I wanted to ask you about. If this guy shows up and tries to move the trailer away from the trailer lot, what do you want done?"

Mason said, "I don't know. I'll have to find out." He nodded to Della Street. "Get Dr. Candler on the line for me, Della."

Della Street put through the call to Dr. Candler's office. After explaining who she was and the nature of the call to Dr. Candler's office nurse, she nodded to Perry Mason and said, "He's coming on the line."

Mason picked up the phone, said, "Hello," and heard a cautious voice at the other end of the line saying, "Yes. Hello. This is Dr. Candler speaking."

Mason said, "This is Perry Mason speaking. I am very anxious to get in touch with Miss Arlene Duvall, Doctor. She told me that she could be reached through you."

"Am I to understand that you are Mr. Perry Mason, the attorney?"

"That's right."

"May I ask why you wish to get in touch with her, Mr. Mason?"

Mason said, "Miss Duvall told me that I

could confide in you, that you were a friend of the family and were like an uncle to her."

"That's right."

"Miss Duvall consulted me earlier in the day."

"Yes?"

"About a certain matter," Mason said, "on which she wished me to take immediate action."

"I see."

"I would like to tell Miss Duvall that the action has been taken and has resulted in at least a partial success."

"It was about the trailer?"

"Yes."

"Surely you haven't located it?"

"We have," Mason said. "It's for sale at a secondhand trailer lot. It has been cleaned of all personal possessions — dishes, clothes, bedding, everything. I think this is information that Miss Duvall would like to have without delay, and if you will let me know where I can reach her I'll try and get in touch with her at once and see what her instructions are."

"I'm sorry I can't give you an address," Dr. Candler said cautiously, "but I can try and get a message through to her. How long will you be in your office, Mr. Mason?"

"Will thirty minutes be satisfactory?"

"I think so. If you'll wait there I'll try and get a message through to her and then she can call you back."

"Thank you," Mason said, and hung up.

Della Street, who had been monitoring the conversation, glanced across at Mason. "Cautious," she said, smiling,

"Playing them close to his chest," Mason said. "However, you can't blame him. How does he know that I'm not a detective calling up and assuming the identity of Perry Mason, the lawyer? After all, he doesn't know me and is not familiar with my voice."

"I see, and by having her call back he would —"

"Verify the number," Mason said. "You'd better plug in the switchboard so you can pick up any calls after Gertie goes home."

"I think she's just leaving," Della Street said and went to the outer office to plug in the line so that any incoming calls would be routed to Mason's private office.

Mason turned to Paul Drake and said, "Paul, I want Thomas Sackett put under surveillance. It will have to be a smooth job. I don't want him to know he's being watched."

"You want him followed day and night?"

"That's right. I want to know where he is and what he's doing every minute of the time. And I want you to find out all you can about a job pulled on the Mercantile Security when a truck shipment of nearly four hundred thousand dollars was —"

Drake snapped his fingers. "That's it!"

"What is?"

"That name, Duvall. He was the guy who juggled packages. They sent him up. Is she any relation?"

"His daughter."

"Oh, oh!"

"Find out everything you can, Paul."

"How soon?"

"Fast."

"Well I'll be darned," Drake said. "Can you feature that? It was her dad who did the job, eh?"

"He got the credit," Mason said dryly.

"He got the cash," Drake corrected.

Della Street returned to the office, said, "Everything's plugged in." She made a dive for the phone as it started ringing. "We'll probably be deluged with calls for the next thirty minutes, Chief. I —"

She picked up the receiver and said, "Hello," then, after a moment, her eyes widened and she nodded to Perry Mason.

"Arlene Duvall?"

She nodded.

Mason picked up his phone.

Della Street said, "He'll talk with you, Miss Duvall. He's right here. Hold the line."

Arlene Duvall's voice was very different from that of Dr. Candler. She made no attempt to control her excitement.

"You have something on the trailer? Did I understand Dr. Candler to say you'd found it?"

"The trailer has been located, Miss Duvall."

"Where is it?"

"It's at the Ideal Trade-In Trailer Mart."

"At the Ideal?"

"That's right."

"Why, I . . . I —"

"You know the place?" Mason asked.

"Why, of course. That's where I bought the trailer."

"When?"

"About six months ago."

"Well, it's there now — offered for sale on a consignment basis."

"Who left it?"

"The name which he gave the manager of the place was Howard Prim. The address which he gave was fictitious."

"Yes, yes, of course. He — what's the condition of the trailer?"

"There are no personal belongings left in it."

"No, no, I mean the trailer itself. Has anyone ripped away the woodwork anywhere?"

"Apparently not."

"Mr. Mason, it's *very* imperative that I get to that trailer at once. Can you . . . can you meet me there?"

"When?"

"Just as soon as you can get there. I'll be waiting."

"Do you," Mason asked, "have anything in your possession that would indicate that you own the trailer, the registration certificate or — ?"

"I have nothing, Mr. Mason. I was left with

nothing except the key to my car and the key to the trailer."

Mason said, "Of course, if you bought the trailer there and the man who sold it to you is there . . . well, I'll drive down and meet you there."

"Right away?"

"Right away," Mason promised.

He hung up the telephone, said to Paul Drake, "Paul, I'm not going to tip my hand in regard to Sackett for a little while at least. I think this may be a case where I shouldn't let my client know *everything* that we know."

"As far as I'm concerned," Drake said, "you're my client. I give information to no one else. You give it out as you want to and to whom you want to."

Mason pushed his swivel chair away from the desk, said to Drake, "Get your men on that other job right away, Paul. Tell the two men who have the trailer under surveillance to keep on the job. Follow that trailer no matter where it goes."

"You think your client can establish her title and move it?"

"She should be able to. Since this outfit sold the trailer in the first place, they'll probably have a record of the original transaction and we shouldn't have much trouble."

"Seems strange a thief would take it back to that same place," Drake said.

"It's a coincidence," Mason admitted.

"You said it," Drake commented dryly.

"Of course, after all, there aren't too many of these trailer sales outfits as big as the Ideal."

"It's still quite a coincidence," Drake said.

Mason nodded to Della. "Ready, Della?"

"Ready," she said.

Drake wriggled himself out of the chair. "I take it," he said, "I'm being thrown out."

"On your ear," Mason told him, holding the door open.

"Well, that always helps," Drake said, grinning. "I'll be seeing you."

"Keep on the job personally until nine-thirty," Mason told him. "I may want to get in touch with you after we've gone down to the trailer place. And I'd like to have you get everything you can on that bank job."

"I'll stay until ten," Drake promised.

Paul Drake walked down the corridor as far as his office, which was on the same floor as Mason's but nearer the elevator.

"Okay," he said, "I'll get on the job."

The lawyer and his secretary descended in the elevator and entered Mason's car in the parking lot reserved for tenants.

Mason eased the car out into the congested traffic of the afternoon rush hour.

"How long will it take us?" Della Street asked.

"Twenty minutes at least."

Della Street raised her eyebrows. "Your new pledge of careful driving?"

Mason nodded.

"The automobile, Della, has become a very

deadly weapon. Too many people with too many automobiles are going places at the same time."

"Well, your reformation will enable me to relax," she said, settling back against the seat. "I won't have to keep one eye peeled for a traffic cop."

"From now on," Mason said, "the traffic cops are my friends. I want more of them. If I'm going to be law-abiding, I'd like to have the other man law-abiding, too. What do you think of our new client, Della?"

"Poor kid," Della said. "She certainly was placed in an embarrassing position."

"Wasn't she!"

"Chief, you sound skeptical."

Mason slowed as the light was changing, brought the car to a stop on the amber light, and said, "When you stop to figure the cold, hard facts, we have a girl whose father was convicted of embezzling nearly four hundred thousand dollars. She drives an expensive car and lives in an expensive trailer. She does not work. She prances around barefoot in the dewy grass, letting the sunlit breezes caress her bare skin."

"Nice work if you can get it," Della Street observed.

"Now, Della, let's look at it from the viewpoint of the parole board. You have Colton P. Duvall in prison on an indeterminate sentence. He claims that he was innocent, that he was falsely convicted. The circumstances are not entirely clear. You are concerned as a member of the board with just how long you are going to keep Colton Duvall in prison. Perhaps you are even considering granting a parole. So you get in touch with the police officers who did the investigative work on the case and ask them for their opinion. They tell you about the daughter driving the expensive car, living in the high-class house trailer, doing no work, and yet apparently having plenty of money."

"Well, when you put it that way," Della Street said, "she . . . good Lord, Chief, her own actions are keeping her father in the penitentiary."

"Provided," Mason said, smiling.

"Provided what?"

"Provided the Adult Authority, which in this state has the same duties and functions as the Board of Pardon and Paroles in most states, has any intention, no matter how remote, of granting parole. It would almost seem as though Arlene Duvall was trying to keep Colton Duvall in prison rather than getting him out. Surely from the viewpoint of the authorities, the daughter's actions must be exceedingly exasperating to say the least."

"Very definitely," Della said.

"On the other hand," Mason said, "they could be a very alluring form of bait."

"In what way?"

"Duvall goes to prison," Mason said. "He is given to understand, perhaps not in so many words, but nevertheless given to understand, that if he wants to disgorge the loot he will be given parole. He apparently has no intention of disgorging the loot. He's going to wait them out. So they finally come to the conclusion that he's going to sit tight. Then the daughter starts living without visible means of support, an ideal existence of complete leisure. Wouldn't it be natural for the parole authorities to say, 'Control of the money seems to have passed from the father to the daughter. How about letting this man out and keeping him under close surveillance? We'll watch every move he makes. We can't help it if his daughter spends money, but if *he* starts spending money we'll get him on the carpet, violate his parole and *perhaps* be able to get the daughter as an accessory. Then we may be able to find where the money's hidden and get some of it back!"

Della Street thought things over. "Someone seems to be playing a very deep game," she said at length.

"Exactly," Mason agreed.

"And where do *you* fit in that scheme?" she asked.

"I might be intended to play the part of a pawn."

"By being expendable?"

"That's right."

"Well, be careful."

"I intend to be."

Mason turned the car in to the freeway. For

another ten minutes they proceeded in swift silence. Then Mason turned off on a cross street, drove half a dozen blocks and turned in at the Ideal Trade-In Trailer Mart.

Mason parked his car and walked over to a street where there was a long line of house trailers on display.

"What won't they do next?" Della Street asked as Mason stopped to look at one of the demonstrators. "The way they've managed to conserve space, to give you every convenience, and yet keep the whole thing so compact, it's wonderful — a real home on wheels!"

A salesman entered the trailer, smiling affably. "How about it? You folks in the market for a trailer?"

"We'd like to see the manager," Mason said.

"Jim Hartsel?"

"Is he the manager?"

The salesman nodded.

"Where can we find him?"

"This way, please."

The salesman led them down the street of trailers, turned to the left.

Mason said to Della Street, "You have your notebook and pencil, Della?"

"Never without them — except in the bath."

Mason said, "When Arlene Duvall comes here she may come in a taxi. She may be driving an automobile. If she's driving an automobile I'll leave it to you to get the license number."

Della Street nodded.

The salesman paused before a small building. "Here's the office. You'll find Mr. Hartsel inside."

"Thanks," Mason said, and held the door open for Della Street.

Hartsel, a broad-shouldered, barrel-chested individual with the build of a grizzly bear and the eye of an auctioneer, sized them up.

"Hello, folks. What's the beef?"

"The beef?" Mason asked.

"Sure," the man said, grinning infectiously. "When people come in ready to close the deal on a trailer they have smiles all over their faces. They've reached the important decision in their lives. They're going out on the road and play gypsy. They're going to begin to really enjoy life. When they come in with faces grim and manner determined there's some sort of a beef.

"Now what is it? Did you buy a house trailer from us and is something wrong with it?"

Mason laughed. "I'm Perry Mason," he said.

"The lawyer?"

"That's right."

Hartsel gripped Mason's hand with thick, powerful fingers.

"Certainly glad to meet you."

"And this is my secretary, Miss Street."

Della Street started to extend her hand.

"Advise you not to, Della," Mason said, rubbing his own hand.

"Well now, you didn't do so bad yourself," Hartsel said. "I did a lot of wrestling and my course on salesmanship said to give a cordial handclasp. In my book that means just a little better than the other man gives. I wasn't able to trump your ace a bit. How do you do, Miss Street. I'm pleased to meet you. Sit down folks and tell me what's the trouble. Have I violated a law or something?"

"Do you know an Arlene Duvall?" Mason asked.

"Duvall . . . Duvall . . . the name's familiar somewhere . . . oh yes."

Suddenly Hartsel grinned.

"A joke?" Mason asked.

"Well, let's say a pleasant memory," Hartsel said. "A nice little girl. Bought a Heliar trailer. Paid for it in cash."

"What do you mean by cash?" Mason asked.

"Cash. C-a-s-h."

"Check or — ?"

"No check — cash. Cold, hard, coin of the realm. Crisp one-hundred-dollar bills."

"Do you," Mason asked, "know anything else about her?"

"Not when they pay for trailers in cash right on the barrel head. I don't have to know anything else about them. What about her? Don't tell me she's robbed a bank or something."

Mason started to say something, then checked himself.

"Well, what is it?"

"The Heliar trailer that you sold her has been stolen."

"The deuce it has! Insured, I hope."

"I don't know," Mason said. "My interest lies primarily in recovering the trailer."

"Well, what can I do for you?"

"Turn it over."

The smile faded from Hartsel's face.

"Now *wait* a minute."

"No, no," Mason said, "I don't intimate that you stole it, but apparently you purchased it."

"Oh, so *that's* it," Hartsel said. "Someone telephoned a while ago, wanted to know if we'd taken in a Heliar trailer today. I didn't buy it. I have it on consignment. As a matter of fact I happen to have the card right in front of me — a man by the name of Prim — at least that's the name he gave me. Wanted to put it on consignment, gave me a telephone number and an address. I took the precaution of taking the license number on his jeep. I haven't looked it up yet."

Mason said casually, "The jeep may have been loaned him by a friend."

"Want to take a look at the trailer?" Hartsel asked.

Mason nodded. "I expect the owner will be here momentarily. She was to meet us here."

"Well, we can go out and take a look at the trailer," Hartsel said. "Of course, Mr. Mason, I know you and know your reputation, but I'm going to check on this. We have records here you know — manufacturer's body number and all that."

Mason nodded.

"Let me look that deal up," Hartsel said.

He walked across the office, swung back the door of a big safe, pulled out a filing drawer, ran through the files until he came to a card, and then jotted information down swiftly in a notebook.

"All right," he said, "we can —"

He broke off as the door opened and Arlene Duvall said, "Well, good evening everyone. I was delayed in traffic — it's terrible."

"Well, well, well," Hartsel said. "Miss Duvall! How *are* you?"

She came forward and gave him her hand. "Doing fine."

"Well, you certainly look it."

Hartsel released her hand, took the wrist and held the hand out for Della Street's inspection.

"See, Miss Street, no wounds. In dealing with the opposite sex I'm gentle as a summer breeze. It's only when someone grips that I grip back. Mr. Mason was telling me about your trailer, Miss Duvall."

"Yes, it was stolen."

"And I seem to have it."

"That's what Mr. Mason told me."

Hartsel said, "I'm wondering if someone would kindly tell me how Mason knew about all this?"

"She paid me to find out," Mason said.

"Not the police?" Hartsel asked.

Arlene Duvall shook her head.

Hartsel hesitated a moment, then said, "Well, let's take a look. I'll let you know right quick if it's the same trailer."

Hartsel led the way down one of the back streets of the trailer display, keeping up a running fire of conversation. "Keep my jobs that are on consignment in the back part here. Of course, we try to sell them, but usually the profit isn't quite as good as on the ones we own outright, and, of course, when it's a question of bringing in money and getting a turnover I like to turn over my own capital. By the time you come to the section where the trailers are on consignment you have walked past some mighty inviting trailers. I don't know whether you folks are in the market. You should have a trailer for getting away, Mr. Mason. I suppose that wherever you go you're pestered with people who want to talk about their problems and your cases. Now here's a twenty-five foot job that would tow along behind your car like a whisper. You'd hardly know you had it. Light as a feather and yet it's strong and sturdy — insulated with Fiberglass so that you can park it right out in the burning sunlight on the desert with the inside as cool as a cucumber, just as though you were inside an adobe house. Want to take a look at it?"

"Not today."

"Well, don't mind me," Hartsel told him. "I always have to make a pitch. I'm not really trying to sell you a trailer, I'm just keeping my line in shape. Well, here we are. Here's the Heliar."

"Locked?" Mason asked.

"Oh, certainly. We always keep our consigned trailers locked. In fact, we lock all of them except the ones that are on display."

"I'll open it," Arlene Duvall said, taking a key from her pocket.

Hartsel, who had produced a key, promptly stepped back and waited for Arlene to fit the key in the lock.

She turned the latch and the door swung open.

Making no attempt to conceal her anxiety, Arlene jumped up and into the interior of the trailer.

Mason took Della Street's elbow and assisted her up the step, then climbed in. Hartsel brought up the rear.

"This is it," Arlene said.

"Well, let's just take a look," Hartsel said.

He located a metal plate back of the door, rubbed his finger along the plate to bring out the number and compared it with the number in the notebook.

"Sure seems to be it," he conceded.

He opened a closet door, peered inside with a flashlight and checked another piece of metal.

"This is it. Same number anyway."

"Aside from the number," Mason asked Arlene Duvall, "are there any other identifying features?"

She said, "In that compartment, the little built-in vanity case by the side of the bed, the one with the mirror on it, I spilled a bottle of ink. I never did get the stain entirely removed."

Hartsel lifted the mirrored, hinged cover, said, "Okay, sister, you win. Here it is. Anyone else want to take a look?"

Mason and Della Street stepped forward and looked.

"When was it taken?" Hartsel asked.

"This morning."

"Well, they sure worked fast. It's cleaned out slick as a whistle."

Arlene Duvall nodded.

"So what are you going to do?" Hartsel asked. "I don't want to hang on to it, but I just don't want to turn it over to you. I suppose, of course, you've notified the police?"

She shook her head.

"Well, you'd better."

"Why?" Mason asked coldly.

Hartsel sized him up. "Well," he said, "suppose this man Prim comes back here and asks me where his trailer is and I tell him that I've delivered it to Miss Duvall because it was a stolen trailer. Then suppose he gets rough about it."

"He won't."

"But suppose he does."

"Well," Mason said, "*you* know it's Miss Duvall's trailer."

"I know it's the trailer I sold her, that is, it

has the same numbers on it and there's nothing to indicate the plates have been tampered with in any way, but suppose he says he bought it from her. You see the position I'm in. If he shows up and makes a squawk and I say, 'Let's call the cops' and reach for the telephone, then I'm in one sort of a position, but if I just have to sit there and twiddle my thumbs I'm in another position and that's a position I don't like."

"However," Mason said, "suppose that I, as Miss Duvall's lawyer, tell you that you are keeping stolen property in your possession. Then what?"

"Wouldn't bother me at all," Hartsel said. "Not in the least. I'd tell you to go to court and start rolling your hoop. Bring a suit in replevin, or whatever you want."

"Together with damages for its detainer."

"Oh sure. You'd ask for damages," Hartsel said, "but all I'm asking is that you call the cops. That's the reasonable thing to do. I'd tell that to a judge or a jury and that'd be all there was to your lawsuit for damages. It'd go out the window. That's all I'm asking you to do. If the trailer has been stolen let's notify the police."

"Miss Duvall doesn't want the notoriety."

"Phooey! There wouldn't be any."

"There might," Mason said.

"Why?" Hartsel asked, suddenly suspicious.

"Because when the trailer was stolen," Mason said, grinning, "Miss Duvall was engaged in sun-bathing. That's how it happened the persons who took the trailer were able to drive off with her car and the trailer."

"Car too?" Hartsel asked.

Mason nodded.

"Then it *sure* is a case for the police," Hartsel said.

"And the newspapers," Mason pointed out.

"That's her hard luck, not mine."

"All right," Mason said, "let's forget that the trailer was stolen."

"And do what?" Hartsel asked.

"I'll buy it," Mason said. "What's the price on it?"

"The price he wanted was twenty-eight ninety-five," Hartsel said. "I offered him two thousand. I'd have put it on sale at twenty-four hundred and turned it within thirty days. Twenty-eight ninety-five is just a little high. Perhaps if you care to make an offer I'll —"

"No offer," Mason said. "I'll buy it at his price. Twenty-eight ninety-five. Give him a ring and tell him to come on down with his registration slip and we'll close the transaction."

"Now wait a minute," Hartsel said. "That doesn't make sense. If he's stolen the trailer —"

"When he comes down here," Mason said, "if he comes down here, I'll put him under arrest as a citizen and *then* we'll call the cops."

"Now that *does* make sense," Hartsel said. "Come on. We'll go to the office and give him a ring."

They stepped out of the trailer. Arlene Duvall locked it and they started back toward the office.

After they had gone some fifteen or twenty steps Della Street, who had been watching Arlene Duvall, said quietly, "Didn't you have a purse, Miss Duvall?"

"Oh, good heavens," Arlene said. "Of course. I put it on the bed in the trailer while we were looking at the interior of that vanity case for the ink stains. I'll get it."

She whirled and ran to the trailer. Hartsel looked after her admiringly.

"Now there's a girl who really runs," he said. "Knees together, elbows close to the side, holds up her skirts so she has plenty of knee action, and really covers the ground. She runs like a deer. Wonder if she's ever had any athletic training."

"Probably a natural athlete," Della Street said, watching Arlene Duvall fit the key to the door.

"Well," Mason said, "we'll go on to the office and you can call Prim."

Hartsel waited for a moment, slowly turned back toward the office, walked a few steps, then abruptly stopped. "I should be sure that she locks the thing up," he said. "As long as it's in my possession I have a responsibility and . . . well, we'll just wait, if you don't mind."

They waited.

Mason lit a cigarette.

"Well, it's taking her a time to find that purse," Hartsel said.

"Probably it wasn't on the bed," Della Street said. "She may have left it in one of the closets and —"

Abruptly Hartsel started walking toward the trailer with long purposeful strides that made Mason and Della Street hurry to keep up.

They had almost reached the trailer when Arlene Duvall jerked open the door and came out.

"Thought we'd lost you as well as the purse," Hartsel said, unsmilingly.

Her slate-colored eyes regarded him with disarming candor.

"Oh, for heaven's sakes, I had no idea I was holding up the procession. Did you ever know a girl who could pass up a mirror? When I got one look at my face I made a dive for my compact. I'm afraid I've been traveling too fast this afternoon to pay much attention to personal appearance."

Hartsel, suddenly reassured, grinned and said, "You have something there. You'd be surprised at how many women inspecting a trailer look over the kitchen facilities, then pause in front of one of the full-length mirrors, look themselves over, pull out a compact and go to work. Okay, let's lock the door. Well, just to be on the safe side, suppose *I* lock it with *my* key."

He locked the trailer door.

"That, I take it," Mason said, "is the key you got from Prim?"

"Sure, he left the key with the trailer. Why?"

"Oh nothing," Mason said, "I was just wondering."

"Say, wait a minute," Hartsel said. "You have a point there. If he'd stolen the trailer how did it happen he had a key for it?"

"He had to have a key to get in. I'd left it locked," Arlene Duvall pointed out.

"Well, where did *he* get his key?"

"Perhaps one trailer key will unlock all the other models of the same make," Della Street suggested.

"Not with the Heliar," Hartsel said. "That's a pretty classy job. They pay a lot of attention to that job. It's one of our best-made trailers on the market."

"Well," Mason said, "he undoubtedly had a key since he gave you one, and since it works, suppose we ask *him* where he got it?"

"Yes," Hartsel said, "I think that's next in order. Let's go telephone."

They returned to the office. Hartsel consulted the card, picked up the telephone, dialed the number, then, after a moment, said, "Hello. May I speak with Mr. Prim, please. This is Mr. Hartsel at the Ideal Trade-In Trailer Mart."

They heard squawking sounds on the telephone, then Hartsel said, "But he left this number. Doesn't he stay there? . . . Howard

Prim. Don't you know him? . . . Okay, okay, I'm sorry."

Hartsel dropped the telephone back into place and said, "Well, there's no need for them to get sore about it. It's a private residence. They say that's the second call they've had this afternoon both from people asking for Howard Prim. They've never heard of him."

"Any chance you got the number wrong?" Mason asked.

"No chance that *I* got the wrong number. *He* may have had it wrong. Here's the card with the number he wrote down. That's in his own writing, together with the address."

"Did you," Mason asked, "check the street?"

"You mean the address?"

"No, just the street," Mason said. "I don't think there is any such number on that street. As I remember it, it's a short street and —"

Hartsel took out a map of the city, checked on the street and the numbers, then consulted the alphabetical index of streets, folded the map and said to Mason, "Okay, you win. I want a receipt for the trailer and a statement that you're assuming the responsibility for delivering it to your client. I'll take your assurance that it's stolen. Your credit's good. I want a written statement, however, signed by you as part of the receipt."

"Draw it up," Mason told him. "I'll sign it."

"When are you going to take the trailer?"

"Right now," Arlene Duvall said.

"But what about a car? You say yours was stolen."

"I have a car," she said.

"With a trailer hitch?"

"With a trailer hitch. It's all ready to go."

"Okay," Hartsel yielded. "I prefer to have you call the cops on this, but if you don't want to it's okay, only I'm going to make that receipt plenty tight so it'll protect me."

Mason said, "If you confine your statements in the receipt to the fact that you are delivering the trailer to Arlene Duvall on the strength of my assurance that the trailer was stolen from her and that she is the true owner, and include in there a statement that you have checked the number of the trailer with the number of the trailer you previously sold Miss Duvall, I'll sign it."

"Fair enough," Hartsel said, and started writing.

Hartsel placed a sheet of paper on the desk, wrote a few lines, hesitated, wrote some more, then finally sent his pen dashing over the paper.

He handed the document to Mason.

"You're a lawyer. Let's see if you'll sign *that.* I have always been given to understand a lawyer will never sign anything the way it's written."

Mason whipped out his fountain pen and said, "I'll sign it without reading it."

Hartsel looked at him in amazement.

"Chief," Della Street said in a low voice, "you haven't even read it?"

"I've signed it," Mason said. "Now then, Della, will you please copy this in a notebook. I'm willing to sign anything but I want to have a copy of what I've signed."

Mason held the document so that Della Street could see it as she took shorthand notes; then Mason casually tossed the document over to Hartsel.

"All right, Miss Duvall," Mason said. "Go hook onto the trailer."

"On my way," she said.

Hartsel slowly got up from his desk. He shook his head. "I can't get over it," he said. "A lawyer signing something without even reading it. I thought you tell your clients never to do that."

"We do," Mason said.

Arlene Duvall hurried down the steps from the office. Hartsel went to the door and called to one of the assistants, "Help Miss Duvall hook on that Heliar trailer, Joe."

"She bought it?" the man asked.

Hartsel grinned. "Twice," he said and went back into the office. "Signed it without reading it," he muttered under his breath incredulously.

"Well, if it makes you feel any better," Mason said, "I can tell you a point of law that may come in handy sometime."

"What?" Hartsel asked.

"A document," Mason said, "in order to constitute an agreement has to be signed, sealed and delivered. In this state the signature imports a seal, but a document is valueless unless it's delivered."

"Well?" Hartsel asked.

"And while I didn't read it *before* I signed it, I read it after I'd signed it, while I was holding it for Miss Street to copy."

"And you mean that if there had been something in there that you couldn't go for you'd have refused to deliver it?"

"Exactly. I'd have torn it up," Mason said.

Hartsel grinned. "Now I feel better. You jarred me when you signed it without reading it. I didn't think you'd sign it the way I'd put that guarantee in there."

"And if I'd quibbled with you about it," Mason said, "you wouldn't have delivered the trailer."

"You're right on that," Hartsel admitted, smiling. "I guess you'd have made a darn good trailer salesman, Mr. Mason."

He got up and extended his hand.

"This time," Mason said, "let's both be reasonable and use half as much pressure as we did the first time."

"You set the pace," Hartsel said.

The two men shook hands.

Mason and Della Street walked back to the lot where Arlene Duvall, backing her car with the skill of one who has had a great deal of trailer experience, centered the ball right under the socket on the trailer hitch. The mechanic dropped the trailer into position, adjusted the chain with the locked link, and said, "The socket on the direction lights, stop lights and electric brakes won't fit, Miss —"

"I have a Heliar socket here," she said, opening the glove compartment. "Put it on the wiring on the car."

"Well," the mechanic said, surprised, "you sure thought of everything, didn't you?"

"You'd be surprised," Arlene Duvall told him.

"I am," the man announced dryly.

While the mechanic was scraping the ends of the wire to make the connection Mason walked over to his client.

"Any plans?" he asked.

"Yes," she said. "I want you to handle my affairs, and Dad's. I think you're making a swell start. Go ahead from here."

"You may not care for my methods when you've seen more of me."

"Why?"

"I serve justice."

"I like what I've seen so far."

"Suppose your dad really was guilty?"

"He wasn't."

"You want me to unscramble that case?"

"Definitely."

"You're taking the trailer with you now?"

"Definitely."

"It has just occurred to me," Mason said, "that you are rushing out with a trailer that has been stripped. There's no bedding, no pillowcases, no sheets, no towels, no soap, no provisions."

"How right you are."

"And yet you intend to start out in it?"

"At once."

"And spend the night in it?"

She nodded.

"And when do I see you?"

"Tomorrow morning at nine-thirty, when I bring you your retainer. And thank you very much."

Mason said, "If I'm going to represent you I'll need a lot of information."

"From me?"

"You and others. I'll have to hire detectives."

"Go ahead. Hire them."

"It may run into quite a bill."

She met his eyes. "Let's get one thing straight, Mr. Mason. If you can help my dad, I'll authorize you to take any steps that may be necessary."

"That's all right, but the expense —"

"Did I say anything about expense."

"No. I'm the one who's talking about expense."

"Well quit talking about it. Do what you have to."

"I'm retaining the Drake Detective Agency. Paul Drake does my work. It was through him we located the trailer."

"Fine. Hire as many people as you need."

"And what's the limit?"

She said slowly, purposefully, "There isn't any."

Abruptly she extended a lean, browned hand, gripped Mason's hand. "There's no need for you to wait."

"This is rather an unsatisfactory point at which to terminate our conversation."

"For you, perhaps, but not for me. Go ahead. Do what has to be done."

Mason, somewhat angrily, said, "Remember what I told you. There's a big reward out on that money. If you try to cut corners with me I'm going to make my fee out of the reward."

"I have an idea you'd do it, too."

"I would."

The mechanic said, "All ready, miss."

She smiled at the lawyer. " 'Bye now. See you tomorrow."

• 4 •

It was a little before nine when Mason and Della Street entered Drake's office.

Paul Drake sniffed and said, "I detect the well-fed aroma that exudes from your satisfied faces."

Mason lit a cigarette. "It's a great world, Paul."

"It is for you," Drake said, snapping open a box and dropping a pill of bicarbonate of soda in his palm. He walked across to the water cooler, trickled water into a paper cup, took the soda pill.

"That bad?" Mason asked.

"It's catching up with me," Drake said. "Sitting here on the end of a telephone, running men out on jobs, supervising them, chaperoning them, correcting their mistakes, doing their thinking for them, correlating their reports, arguing with clients, running down to hole-in-the-wall restaurants, grabbing greasy fried food, gulping it down, hurrying back and trying to find out what's been happening during the few minutes I've been gone."

"You're working too hard, Paul."

"You said it."

"What's new with our little sun bather?"

"She's driving a car furnished by a rental agency. She hooked onto her trailer and went to one of the big marts where they have parking space and all sorts of things, a regular drive-in department store so to speak."

"Your men didn't have any trouble following her?"

"Hell," Drake said, "we were in a procession."

"Others?"

Drake nodded.

"What happened?" Mason asked.

"Well, your little friend bought blankets, sheets, pillowcases, tablecloths, silverware, towels, soap, provisions. Boy, she sure went on a shopping spree and she did it fast. You'd have thought she'd rehearsed the whole procedure or else had done it so many times before it was a habit."

"Did she have a shopping list?" Mason asked.

"Not a sign of a list. She went through those departments like a whirlwind through a pile of autumn leaves. She had clerks scurrying around putting stuff in cartons, trotting out to the trailer like those pictures of African natives on a safari."

Mason glanced at Della Street. "Did she pay for that stuff or have it charged, Paul?"

"She paid for it."

"What with? Check or — ?"

"Cold, hard cash."

"Did she seem to have plenty?"

"She was just like Santa Claus. She scattered money around like green confetti. She never asked about price — she just pointed. This and this and this and this and some of that and a dozen of those and what's your best grade of so-and-so."

Mason frowned.

"So," Drake said, "she had the trailer all provisioned. I bet it took her hours to put the stuff away. Boy, she sure was all fixed up. Virgin wool blankets, down-filled quilts, dishes, silverware, cups, saucers, coffee pots, finest quality frying pans, double boilers, a whole supply of canned goods — everything."

"And then what?"

"And then she drove away," Drake said, "and two of my men tagged along. A third one stayed behind."

"Stayed behind where?"

"At the mart."

"Why?"

"Because he had a hunch."

"About what?"

"When your little sun-bathing friend drove away she didn't have all of the procession with her. Part of the procession stayed behind, so one of my operatives played it smart and stayed behind too."

"And what did he find?"

"He found men moving around talking with the cashiers, taking leather folders out of their hip pockets, opening them so the cashier could see the badges and the credentials, and then the cashier would go in to the till and bring out the little green confetti that your client had been scattering around, and the busy little men would produce billfolds and give the cashiers other bills in place of the ones Arlene Duvall had given them. Then they'd put Arlene's bills in their pockets and walk out."

"And what about the men who were shadowing Arlene? Did they have any trouble?"

"Not in the least. Arlene went down to a side road that winds around the back of the Remuda Golf Club, then she turned off on a dirt road, then she swung in on an all but deserted road that goes in back of the golf club, the same road that I scouted earlier in the day, the one where I found the jeep tracks."

"And what did she do there?"

"Parked the trailer, made herself at home. Lit a gasoline lantern, hung it on a hook in the trailer, cheerfully started in making beds, putting food away, getting everything all shipshape."

"And your men stayed there to watch her?"

"Well, not right there, Perry. They're back out on the highway. There's no way on earth she can get out of there with the trailer except by turning around and coming back out of that service road. My men's instructions are to keep the trailer under surveillance. They phone in reports every hour."

"And what about the procession?" Mason asked.

"Only one other man in sight. He's parked

down the road a ways from my men. There were three men in that car. One of the men is in the car at the wheel, waiting and watching to see that the trailer doesn't come out. The other two men disappeared in the brush some place, presumably staked out where they can keep an eye on the door of the trailer so that every time cutie comes out they can follow and see where she goes and what she's doing."

"Not much opportunity for privacy," Mason said.

"Hardly any," Drake observed dryly. "Evidently they feel the situation is coming to a head, Perry. There's an air of great tension as though every one of them is just waiting for something to happen — all except your client. She's as serene as a house finch sitting on a new batch of eggs."

"Do these other men know that your operatives are on the job, Paul?"

"Oh, sure. No chance to keep under cover on a job like that. My men got the license number of their car and they got theirs."

"What car is it?"

"It's an unlisted license. You know what that means."

Mason narrowed his eyes in thoughtful concentration.

"What did you find out about the Mercantile Security job?" Mason asked.

"Have a heart," Drake told him. "We've just got a good start on that."

"I know, but I want to keep abreast of the situation."

"Ever hear of Jordan L. Ballard?" Drake asked.

"Who's he, Paul?"

"He was the bank employee who was working with Duvall at the time the money disappeared."

"What about him?"

"It was his duty to inspect that outgoing cash shipment. At the time he'd made a bet on a horse race and he was paying a lot more attention to the broadcast over a small portable radio than he was to what Duvall was doing."

"But," Mason said, "even so, Paul, he couldn't have got away with the money because he wasn't in a position to touch it. Duvall was packing the money and —"

"That's right," Drake interrupted, "but it seems Ballard lost his job because he'd been negligent. The bank officials didn't think he was in on the deal although they couldn't be sure, but they fired him on general principles — and, of course, under the circumstances Ballard couldn't get another job anywhere in the banking business."

"What became of him, Paul?"

"Well, as it turned out, it was the best thing that ever happened to Ballard. He was kicked around for a while and I guess he got pretty hungry. Finally he got a job in a service station. He saved some money. The owner of the service station got sick; Ballard bought him out. Then Ballard borrowed money, branched out and put in a big line of tires and accessories. After that he had an opportunity to buy the corner where the service station was located. He paid a few thousand dollars down and agreed to pay a thousand dollars a month. Then one of the big department stores, looking for an outlying branch, picked on that locality and now Ballard is still working, but apparently he doesn't have to."

"Where is he?" Mason asked.

"He runs a super service station at Tenth and Flossman."

Mason made a note of the address. "What else, Paul?"

"Well, you probably know about it. Five thousand dollars of the stolen money was in numbered bills."

Mason nodded.

"That was just a coincidence. It seems the police were working on a blackmailing deal at the time and —"

"Yes, yes, I know," Mason said.

Drake looked at him and said, "You seem to know quite a bit about it."

"Just the general facts," Mason said.

"Well, of course, the way the police figure it, Duvall was in quite a predicament. He got away with nearly four hundred thousand dollars. Five thousand dollars of those bills were ones on which the police had the numbers.

Duvall doesn't know which of the stolen bills are listed with the police."

Mason said, "Five out of four hundred. In other words, if he put his hand in the pile of cash and took out a bill there'd be one chance in eighty that he'd get hold of a bill of which the police had the number."

Drake nodded.

"And," Mason said, "if that was spent in the ordinary course of business the chances are about one in a hundred that it would turn up in the hands of the police. Therefore there's only about one chance in eight thousand that —"

"Your figures are wrong," Drake interposed. "The police make spot checks. They'll go for two or three months without making a move, letting Arlene Duvall spend money. Then when they have her lulled into a false sense of security the police will suddenly put on a bunch of men, just like they're doing tonight, and check every bill that is spent."

"They think the daughter has the money?"

"Sure," Drake said. "How else does she live without working? How does she buy cars, trailers, pay cash for everything?"

"How about the income tax?" Mason asked. "Haven't they tried to reach her through the income-tax people?"

"Of course they have, but they can't get to first base."

"Why not?"

"Because," Drake said, "there's something in

the background, Perry. The income-tax people simply state that her affairs are in order and let it go at that."

"That's strange," Mason said.

Drake nodded.

"Now there's one other thing," Drake went on, "that you should know. The police, of course, aren't releasing any information, but the story is that the fellow who made the demand for the blackmail money wanted five thousand dollars in tens and twenties — and that stands to reason. Even if there wasn't that kind of a rumor out you'd figure that was what would have happened."

"Yes, that sounds reasonable," Mason said.

"Now the big bulk of money that was in the shipment that was taken from the Mercantile Security was in hundred-dollar bills. Also, there were a hundred thousand-dollar bills. The rest of it was mostly in five hundreds and fifties and very few small bills. So, looking at it one way, if Arlene Duvall is smart she can spend the larger bills and be reasonably safe."

Mason's eyes were cold. "You keep insisting it's Arlene."

Drake grinned. "Be your age, Perry. Incidentally, Perry, a messenger boy brought in an envelope for you a short time ago."

"For me?"

"That's right. He said it was something you were to have before morning."

"How did he happen to bring it here?"

"He didn't say. He — It's around here somewhere, just a typewritten envelope . . . oh yes, here it is."

Mason took the envelope from Drake, a plain stamped envelope.

Mason regarded the typewritten address. "Evidently intended to mail this to me and then sent it up here instead. Well, we'll see what it is. Probably some more grief."

Mason took out his penknife, opened the blade and slit open the edge of the envelope.

Drake's phone rang and Drake picked up the receiver, said, "Hello, yes. . . . Hey, wait a minute. Give me that again. . . ."

Drake motioned warningly to Mason.

Mason glanced at the contents of the envelope, then turned his back to Paul Drake, motioned to Della Street, and extracted from the envelope two pieces of currency, one a five-hundred-dollar bill, the other a thousand-dollar bill.

There was a typewritten note in the envelope. Della Street moved over to read it as Perry Mason held it.

The note read:

> I promised you'd have this by nine-thirty. I may not be able to get to your office tomorrow so I'm sending it now.

The note was signed on the typewriter simply with an initial, a capital "A."

Mason glanced at Della Street, placed a warning finger to his lips, put the bills and note back into the envelope, slipped the envelope into his inside coat pocket and turned back to Paul Drake.

Drake hung up the telephone as Mason turned and said, "Now here's something, Perry. Ballard, the man I was telling you about, has been in touch with the police. He gave them some information this morning that seems to have triggered this whole flurry of activity."

"What was the information, Paul?" Mason asked.

"My contact can't find out, but he knows that it started the bank detail going around in circles. He thinks it was something damned important. And here's the point, Perry — Ballard may be down at his service station right now. It seems he drops in about this time every night to check the day's cash, close up the cash register and leave just enough money for the station to keep on operating through the night."

Mason said thoughtfully, "It would be swell if I knew what he'd told the police." He glanced at Della Street, said abruptly, "Come on, Della. I'm going to drive you to your apartment."

He turned to Paul Drake, "Stay on the job until midnight if you can, Paul. I wouldn't be surprised if we had more developments within the next few hours."

Mason drove Della Street to her apartment. "See you in the morning, Della."

"Chief, if you're going to see Ballard and learn anything, let me know, will you?"

"Not tonight. You'd better roll in and get some sleep."

"Meanie! I want to know — and don't go carting all that cash around with you. You'd better let me keep it."

"Not a chance," he told her. "This case has me worried. I never thought I'd get concerned over the mere fact that a client actually paid a retainer fee when she said she would."

"It's the way she does things, Chief. Those big bills! It seems she's trying to jockey you into some sort of a trap."

"Darned if it doesn't," Mason admitted.

"Let me keep them."

"Then you'd be in the trap. No, I'll handle this end of the deal. You get some sleep, Della."

She waved good night from the door of the apartment house and Mason drove to Tenth and Flossman, pulled in to the station in front of one of the gas pumps, said to the attendant, "Fill her up. Is Ballard around tonight?"

The attendant indicated a man who was in at the desk checking a roll of adding-machine paper on which there was a list of figures.

Mason walked in, waited until the man looked up, and said, "Mr. Ballard?"

"That's right."

"I'm Perry Mason."

"The lawyer?"

"That's right."

"I've heard a lot about you. Sure glad to meet you. What brings you out here?"

"I was interested in finding out a few facts concerning a matter you probably don't care to talk about."

"You mean that Mercantile Security job?"

"That's right."

"I'm not embarrassed about that — not any more. They gave me a raw deal, but it sure turned out to be a blessing in disguise. The only thing is that I can't see where it's any of your business."

"A lawyer has lots of business."

"I suppose so."

"May I ask you a couple of questions about it?"

"Why?"

"Certain information might make a lot of difference to a client of mine."

"Then I'd have to know who the client was."

"You know I can't tell you that. Now look, how about that bet you made? Were you in the habit of playing the horses?"

"Depends on what you'd call a habit."

"But this occasion was unusual?"

"I'll say it was! I had a hot tip and I cleaned up."

"Your horse won, eh?"

"I'll say he won! Paid off twenty-two seventy-five on a two-dollar bet, and I had a hundred bucks right on his nose."

"Well, that's something," Mason said.

"I won the bet," Ballard went on. "And it cost me my job. For a while I thought I was all finished, but I worked out of it all right. Now I'm fairly well fixed. If I'd kept on at the bank I'd have still been in the same old treadmill."

"I'd like to talk with you about what happened that day," Mason said.

"Why?"

"Well, I'd like to get the picture in my own mind."

"It isn't much of a picture. Look up the old newspapers and you'll have the whole story — that is, almost all of the story."

Mason jerked his thumb toward the gasoline pump and said, "I'm having my car filled up. Are we in any hurry?"

"No," Ballard said, sizing up Mason and pushing back a paper on which he had been copying figures.

The man stood up and Mason saw that he was rather short-legged, although he had broad shoulders and a good head. He was perhaps fifty-five years old, with steady gray eyes and bushy eyebrows. His hair was shot with gray, and there was about him the incisive air of one who is accustomed to dealing in figures, where a result is either right or it's wrong, where there is no such thing as an approximation but only an answer.

Mason, lowering his eyes to the pad of paper on which the figures were written, noted that each figure had been written with copperplate accuracy.

"I'm just getting ready to close up," Ballard said. "I try to take cash by ten o'clock every night. I leave just enough money for the boys to use in making change. The stick-ups take place around midnight. I don't leave anything for the stick-up artists to work on. When that information gets around they don't bother us so much."

"I see. Want to tell me about the Mercantile Security?"

"I'd have to know a bit about why you wanted the information."

"I want to find out who really was guilty."

"You don't think it was Duvall?"

"The law thinks so."

"But you don't?"

"I haven't anything to think on as yet — I'm trying to keep my mind open."

"I see."

"Perhaps if we didn't talk about the money we could talk about Duvall. What sort of a chap was he?"

"There's a question."

"Where's the answer?"

"There isn't any."

"Why?"

"You can't classify him. You can't label the guy."

"Could you try?"

"Well, he was a quiet, cheerful sort of a chap. He had a lot of friends and he was all wrapped up in his daughter. His wife had died when the girl was ten years old, and Colton Duvall had made a career out of raising the girl, being both a father and mother. And if you ask me, that's an impossible job."

"Didn't turn out so well?" Mason asked.

"That depends on what you mean by well. Duvall had ideas. He thought people could never be thoroughly at ease unless they were really natural. He thought that all of the conventional gambits of politeness and etiquette were a species of hypocrisy."

"Why?" Mason asked.

"He said that people should be thoroughly natural and their conduct would then reflect their personalities instead of conforming to some ritual or convention that had been laid down in a book."

"A little cracked?" Mason asked.

"Not cracked. The guy was plausible as could be. Listening to him you'd find yourself nodding your head when you should have been telling him straight out that that was no way to raise a daughter."

"Did the daughter like him?"

"Worshiped the ground he walked on."

"What about the money? Did Duvall get it?"

"I don't see how he could have. When you come right down to it I don't see how anyone could have."

"Mind telling me why?"

"Because of the various factors, all the checks and precautions. It was just an impossibility."

"Yet it happened?"

"That's what they say."

"Duvall couldn't have done it?"

"No one could have done it. It was like watching a magician on the stage. He does things that couldn't possibly happen, yet you sit there and see them happening."

"Perhaps if you'd tell me what did happen I might suggest a solution," Mason ventured.

Ballard hesitated, then said, "It was about two o'clock in the afternoon. In those days there was a big Government payroll at Santa Ana, and we had to ship enormous quantities of cash to take care of it. They had an aviation center there and a huge personnel. Also our Santa Ana branch did quite a business. We'd be moving cash back and forth two or three times a month.

"Well, the way we moved cash was foolproof. We had specially built trucks with the cash compartment separate. Only the supervisors and checkers had keys to the cash compartment. The driver of the car didn't have a key. That was worked out so in case someone should stick up the driver along the road, they still couldn't get into the cash compartment. There was also a short-wave radio on the car that people didn't know about. It was tuned in on police signals and if anyone tried to stop the car en route the driver only needed to press a button and it would start a phonograph recording playing over the police network giving the number of the car and stating that it was in trouble. Then all the police had to do was call the dispatcher's office, give them the number of the car and the dispatcher would be able to tell police where the car was headed and about where it would be."

"Go on," Mason said.

"The way we'd ship cash," Ballard continued, "was to have the cash shipping clerk make up the cash shipment while a checker watched him. Prior to that time the bank would have telephoned for one of the armored cars. The car would pull in at the curb. By that time the shipment man and the checker would have put the cash in a box which was wrapped in special paper, and sealed with red wax. The cash shipment man would put *his* seal on, and the checker would put on *his* seal. Then the two of them would take the cash out and put it in the armored car after two armed guards had made certain it was safe to bring out the cash.

"Well, after a while, after you've shipped so many millions of dollars you get so you handle that stuff just like you'd handle a shipment of carrots or any other merchandise you were handling."

Mason grinned appreciatively.

"Well, I had my bet on the race that afternoon and, as luck would have it, Duvall was loading that big shipment of cash just as the race came on. Well, what would you have done, Mr. Mason? I was working on a small salary and I had a hundred dollars on that horse's nose. I knew that if he won I'd clean up. You take a man working on a small salary, with costs going up all the time, and a hundred dollars is pretty hard to lose. On the other hand, give him a thousand dollars extra and that's *really* something. That race meant a lot to me."

Mason nodded.

"I stepped back into the glass-enclosed office. I could still watch Duvall, and I swear, Mr. Mason, he was picking up the packages of money all right, checking them and dropping them into the box. We'd already counted the money into packages. The only way I can figure it out is that he must have had a file of canceled checks that he'd previously collected from the nearest filing drawer. Then he picked up the money and moved it over to the box. He kept his body between me and the wastebasket that was down underneath the counter. He must have dropped the money into the wastebasket and put the canceled checks in the box.

"But I'll tell you one thing, Mr. Mason, he certainly fooled me. It was the slickest job I've ever seen. It was done casually and naturally. Of course, I was listening to the race and when they began to come around the stretch I was plenty excited. It was a photo finish and I had to wait a little while to be sure my nag had won. I lived a thousand years while I was waiting for the results of that race to be confirmed, and when it finally turned out I had won I was quivering all over, and just as wet with sweat as though I'd been out doing hard work."

Mason nodded sympathetically.

"Well, Duvall, of course, knew what I was doing, but he didn't say anything and I didn't either. He was covering for me and I was grateful. I had no reason to be suspicious. I'd been working with Duvall for five years. During that time we'd shipped Lord knows how many million dollars in currency. So I just put my seal on the package and Duvall and I went out and loaded it in the wagon. I used my key to open the cash compartment, we shoved the box in, made note of the time the car started off and notified the dispatcher. Then we went back to our work. I couldn't concentrate much the rest of the afternoon. I was spending that money I'd won on the horse race. I wanted a new fishing rod and one of those spinning reels. I'd been planning on a vacation. I used to be a great fisherman."

"Still fish?" Mason asked.

"Don't have the time. I certainly would love to. When you get to working for yourself it's pretty tough."

Mason said, "I see my car is ready. I'll go out and pay up and move it away from the pumps."

"Which way you going?" Ballard asked.

"Out toward Beverly Hills."

"Say, look, could I grab a ride with you? My car's laid up and I was figuring on a taxi. It's pretty late and I'm carrying a fair amount of cash with me, so I don't like to walk the four blocks down to the bus line or the five blocks from the bus line home, and —"

"Sure thing," Mason interposed. "Come on, get in."

Ballard hurriedly stuffed the pad of figures, the roll of adding-machine tape and a canvas bag in a small black satchel. He took a snub-nosed revolver out of the satchel, put it in his coat pocket and jumped into Mason's car.

"Hope I don't frighten you, Mason, but there have been a lot of service station holdups, so the police suggested I'd better keep this thing with me at all times, and if —"

"Sure, I understand," Mason said, easing the car out into traffic.

"Seems as though a lot of these young punks don't want to work," Ballard went on. "They've been raised in the school of getting something for nothing, and they sure are a trigger-happy lot. I never had any kids — the wife died soon after this bank business. It seemed like bad luck hit me all at once — and hard."

"Anything else about Duvall?" Mason asked after a few minutes.

"You know it all now," Ballard told him. "When the clerk in Santa Ana opened the package all that was in there was canceled checks."

"Or so he said," Mason observed.

"Well, he said that's what was in it, and he was right.

"There's one thing that clinches the case. The canceled checks that had been substituted for the money came out of files in our Los Angeles bank. Some of those canceled checks were ones the clerks had put in the files within an hour of the time the shipment went out. So that showed what had happened."

Mason digested that information. "Well, Ballard," he said after several minutes, "that would seem to put the responsibility quite definitely between you on the one hand and Duvall on the other."

"That's right," Ballard admitted. "That's the way the police figured it."

Again they rode in silence. At length Ballard said, "Of course, if *I* had taken the money out, Duvall would necessarily have been my accomplice. It would have been a two-man job. We'd have split it. But if Duvall had taken the money out I could have been negligent. There's no dispute that Duvall was the one who had the responsibility of putting the money *in* the package. He said he did put the money *in the package*."

"And it was your duty to watch him do it."

"That's right."

"And if you had neglected that duty Duvall could have got away with the money."

"I did and he did."

"Well, in any event, he could have."

"That's right."

"But if you had arranged for the theft Duvall

must necessarily have been in on it?"

"That's right."

"How about a switch?" Mason asked. "How about switching packages?"

Ballard shook his head. "No chance. It had to be either Duvall or me, and it couldn't have been me unless Duvall was in on it."

"Why do you say there was no chance of switching packages?"

"Because the driver never stopped the car from the time he left our bank until he got to the branch bank at Santa Ana, because even if he had stopped he couldn't have got at the money compartment."

"Suppose he had a key?"

"He didn't have one."

"But suppose he had had one? Suppose he'd been able to get a key and —"

"All right, I'll answer that one," Ballard said. "Suppose he'd stopped the car. Suppose he had a key. Suppose he had packages all ready to switch. He still couldn't have done it."

"Why not?"

"Because if he'd substituted newspapers or books or anything of that sort he might have been able to make the switch, but remember that the box was filled with canceled checks that had been taken from a file *inside* our bank. The drivers never get inside the bank."

"That driver couldn't have come inside?"

"Impossible. Nobody comes in through that side door. That's a shipment door."

"And the checks couldn't have been prepared in advance?"

"No, they were checks that had been cashed and were filed within an hour of the time the shipment was made."

Mason said, "That makes it look like Duvall, doesn't it?"

"It had to have been Duvall. And then, of course, they caught Duvall with some of the stolen money in his possession."

Mason said, "I understand they have the numbers of five thousand dollars in bills."

"That's right."

"Who has those numbers?"

"That list of numbers," Ballard said, "is one of the most confidential pieces of information in the entire case. The FBI has the list. That list is guarded so closely that there's no opportunity to find out anything about it. Even the most trusted police officers don't know it. If they run on to money they think is suspicious they're instructed to buy up that money right on the spot. They bring the bills in, the numbers are copied from the bills and put on a confidential sheet which goes to the chief of police, and the FBI. They make their comparisons."

"But they did find some of that money?"

"They don't take me into their confidence. You can give them information but they don't give out any."

"You have given them some?" Mason asked.

Ballard said, "Look, Mason, you're a square

shooter. I'm going to let you in on a secret. There were some thousand-dollar bills in that shipment. The police now have the number of one of those thousand-dollar bills."

"How come?" Mason asked.

"Because I happened to remember it. When the thousand-dollar bills came out of the vault for shipment they were in a package. Remember that I had bet on a horse race. I was looking for omens, wondering if I was going to be lucky. The race was due to start in a few minutes. I picked up one of the stacks of thousand-dollar bills and the number on the top bill was 000151. The horse I was betting on was 5. I took that as an omen. It meant that the horse was coming in first and there'd be no other horse anywhere near him. It was a foolish idea of course, but I can understand how gamblers get — using any little thing as an omen. Well, anyway, this enabled me to remember one of the thousand-dollar bills, although it only occurred to me when that young chap was questioning me."

"What chap?" Mason asked.

"He's from the police. He may be FBI. I don't know just what his connection is except that he's police. He's been back half a dozen times, patient, courteous but insistent, asking me to go over all the events of the day.

"I'd tell him about everything I did — and then just a few days ago when he was here I remembered about looking at that package of thousand-dollar bills and seeing the number 5 bracketed by two ones with no other number on the bill."

"You're certain about the numbers?" Mason asked.

"Oh, absolutely. As soon as I recalled the incident the numbers were very vivid in my mind."

"And that's the only one of the thousand-dollar bills that the police have the number on?"

"As far as I know, it is, Mr. Mason. Like I told you, they work me on a one-way street. I give them information — they don't give me any."

"Well, thanks," Mason said. "I'm trying to get it cleared up myself, just as the police are."

They were silent for several minutes; then Ballard asked casually, "What do you find out about Duvall's daughter? What's she doing now?"

"I don't even know whether she's doing anything," Mason said.

"She was a pretty good secretary I understand. Well, I guess the police kept an eye on her and that bothered her. Turn off at this next signal light if you will, Mr. Mason, turn to the right and go about five blocks, then turn to the left. . . . Here's the house, Mr. Mason, on the corner. A little bungalow. I should have put it on the market right after the wife died, but at the time I couldn't find a buyer, and now values are going up and I don't want to sell. If I rent it, the property will probably depreciate just about the amount of the difference between the rent I'd get and what I'd have to pay. Shucks, I'm running along here like an old windmill. Somehow you seem to make a man want to talk. I haven't talked this much in months."

Mason stopped the car, said, "Thanks a lot, Ballard. I appreciate your telling me about all this."

Ballard turned the handle on the car door, then said, "Say, would you like to see a picture of one of those armored trucks? It would give you an idea of how the things were put together."

"I certainly would," Mason said. "Do you have one?"

"I've got some snapshots in here of the old banking days. My wife was a shutter bug and she took some pretty good pictures. I have them in the album. Come on in. Drive right up in the driveway. That'll put you right close to the front door."

Mason parked the car in the driveway, entered the house with Ballard. Ballard switched on the lights, indicated a chair for Mason, brought out a book of photographs, a big album consisting of double plastic pages with enlarged photographs held in place between the pages.

Mason studied the pictures carefully.

Ballard said, "I don't know how you feel, Mr. Mason, but every night when I get home I find it helps me to relax if I have a good stiff Scotch and soda. I wonder if you'd care to join me?"

"I certainly will," Mason said, "only don't make mine stiff. Make it very, very light. When I'm going to drive a car I never take more than one drink and I have that very light. Just flavor the soda with Scotch if you will."

Ballard excused himself and went out in the kitchen to mix the drinks.

Mason, left to himself, pulled out the envelope Paul Drake had handed him, reached inside and pulled out the contents.

The lawyer glanced at the door to the kitchen where Ballard was mixing drinks, then swiftly turned the thousand-dollar bill so he could see the number. It was 000151.

Mason put down the photograph album, stepped swiftly to the big, plate-glass window. Heavy drapes had been pulled. Mason stepped behind those drapes, saw that there was a roller curtain shade over the top of the window.

The lawyer pulled the shade down some two feet, placed the two bills up against the roller, then snapped the shade back to its original position.

He had barely returned to his chair, picked up and opened the album when Ballard kicked open the swinging door from the kitchen, carrying two tumblers.

He said, "I took you at your word, Mason.

The light-colored one is for you. I made mine heavy."

"Thanks," Mason told him.

"Now those pictures," Ballard went on, sitting down and preparing to enjoy his drink, "go back to the old banking days. That's my wife there — second from the left, taken just a few months before she died. Now here's a picture of the very car that figured in the transportation. Car 45. See the number? And there's Bill Emory, the driver of Car 45."

"Where's Emory now?" Mason asked.

"Still driving as far as I know. He was, the last I heard. He wasn't involved in any way. He's young yet. He hadn't been out of school very long when that picture was taken. He was quite an athlete in school . . . basketball player . . . pole vaulter . . . the police sure had him sweating blood. He was one scared kid."

"By the way," Mason said, "do you know Dr. Holman Candler in Santa Ana?"

"Sure. He's a friend of Colton Duvall. He was the official bank doctor. He was Duvall's personal physician. He's a pretty able doctor, too. He circulated a petition to get Duvall out — sent his office nurse around to get the signatures of various bank officials. I signed it myself, but I told her my name on it would hurt more than it would help. She said she had a list of names she wanted on there and mine was on the list, so I signed. She sure is good-looking — — quite a dish. Incidentally, and this is confidential, it was through her I got that tip on the horse race. Some patient of Doc's had handed the tip to Doc, but he didn't know what to do with it. Don't believe he ever gambled in his life. He was personal physician to Edward B. Marlow, the bank's president. Well, that nurse got my signature and what's more I'll bet she got every signature she went after — but that sort of stuff doesn't do any good.

"They're not going to let Duvall out on parole until he kicks through with that money, or at least a substantial part of it. He might be able to hold out thirty or forty thousand dollars by telling them that much of it had been spent or something, but they're not going to let Duvall out as long as he has nearly four hundred thousand dollars stuck away. You could present a petition signed by every man, woman and child in the State of California and they'd still keep him in."

"Well," Mason said, finishing his drink, "I must be getting on. Thanks a lot."

"So soon!" Ballard exclaimed. "Why, you just got here."

Mason smiled, got to his feet. "I have a late appointment," he said. "Thanks for your help and your hospitality."

"Wish you'd stay for another drink," Ballard said.

"No, thanks, one's my limit when I'm driving."

Mason said good night, got in his car, eased

out of the driveway and drove to his apartment house.

As he swung the car down the ramp to the garage, the night attendant made an almost surreptitious motion with his hand, waving Mason back.

Mason slammed on the brakes, brought the car to a stop, snapped it into reverse and started backing out.

Before he was able to reach the street a man came running up the ramp and pulled up alongside the car door.

"Perry Mason?" he asked jerking open the door of the car.

"What do *you* want?" Mason asked.

The man handed him a folded legal document. "Subpoena to appear before the grand jury at ten o'clock in the morning. This is a subpoena duces tecum. Bring any and all bills, money, or other legal tender that you have in your possession paid to you by Arlene Duvall. Good night."

The man slammed the car door shut, turned and walked back down the ramp. Mason took off the brake, kicked the car out of reverse and eased down the ramp.

The night attendant said, "I'll take it, Mr. Mason," and then in a low voice, "What was he? A process server?"

"That's right."

"I thought so. I tried to warn you but there was no way I could get out to head you off."

"It's all right," Mason said. "He was bound to get me sooner or later."

"Gosh, I'm sorry, Mr. Mason. But, I couldn't leave the place, and anyway, he'd have become suspicious if —"

The process server walked past them and started up the ramp.

"Don't be sore at me, Mr. Mason. I'm just doing a job."

"I'm not sore," Mason told him, "but I wish you'd given me more notice."

"I didn't have any more notice myself. Hamilton Burger, the district attorney, handed me that subpoena not over an hour ago and said, 'Serve this tonight, and be damn certain you hand it to Mason personally.' That's all the notice I had.

"Well, I'll be shoving along. Glad you don't have any hard feelings. Lots of 'em do. My partner had one to serve on . . . on another guy. I was glad I drew you. You're a lawyer. You know how those things go. You ain't going to get sore. It's just part of my job.

"Well, good night and thanks for being so decent, Mr. Mason."

The man walked up the ramp to the street.

When he had gone the garage attendant said, "I was trying to think of some way I could tip you off, but I couldn't figure anything that was worth a damn. He had a star as big as a dinner plate. If it hadn't been for that I'd have socked him."

Mason said, "That's all right, Mike. There was nothing you could do. Now I'm going to have to go out again."

Mason turned his car, drove slowly up the ramp to the street, then to a service station where he telephoned Paul Drake's office.

"Paul still there?" Mason asked the night switchboard operator when the call was put through.

"Yes, he is, Mr. Mason. Shall I put you through?"

"Please."

A moment later Drake came on the line and said, "I was just going to call you, Perry."

"What happened?"

"That fellow Jordan L. Ballard I told you about."

"Oh yes," Mason said. "I —" He caught himself abruptly.

"You what?" Drake asked.

"Tell me *your* news first," Mason said.

"The guy's dead."

"What!" Mason exclaimed.

"That's right. If you haven't talked with him you're never going to talk with him now. It's a shame, too, because he had some information that he gave the police and . . . well, hell, Perry, for all I know that may have brought about the fatal result."

"What happened, Paul?"

"It's still happening. I can only give you the high spots. My contact down at police headquarters picked up the radio call and relayed it in."

"Okay, okay, give me what you have."

"Not too much. It seems that for some reason the district attorney's office had the idea that Ballard might have some money he had received from Arlene Duvall. Evidently some sort of a tip went out, but no one knows where it came from."

"All right, what happened?"

"Well the district attorney started serving subpoenas duces tecum on witnesses ordering them to appear before the grand jury and telling them to bring with them any money in the form of currency that they had received from Arlene Duvall."

"I'll discuss that phase of the case with you later," Mason said. "Right now give me the dope on Ballard. It may be *very* important."

"Well, this process server started out for Ballard's house with a subpoena duces tecum. He got there and found the front door about half open. He rang the doorbell, got no answer, and then something made him suspicious. He went on in and found Ballard's body lying sprawled on the kitchen floor. Apparently he'd been mixing a drink for some visitors at the time. There were three glasses, ice cubes and bottles on the kitchen sink. Apparently someone clouted him from behind. Then, after he fell over, the person made sure a very good job had been done by plunging a carving knife into Ballard's body three or four times. He then went out and left the knife sticking in Ballard's back.

"Naturally police are swarming all over the place."

"Any fingerprints?" Mason asked.

"Have a heart, Perry. The flash just came in this minute. I got what details are available. The police are out there working on the job now. Heaven knows what they're finding or what they will find. Naturally they aren't going to take *me* into their confidence. We can get some of the stuff from the newspapers, some of it from my contact at police headquarters, some of it we'll have to guess at.

"The reason I thought it would be important to you is that I felt the motive for his death might well be tied in with the information he had given the police — whatever it was about that Mercantile Security case."

"Thanks a lot, Paul," Mason said. "Keep on the job. Find out everything you can about it. I'll call you back in an hour."

Mason hung up, drove to a newspaper office and prevailed upon a friendly employee to open up the morgue of clippings and spent half an hour reading contemporary accounts of the theft of the big cash shipment from the Mercantile Security.

At the end of that time he called Paul Drake again. "Anything new yet, Paul?"

"Not much. Wait a minute, here's a call

coming in on the other line. Hold on a minute, Perry."

Mason hung on to the telephone for some three minutes, then heard Paul Drake's voice again. "Hello, Perry. You on there?"

"Uh-huh."

"Well, I guess the fat's in the fire."

"What happened?"

"Your little girl friend is mixed in this thing up to her cute little eyebrows."

"All right, give."

"It's a long story. I only have the high lights."

"Give me those high lights."

"Okay. I had two of my men out there at the golf club. One of them stayed with the car. The other one started to walk over to the service station on the boulevard to telephone in a report to me. He walked over the golf course for a short cut and while he was cutting across the edge of the fairway he noticed a figure ahead of him, running along rather lightly but covering territory. He decided he'd get up close and take a look without letting her know he was behind. It turned out to be Arlene Duvall."

"All alone?"

"All alone. Apparently she'd managed somehow to ditch the police shadows."

"Okay, what happened?"

"My man did some fast thinking. He followed Arlene Duvall out to the highway. That all-night service station on the boulevard is about a block from the golf club. She went there and made a telephone call.

"My man went out in the street and tried to flag down a passing car. It was quite a job at that time of night because few of them wanted to stop, but finally one of them did. My man identified himself, showed his credentials and asked the driver if he wanted to make twenty bucks. The man said he did, so my operative told him to park at the curb and when Arlene left there to follow — it was that simple."

"Where did she go?"

"First she got a taxi. That's what she was phoning for."

"Then what?"

"The taxi took her out to Ballard's house.

"Now when she arrived some other fellow was there. A car was parked in the driveway and my man heard voices, men's voices. Arlene heard them, too. She didn't want to go in."

"So what did she do?"

"Evidently this upset her plans. She returned to the taxi and paid it off. Then she walked around to the back of the house and waited.

"My man could see someone was in the living room. He got a glimpse of him but couldn't recognize him. The guy went to the living-room window and lowered and raised the roller shade — evidently a signal to someone, the way it looks now. He pulled the shade down about two feet, then after four or five seconds, rolled it back."

"Your man get a good look at this fellow?"

Mason asked, his voice carefully controlled so as to betray no emotion.

"Apparently not. The drapes were drawn tight. This guy just popped through the drapes, let them fall back into position, signaled with the window shade and then popped back through the drapes.

"Then, after only a few minutes the man came out, got in the parked car and drove away. My man had assumed all along that it was Ballard's car because there was only one car, but apparently it was this other guy's. That's where my man fell down on the job, Perry. I've tried to din into their minds that they should never take anything for granted, but because this car was parked in the driveway, because there wasn't any other car, he assumed it was Ballard's car and didn't take the license number."

"Go on," Mason said.

"Well, right after this man came out and drove away, Arlene went in."

"How did she go in?" Mason asked.

"That's it, Perry. That's the bad part of it. She went in through a back window."

"The devil!"

"That's right."

"Then what?"

"She was in there about five minutes and then she came out through the front door in a devil of a hurry. She was almost running. She didn't close the door behind her."

"She was walking fast?"

"Running would be more like it."

"Your man followed her?"

"He followed her for about seven blocks. He should have left his car and followed her on foot, but you never know what to do in a situation like that. Well, somehow she got the idea she was being tailed and she ditched him."

"How did she do that?"

"It's easy enough at night if you know you're being tailed and someone is following you in a car."

"Just what *did* she do?"

"Simply walked up to one of the houses as though she was going to ring the front doorbell. But she didn't ring the front doorbell. She didn't go up to the front door at all. She abruptly circled around to the back of the house. When she got in the back yard she must have taken the alley and . . . well, no one knows where she went after that."

"Your man tried circling around?"

"He tried every trick known to the trade. That's why he was so late sending in his report. He didn't want to leave the place. He spent five or ten minutes circling the block. Then he increased his circle and covered a group of six blocks."

"All without picking up a trail?"

"Not a sign of a trail."

"No chance she actually went in a house somewhere, Paul?"

"I don't think so. My man says the house was dark and well, if she'd been going in she'd have gone to the front door. She started boldly right up the steps to the front porch, then suddenly circled and ran around to the back."

"Your man feels she knew she was being tailed?"

"That's right. The way she acted, the fact that she started to run when she started around to the back porch — it's an old dodge, Perry, but there's not much way of countering it."

Mason said, "I want to think this over, Paul. What's your man's name?"

"Horace Mundy."

"Does he know me?"

"I don't think you've ever met him personally. He's seen your picture, of course, and he knows that I'm working on this thing for you."

"Where can I find him?"

"Of course, he doesn't know anything as yet about Ballard's death, Perry, so he wasn't in too big a hurry to phone in a report. He knew his partner would be worried —"

"Never mind that. Where is he?"

"Back at the service station on the boulevard by the golf club. Since he'd had this driver make a flat twenty-dollar rate, he had the driver take him back there so as to save taxi fare and then phoned in his report."

"Okay," Mason said. "I'm going out there to talk with him."

"I'll let him know you're on your way over. Any instructions?"

"Keep on the job, Paul."

"Okay. I'm sitting here swigging coffee and sweating it out."

"That's fine. Keep an ear to the ground. Find out everything you possibly can on Ballard's murder. No chance it could have been suicide?"

"Hell, no."

"All right. Find out everything you can. I'll call you after a while."

"Where will you be?"

"I'm going out to see Mundy. I want to talk with him. One other thing," Mason said, "what are the chances of getting Mundy to forget what he saw?"

"I've been worrying about that, Perry."

"Why?"

"I thought you might ask that."

"Well, what are the chances?"

"Not good."

"Why?"

"I have a license."

"Well?"

"Remember," Drake said, "Mundy was caught in a jam. He didn't have a car. He needed one. He offered that motorist twenty bucks to pilot him around. The motorist was getting a great kick out of it, playing cops and robbers and having a wonderful time. Remember Mundy had identified himself. When

Mundy let the guy go the motorist took the twenty bucks all right, but said he wouldn't have missed the experience for anything."

"Of course," Mason said, "the motorist doesn't know Ballard is dead."

"So what? He'll find it out. He'll remember the address."

"I was thinking about the time element. Can you wait a day before you tell the police?"

"Have a heart, Perry," Drake said. "I'll have to tell them at least as soon as the information about Ballard's death is announced publicly."

"Now wait a minute," Mason said, "you're representing a client. You don't have to tell the police *all* you know. You —"

"This is a murder case," Drake interposed, "and remember that Mr. John Q. Citizen was dragged into it by my man. By tomorrow morning, after he's read the newspapers, he'll be singing like a skylark and if I haven't chirped by that time they'll go after my license.

"It isn't as though we could put this thing in our pocket, button the pocket and forgot about it, Perry. It's going to come out and I don't *dare* wait until the police are told about it by someone else. As soon as there's an official notification on Ballard I've got to be the one to call them."

"And give them Mundy's name?"

"That's right."

"And then they'll interview Mundy."

"Of course."

"How much time do I have?" Mason asked.

"I can't guarantee more than an hour or two, Perry."

"Stick around," Mason said. "I'll call you back."

• 5 •

Perry Mason drove his car past the entrance to the Remuda Golf Club.

The long, rambling clubhouse was illuminated by rather weak floodlights. Aside from those floodlights the club grounds were in darkness. The building on the hill seemed a moonlit mirage, floating on a cloud of darkness.

At the boulevard was a lighted service station and along the boulevard there was still considerable traffic.

Mason made the boulevard stop, turned to the right, and then swung his car into the back entrance of the service station, driving over by the water faucets and rest rooms.

He turned off the headlights, switched on the dome light, lit a cigarette, then clicked off the dome light.

A few moments later a man approached the car. "Your name Mason?" he asked.

"That's right," Mason nodded.

"I don't think I've met you."

"Are you Paul Drake's man?"

The man didn't answer the question immediately but said, "In this business we have to play them close to our chest."

Mason took out his wallet, presented the man with one of his business cards, showed him his driving license.

"Okay," the man said. "My name's Mundy."

He took a leather folder from his pocket, presented his own credentials.

"Want to get in?" Mason asked, opening the door.

The detective slid into the car on the seat beside Mason.

Mason said, "I may be rather short on time. Paul Drake gave me most of the details. I want to got a few more from you. Did you at any time see the person in the house so you could recognize him?"

"You mean the man who was in there when Arlene Duvall's cab drove up?"

"That's right."

Mundy shook his head. "I can describe him generally, and that's all. I never did see his face."

"When did you see him?" Mason asked. "When he left the place?"

"That's right. When he went out the front door and got in his car. I saw him once before that."

"Where?"

"He pulled back the drapes on the big window, then lowered the shade. You know what I mean — the roller curtain shade over the top of the window."

"Go on," Mason said, his voice without expression.

"Well, I don't know what he was doing. He

pulled the shade down — oh, maybe eighteen inches or two feet — and then stopped. I couldn't figure what he had in mind. I thought perhaps he was going to pull the shade all the way down. But he didn't. He stood there for a minute and then put the shade back up. It must have been some sort of a signal."

"Then what?" Mason asked.

"Then he stepped back through the drapes into the lighted room and the drapes fell back in place."

"You didn't see the man's face?"

"No. I just had two brief glimpses of his figure silhouetted against the light in the room."

"Can you describe him?" Mason asked, again keeping expression from his voice.

"Well, he was tall and . . . well, he was well-built. Good shoulders, narrow hips."

"How heavy?"

"Oh . . . something about your build, Mr. Mason, something like that. What do you weigh?"

Mason said, "The police are going to ask you about him. You won't have an opportunity to use me as a model at that time. You'll have to figure age, height and weight to the best of your ability."

"Well, I can't help them a great deal."

"You saw this man again when he came out and got in his automobile?"

"That's right."

"The same man?"

"Of course . . . now wait a minute . . . I couldn't swear to it. The build was the same and . . . well, something about the way he walked."

"Now you weren't alone."

"No, that's right, I had this motorist with me."

"What's his name? Did you get it?"

"Sure I got it. I paid him twenty bucks for tailing the taxicab and driving me around, I had him sign a receipt so I'd have a voucher for Paul Drake."

The detective took a folded piece of paper from his pocket. "Here it is," he said, exhibiting a receipt for twenty dollars bearing the signature and address of James Wingate Fraser.

Mason copied the name and address in his notebook.

"How was Fraser?" he asked.

"How do you mean?"

"Co-operative or — ?"

"He was having the time of his life, Mr. Mason. He'll have something to talk about for the next ten years."

"You think he'll talk?"

"Will he talk! I'll bet he's talking about it right now."

"He was alone in the car?"

"That's right."

"Know anything about him, about his background or anything?"

"No. He was a good driver. I checked his

name with the registration certificate on the car, and I jotted the license number down opposite his name on the receipt."

"So I noticed," Mason said. "Where was he when you saw this man moving through the drapes and pulling down the shades?"

"He was parked up the street about half a block."

"Could he have seen the man?"

"No. Well, only a glimpse. He was too far away and on an angle."

"Did he see the man when he came out?"

"Yes. He had a better view of him than I did."

"Could you describe the car this man was driving?"

"That I couldn't, Mr. Mason. It was a dark-colored sedan. Not too big, not too small, something about the size of this car."

"You couldn't tell the make or model?"

"No. It was dark there in the driveway and to tell you the truth this man surprised me. He got in the car and drove away. I chalked up an error against myself on that job. Drake knows it and I know it. I'm sorry it happened. But there's no use trying to kid *you*.

"I just took it for granted that the car parked there in the driveway belonged to the man who owned the house. At the time I didn't know who the guy was. I still don't know. I got the address and that's all. I was interested in this Arlene Duvall."

"The man's name was Jordan L. Ballard," Mason said, "and for your information he's dead."

"Dead!" the detective exclaimed.

"That's right, he was murdered."

"Who killed him?"

"Circumstantial evidence points to Arlene Duvall."

"Well, I'll be damned."

"Therefore," Mason said, "it becomes absolutely imperative that you get this thing straight. You're going to be interrogated by the police. You're going to have to tell them your story."

Mundy nodded.

"The police are going to keep banging away at you. You saw this man leaving the house. You saw the man standing at the window, pulling the roller curtain shade down and up. What do you *think* he was doing?"

"Gosh, Mr. Mason, I haven't the faintest idea. He must have been doing something. He may have been giving a signal to Arlene Duvall. I don't know."

"Was she where she could see the signal?"

"At that time I think she was."

"Where was she?"

"She left the taxi and went up the front steps to the house. She listened there for a minute. Evidently she could hear people talking. She didn't like that so then she paid off the cab and walked around the house."

"Now you say she walked around the house. What do you mean by that?"

"Well, she went around the house on the street side."

"Keeping on the sidewalk or in the grounds?"

"Right on the sidewalk. That's a corner house. The window that this man appeared at was the window on the side street, but the main living-room window."

"And she had a good view of him?"

"Well, I don't know as you can say anyone could have had a *good* view of him. He came through the drapes and I just had a flash of his figure silhouetted against the lighted room as the drapes were falling back into place. Then you could see him standing there at the window fooling around with that curtain. He *must* have been signaling her."

"And she saw him?"

"She was walking by on the sidewalk at the time. She had a lot better view of him than I did."

"But Fraser didn't have a good view."

"No. He might have seen a brief flash of light on the window when the drapes were pulled back and then dropped back into place, but that's all."

"And then what did Arlene Duvall do?"

"She kept on walking around to the back of the house. It's a California-type bungalow on a deep lot. She walked into the back and was concealed by the shadows. I couldn't see what she was doing for a few minutes, so I walked over to where I could get a view."

"How long was she there?"

"Maybe three or four minutes. Then she came back into my sight again just as the man was leaving by the front door. That's why I didn't pay more attention to the man. I was trying to keep my eye on her."

"First she went up the front steps?"

"That's right."

"Then came down and paid off the taxicab?"

"Then started walking around the house on the street side?"

Mundy nodded.

"And when she was on the sidewalk just opposite the window the drapes were pulled to one side and this man stood there and fumbled with the curtain. Is that right?"

"I *think* it was while she was passing by the window, and I don't think you can say the man fumbled with the shade. He pulled it down and then let it back up."

"How long was it down?"

"Oh, three or four seconds perhaps. Not very long."

"You think it was a signal?"

"What else could it have been?"

"*I* don't know," Mason said. "I'm trying to get it from *you*. The police are going to ask you about it. Now let's get back to Arlene Duvall. What did she do?"

"After the man had driven away she dragged a wooden box out from the back some place and put it up by the kitchen window. She climbed up on the wooden box and looked in."

"For how long?"

"For quite a little while. Oh, maybe seven or eight seconds. She seemed to be studying something inside the house."

"Then what did she do?"

"Then she raised the window."

"How?"

"Just used her fingers. Apparently the window wasn't locked. She fooled around with it for a moment, then raised the window. She grabbed the sash of the window with her hands, and threw her right leg over the window sill. Then she ducked her head under the window and eased into the kitchen."

"Then what?"

"Well, she was in there maybe five minutes altogether. Then she came running out the front door."

"You were trying to cover both front and back of the house?"

"As best I could. I was trying to concentrate on the Duvall girl. After she got in the window I made arrangements with Fraser to flash the car lights if she came out the front of the house."

"She did?"

"That's right."

"He flashed his lights, so I ran around the

front of the house. He told me that she'd hurried down the front steps and was running down toward the corner. I jumped in the car and he cruised down and picked her up. He was a little clumsy about it. He got a little too close, then slacked off abruptly and acted self-conscious, put his lights on the dim and pulled into the curb and . . . well, he ranked the job, that's all."

"You think she knew she was being tailed?"

"Right then she knew it."

"What did she do about it?"

"She walked another two or three blocks, evidently thinking out a plan."

"You followed her?"

"Not right close. We turned out the lights and eased along behind. Then when we saw her turn into a yard we turned the lights on bright and came up fast."

"You have the number of the place where she turned in?"

"That's right. I've got everything in my notebook."

"Now how did she got out of the trailer without anyone picking her up?" Mason asked.

"That I don't know. I was cutting across by the golf club to come over here and telephone when I saw this figure ahead of me. I saw it was a woman. I ducked down so I could see her against the skyline and then followed along. It was Arlene Duvall all right. She came over here to the service station and telephoned."

"You weren't watching the door of the trailer?"

"No, we weren't, Mr. Mason. We figured there was no other way for her to get out. But I think the two other detectives who were staked out in there were where *they* could watch the door of the trailer. They must have been. They disappeared in the brush as though they knew exactly where they were going and what they were doing."

"She isn't in the trailer now?" Mason asked.

"I don't know," Mundy said, "and I bet my partner is wondering what the devil happened to me. I came over to telephone and have been gone so long he must think I've deserted him."

"Well, let's get back to him," Mason said, "and see if there's anything now. If there is you can come back and telephone it in to Drake's office. I'll see you a little later on."

"You aren't coming over with me?"

"I'll drive you over but I won't stay."

"Okay, that's swell. It's quite a walk across the golf club."

"Anyone see you or Miss Duvall when you were crossing over?"

"I don't think so. There's a watchman there at the club. He's a fussy old fuddy-duddy. He putters around the place with a flashlight once in a while and punches a time clock every hour, but I have an idea he's just an old pensioner that they keep there to watch out for fire and just make the members feel good knowing there's a watchman on duty all night."

"All right," Mason said. "Let's go."

"In case you don't want those other fellows to spot you or the car you can drop me off at —"

"I don't care if they spot me," Mason said. "I'll give them one of my cards if they get curious."

Mason started the motor and again switched on the headlights.

"You drive around the other side of the golf club," Mundy instructed, "then take a dirt road that swings in back to another dirt road. There's a little, narrow service road that turns off that. We're parked on the dirt road just this side of the service road."

"Wouldn't you be right in the path of her headlights if she came out with the trailer?" Mason asked.

"We would if we stayed there," Mundy said. "But the minute we heard her start the car we'd get our car back out of sight. What's more, I don't think she can come out of there with that trailer without using her headlights, and those headlights would make a reflection on the trees and bushes so we'd know she was coming."

"Okay," Mason said. "I think I have the picture."

Mason drove Mundy around to where the car was parked with the other detective in it. Some hundred yards ahead Mason's headlights picked up another automobile parked by the side of the road.

The Drake detective who had been waiting in the car said to Mundy, "Where the hell have *you* been?"

"It's a long story," Mundy said. "I'll tell it to you later. Anything doing here?"

"Dead as a church on Monday," the detective said.

Mason said, "Okay, boys. Keep on the job." He turned his car down the driveway, then backed it so he could turn around and return to the paved road the way he had entered rather than drive past the other car which was parked farther down the road.

• 6 •

Mason drove to the address James Wingate Fraser had written under his name on the receipt he had given Mundy.

It was a well-built, California-bungalow-type house, in a district which was now sprinkled with apartment houses and an occasional small business.

The house was lighted from one end to the other. Three cars were parked in front of the place, with another car in the driveway.

From the interior Mason could hear the sounds of laughter and voices. Several people were talking at once.

Mason found a place to park his car, walked up the steps and rang the bell.

A man came to the door.

"I'm sorry to bother you at this late hour," Mason said, "but I would like to see Mr. Fraser."

"I'm Fraser."

Mason saw that the man was slightly flushed. There was whisky on his breath. He showed that peculiar restraint which comes from having been the life of the party one minute and trying to pick up a cloak of dignity the next.

"Sorry to be bothering you at this hour," Mason said, "but I'd like to talk with you for a few moments. I'm Perry Mason, an attorney."

"Perry Mason, *the* attorney?"

"Let's say I'm *an* attorney."

Sudden, effusive cordiality melted the last vestige of Fraser's dignity.

"Come on in, come on in," he said. "We've got a little gathering of friends here. People that would be just crazy to meet you. My wife was having a bridge party tonight and . . . well, sort of a hen party, and when I came home I telephoned some of the husbands to come over and have a drink. I'd had . . . well, kind of an unusual experience. Come on in, Mr. Mason."

"I'd prefer to talk with you out here," Mason said. "I —"

Fraser said, "Oh, stuff and nonsense! Come on in and meet the people. Hey, Bertha," he called loudly. "You have no idea who's out *here!*"

The babble of voices from the interior of the house suddenly ceased.

"Come on in," Fraser said, taking Mason's arm.

Mason followed Fraser into the house. He shook hands with several men, bowed to their wives, acknowledged introductions, permitted himself to accept a drink.

"Birthday party?" Mason asked, tactfully leading up to the subject he had in mind.

"Just sort of a celebration," Fraser said. "I had an experience tonight. I have now become old C. R. Fraser — the C. R. standing for Cops and Robbers. By the way, Mr. Mason, if it's not impertinent, what is the reason for *your* visit?"

"I wanted to talk with you about the cops-and-robbers chapter in your life," Mason said.

Fraser became instantly cautious. The others gathered around, expressions varying from polite interest to the owlish solemnity of the man who has had one too many and is concentrating with great intensity upon a simple problem.

Fraser said, "I was coming by the Remuda Golf Club when I saw a well-dressed chap out in the road waving me down. Ordinarily I don't pick up hitchhikers at night, but this fellow had an air of quiet respectability about him.

"I slowed the car to see what he wanted and he flashed a badge at me, then showed me credentials — a detective. At first I thought he was a police detective. I guess he was willing to let me think that. He simply told me he was a detective. I found out afterward he was a private detective working for the Drake Detective Agency."

Mason nodded.

"You interested in all this?" Fraser asked.

"All of it," Mason said.

Fraser's wife interposed quickly, "May I ask why, Mr. Mason?"

Mason said, "Frankly, the operative your husband picked up was working for me. He made a report covering his activities and I wanted to check that report because some of it may be important."

There was instant relief on Mrs. Fraser's

face. “Oh,” she said, and then added, “I’m going to the kitchen. Who wants a refill?”

She picked up a couple of empty glasses. The tension seemed to relax.

“Well,” Fraser said with a glibness indicating he had already told the story many times before, “this chap, whose name it turned out was Mundy, wanted me to shadow a taxicab. We played tag around for a while, and then the girl who was riding in the taxicab went out to a nice, quiet residence, got out of the cab, walked up to the porch, listened a minute, came back and paid the cab off and walked around to the back of the house.”

“Why didn’t she go in?” Mason asked.

“Some chap there ahead of her, someone she didn’t want to see, apparently.”

“Any idea who he was?”

Fraser shook his head. “He owned the car that was in the driveway, at least he drove off in it.”

“You saw him come out?”

“That’s right.”

“You didn’t get the license number of the car?”

“Me?” Fraser asked, pointing a finger at his chest. Mason nodded.

Fraser laughed and said, “Hell’s bells, Mason. You’ve got me mixed up. I wasn’t the detective. I’m just old C. R. Fraser, known as Cops-and-Robbers Fraser — that’s me.”

Everybody laughed.

"Go on," Mason said.

"Well, our gal friend — and believe me she was a slick-looking chick —" Fraser glanced apprehensively in the direction of the kitchen — "walked around the building to the back and *I* didn't actually *see* her go in the window, but Mundy, who had left the car and was out where he could keep an eye on operations at the back, said she pulled up a box and climbed in the kitchen window. There she was, pulling up her skirts and tying them around her waist and sliding a well-shaped leg into a lighted kitchen window — and where was old Cops-and-Robbers Fraser, sitting in a goddam automobile where he couldn't see a thing."

Again everyone laughed.

"You saw the front of the house?"

"That's right."

"And you saw a man come out and get in the car?"

"Uh-huh."

"Can you describe him?"

"Tall, well put together, moved very smoothly when he walked, sort of athletic-looking, seemed to be well-dressed."

"How old?"

"The way he walked you'd say he was young, reasonably young."

"Tall?"

"That's right."

"Weight?"

"Hard to tell. He had good shoulders but he

tapered down to the hips. Looked like a man who keeps himself in good condition. He was — shucks, Mr. Mason, he was just about *your* build."

"But you couldn't recognize him?"

"If I saw him again I *might* recognize him, that is, if I saw him the way I saw him there at that house, you know, if he'd come out of a door and walk down a front porch and get in an automobile I *might* —"

"But you didn't see his face?"

"No."

"And you couldn't recognize his face if you saw it again?"

"No."

"How about the car? You said you didn't get the license number. Do you know what kind of a car it was?"

"Fairly late model sedan, I'd say. One of the good grade of cars. Not a big ice wagon but a chunky little dynamo of power. Just something about it, the way it was put together . . . well, it was a competent-looking car — the kind they're making these days for real performance."

"You don't know the make?"

"No."

"Nor the model?"

"No."

"See anything else?" Mason asked.

"Well, the chap who was inside there came to the window, pushed his way through the drapes and gave some sort of a signal with the curtain. But I didn't have as good a view as Mundy did. I just saw him, that's all."

"You couldn't recognize him when the light came through the window?"

"No."

"You didn't get a good look at him at that time?"

"Not as good as I got when he came out of the house."

"And what happened after that?"

"Well, he got in the car and drove away, and then Mundy moved around toward the back of the house. I saw him moving up and trying to look in a window; then he came to the car, told me to flash my lights if the girl should come out. Then he went back toward the rear of the house; then the door opened and this girl came out. I gave Mundy a signal and he moved up."

"Could you recognize her if you saw her again?"

"Sure. I looked her over pretty carefully. What's more I saw her face."

"When?"

"A little later on. I guess I botched things up. I was a little too eager. Mundy kept telling me to slow down, but I was afraid she was going to get away so I moved up a little too close. All of a sudden she turned around and saw me — that is, saw the headlights. I got a good look at her face and you could see that she was alarmed. I dimmed the lights right away.

Mundy thought perhaps she felt someone was trying to put on a wolf act, but as it turned out she was hep."

"What did she do?"

"Well, when she came out of that house and went down the little walk leading to the sidewalk she was just about half-running. Mundy came hurrying over to the car after I signaled. He got in and we followed the girl. As I say, she got wise after a few blocks and gave us the slip before we could do anything about it."

"That was the last you saw of her?"

"That's right. We put in half an hour cruising around the vicinity. Mundy was pretty sick about it. We cruised around the block first, then we cruised around two blocks, then we made four blocks, then we just looped around the neighborhood looking for a chance to pick up the girl again."

"What would you have done if you'd found her?" Mason asked.

"Darned if I know," Fraser said. "I was just driving the car. But, believe me, it was an experience. I suppose those things don't mean anything to you — but, well, this was really something in my young life — a real break in the monotony. I'd never seen a detective at work before and . . . I was surprised at how much technique there is in shadowing a person. I was just telling these folks I learned more in an hour or so tonight than I could have learned in a month of study. It seems there's quite a technique. You have to be just so far behind and you can't stay right behind a cab when you're following it. You come up and drop back and turn down a side street and then make a U-turn and come shooting back to come up like you're another car, and all of that sort of stuff so the cabby don't realize he's being tailed and —"

"But you couldn't recognize the man?"

"I never did see his face, but I have a feeling I *might* be able to recognize him if I saw his figure again under the same circumstances. I'd sure like to know more about the background. What sort of a case is it?"

"I'm not at liberty to tell all the details," Mason said. "I'm an attorney and my client pays me to got information, not to give it. I'm sorry."

"Well, sit down and tell us about some of your other cases. Gosh, to think the great Perry Mason has been right here in this living room! This is a night. It really is!"

"I'm sorry," Mason said, "but I still have work to do."

"Can't you have another drink? Even the great Perry Mason can't fly on one wing!"

They all laughed.

Mason edged toward the door. "I'm sorry. I'll have to be leaving. Thanks a lot for telling me about what happened, Fraser."

"Thanks for telling *you* about it!" Fraser exclaimed. "Thanks for giving me the opportunity. This was *really* something. And to think that I took part in a case that tied in with the activities of Perry Mason. If you can't tell me about the case, I suppose I'll have to wait and read about it in the papers."

"Oh," Mason laughed, "it may not be that important."

"Don't kid me. It's important enough for you to come out here at this hour."

"I saw you were up."

"Sure I was up. But how about *you?*"

"Oh, I work late," Mason explained.

He shook hands all around and Fraser escorted him to the door.

"You don't know whether the man who owned that house was alive when that man left or not, do you?"

"Gosh, no. Why, what do you mean? Is — Good Lord, don't tell me —"

"That's why I called on you at this hour of the night," Mason said. "The man was murdered. Don't go to bed. Police will be calling any time now."

"Oh, my good Lord," Fraser exclaimed, hanging on to the doorknob as though to support himself. "You don't . . . you can't mean that — ?"

"I was just telling you not to get into bed," Mason said, and walked away.

• 7 •

Mason drove to a service station telephone and called Paul Drake.

"How are you coming?" Drake asked.

"Not good."

"How much more time do you need? I haven't —"

"Have your man call police headquarters right away," Mason said. "He can tell police that he checked in with you on the telephone and that you told him about Ballard's murder so that he realized for the first time the importance of what he had seen and hurried to call police headquarters."

"Okay," Drake said, relief in his voice. "I'll send another operative out to tell Mundy to call police."

"Now here's one other thing," Mason said. "I —"

"Wait a minute, Perry," Drake interrupted. "My night operator is in here waving a note at me frantically."

"All right. See what it says."

There was a moment of silence. Then Mason heard Drake's sharp exclamation.

"Go on, Paul. What is it?"

Drake said, "Ballard ran this service station down at Tenth and Flossman."

"Uh-huh. What about it?"

"It's an all-night service station."

"Uh-huh."

"Police went down there to find out what time Ballard checked out. They talked with an attendant. They found that Ballard's car was in the shop. He was planning to call a taxi to take him home. He had too much money to use the bus service — didn't want to carry it with him on the street. The attendant said that *you* showed up and talked with him and that Ballard rode home with *you*."

"The attendant recognized me?"

"That's right."

"Well," Mason said, "that seems to complicate the situation."

"Complicate the situation!" Drake exclaimed. "My God, Perry, you mean that it's true — you mean that you —"

"I mean," Mason said, "that this would be a very good time for you to have Mundy call up the police and tell them about what he saw. Where's Arlene Duvall? Has she shown up yet?"

"Apparently not. My men are down there waiting, and the other shadows are waiting. The only thing is, Perry, that so far we're apparently the only ones who know she isn't in the trailer. The other fellows are staked out down there waiting it out. They seem to think she's still there in the trailer. They're settled down for all night."

"How do you suppose she got out?"

"I haven't the faintest idea. She must have

pulled it pretty slick. If my man hadn't happened to run onto her —"

"He's absolutely certain that it's Arlene Duvall?"

"Gosh yes."

"Okay," Mason said. "Have Mundy call the police and tell them everything that happened."

"Hey, Perry, what are *you* going to do? You're hotter than a firecracker right now."

"I'm going to keep out of sight until I cool off," Mason said. "You'll be hearing from me."

"Perry, what *did* happen? Did you drive Ballard home?"

"Sure I drove him home."

"Then the murder must have been committed just after you left, unless —"

"Unless what?" Mason asked.

Drake tried to make his voice sound facetious but failed miserably. "Unless you killed him," he said.

"That's a thought," Mason said. "Don't pass it on to the police."

"I won't have to," Drake blurted.

Mason hung up.

Mason drove to the Santa Ana Freeway, and eased his car into the stream of late traffic pouring along it.

It was well after 1:00 a.m. when he drove into a service station, consulted a telephone directory, and looked up Dr. Holman B. Candler.

There was an office number and a night number.

Mason called the night number.

After a few seconds a woman's voice answered.

"Mrs. Candler?" Mason asked.

"No. Were you calling Dr. Candler?"

"Yes."

"Will you please tell me what it is? Describe your symptoms, please."

"I'm not sick. I'm Perry Mason. I want to see him about Arlene Duvall. It's important."

There was a moment of silence, then the voice, crisply professional, asked, "Where are you now, Mr. Mason?"

"On the outskirts of town."

"Do you have Dr. Candler's office address?"

"Yes. I got it from the phone book."

"Drive there. I'll have Dr. Candler meet you there. If he isn't there by the time you arrive, park your car and wait. He'll be there within a few minutes."

The phone clicked.

Mason hung up, secured directions from the attendant as to how to get to the address listed in the telephone book for Dr. Candler's office, and stopped at an all-night lunch counter for a hurried cup of coffee before driving to the one-storied building built in the form of a duplex with Dr. Candler having his offices on one side, an oculist and dentist having offices on the other.

Mason parked his car and Dr. Candler drove up almost immediately.

Mason got out of the car as Dr. Candler

fitted a key to the office door.

"Hello, Doctor," Mason said. "I'm Perry Mason."

Dr. Candler whirled with the quick, catlike motion of a man who is under great tension, whose reaction time is quick.

"Sorry I startled you," Mason said, holding out his hand.

Dr. Candler gripped the hand. "I wasn't particularly startled."

"I thought you were, the way you whirled around."

Dr. Candler laughed. "I still retain some of my boxing reflexes I guess — although I haven't done any boxing for years."

"Amateur?" Mason asked.

"Intercollegiate. I was champion of the light heavyweight division. Tall and not too heavy, had a long reach and was pretty fast. Come in, come in, Mr. Mason. I've been looking forward to an opportunity to talk with you. I almost suggested that you stay in your office until I could get in there — when you were calling about Arlene. Did she get the trailer all right?"

"Oh, yes," Mason said, "she got the trailer all right. That was some little time ago."

"Well, come on in and tell me what happened."

Dr. Candler led the way down a long hallway.

"In offices of this sort the atmosphere always seems stagnant with an aura of human misery," he observed apologetically. "I have an air-conditioning unit that changes the air itself and keeps it fresh enough, but there seems to be a psychic miasma that clings to the walls. Too many sick people. That's a hell of a way for a doctor to talk, isn't it?"

"Why?" Mason asked.

"Oh, we're not supposed to be susceptible to psychic influences. We're supposed to be materialists. And yet I don't think any doctor achieves success without being aware of the fact that there are certain things that aren't in the medical books. Sit down, Mason. Sit down."

Dr. Candler, showing evidences of having dressed hastily, settled himself in the big swivel chair and eyed Mason with the shrewd appraisal of one accustomed to sizing up others.

Mason said, "Doctor, I think you know my reputation well enough to know that I wouldn't have called you at this hour of the night except on a matter of considerable importance."

Dr. Candler nodded.

"Now I understand you are very friendly with Arlene Duvall."

Again the doctor nodded.

"As you know, I am representing Arlene Duvall."

"Are you?" Dr. Candler asked.

"What do you mean by that?"

"As I understood it, you agreed to represent her in the event she was innocent, but in the event she was guilty you stated that you would unhesitatingly turn her in and collect your fee from a reward which you expected to receive for recovering the stolen money."

"That is right," Mason said, his eyes suddenly hard. "Is there any objection to that?"

"Not in the least," Dr. Candler said. "It's your privilege to make any sort of an arrangement with a client that you wish, but it is not quite the same as though you were representing her wholeheartedly."

"I'll represent her wholeheartedly if she's innocent."

"Exactly. But suppose you came to the conclusion that she was guilty?"

"Then, as I pointed out to her, I would recover the money and turn her in."

"Now," Dr. Candler said, "you see the point I am about to make. Suppose that she should actually be innocent but there should be some incriminating circumstance which would cause you to believe she was guilty. You would then turn against her."

"I think you can trust my discretion in the matter. I'm not going to jump at conclusions."

"You may not jump at conclusions but it is quite possible that you could lead yourself to a false conclusion."

"You think she is innocent?"

"I'll stake my life on it," Dr. Candler said.

"May I ask the nature of your relationship?"

"I am a friend."

"Is there a romantic attachment?"

Dr. Candler stroked the angle of his chin. "I am not going to get up in the middle of the night in order to be cross-examined on the matter. You may take it for granted that I have a very deep regard for Arlene Duvall. I consider myself a very close friend of her father. I think he had a raw deal."

"You think he is innocent?"

"Of course he's innocent," Dr. Candler said with feeling. "He was made a fall guy because the police and the insurance company couldn't find any other person on whom to put the blame."

"They did find stolen money in his possession."

"So they claimed. However, remember that they didn't find it until some time after the robbery. Undoubtedly the person who perpetrated the robbery was an employee of the bank. He had access to those canceled checks. Why couldn't he have managed to get hold of Colton Duvall's wallet and plant some of the stolen money in it?"

"That, of course, is a thought," Mason said.

"One which should have occurred to you," Dr. Candler remarked acidly.

"It has. I'm keeping my mind open," Mason told him.

"See that you do."

Mason grinned. "The reason that I'm here, Doctor, is because I am for the moment prepared to accept your viewpoint. Now then,

Arlene Duvall is getting money. *Where* is she getting it? Are *you* giving it to her?"

"I'm not, but someone is."

"Who?"

"I don't know. I wish I did."

"Won't she tell *you?*"

"Let's put it this way," Dr. Candler said. "Arlene Duvall has taken me entirely into her confidence. I understand a great deal about her and a great deal about the case, but there is one matter and one matter alone on which she does not confide in me because she has given her promise that she wouldn't."

"And that is?"

"The identity of the person who is giving her the money. I know everything else. I know she is to give you a retainer of fifteen hundred dollars before nine-thirty. I know she'll do it. But I don't know who is giving her the money."

"But you know someone is giving it to her?"

"Yes."

"She has told you that much?"

"Yes."

"Has she confided in you to that extent?"

"Yes."

"And why is this person giving her money?"

"I could answer that," Dr. Candler said. "It would be a guess. I think the strategy is all wrong. I think this person is someone who cannot afford to have his name brought into the case. He is fully convinced of Colton P. Duvall's innocence. Apparently he is just as convinced as I am. He wants Duvall out of prison. As long as the authorities think that Duvall has the money concealed and isn't telling where it is, they'll never let him out of prison. If, however, the authorities feel that Duvall's daughter has found where the money was concealed — and you must remember, Mr. Mason, that the authorities take it for granted that Duvall is guilty — and that the daughter is spending that money, there might then be no further reason to keep the father in prison.

"They would, under those circumstances, consider that by releasing the father they could count on him and his daughter having a settlement, either amicable or otherwise. They would then find Duvall in possession of the money, force him to account for where and how he received that money, and then violate his parole. They might then also be able to hold his daughter as an accessory and would stand some chance of recovering the money. That is the reasoning of the unknown individual who is donating money to Arlene. He is using it as bait for a trap, a trap which he hopes will get the parole authorities to release Duvall from prison."

"I am not inclined to agree with that reasoning," Mason said.

"Neither am I," Dr. Candler snapped. "I think it is utterly asinine. I think it will defeat its own purpose. I have argued with Arlene about it. However, she gave her promise to this mysterious friend, whoever he is, that she would carry out his instructions at least for a period of eighteen months."

"And you believe that story?" Mason asked.

"I believe every word of it, sir, because Arlene told it to me."

"If it had been told you by someone in whom you didn't have so much confidence, in whom you didn't have such a romantic interest, let us say, it would be considered the height of absurdity, wouldn't it?"

"Perhaps."

"Do you have any clue as to the person who is putting up this money?"

"I think he is an official in the bank."

"Do you think he is perhaps the person who engineered the theft in the first place and has perhaps a guilty conscience because Duvall has been incarcerated?"

"That thought has occurred to me," Dr. Candler said, and then added dryly, "a great many times. However, if I had to make a quick guess I would say this mysterious benefactor — if you could call him that — is Edward B. Marlow, the president of the bank."

"Why him?"

"He was instrumental as president of the bank in directing the prosecution of Duvall. He is independently wealthy. He has a conscience. I think he now has doubts as to Duvall's guilt. Yet he could never afford to have his name brought into this phase of the case.

"He has enough pull so he could give money to Arlene, report it as a gift, pay a gift tax on it, and see that the income-tax people kept the information confidential. So far the income-tax officials have kept out of the case and are giving no help and no information to the police.

"You must admit that indicates someone with great influence is in the background of the case."

"Anything else?" Mason asked. "Have you any other clues?"

Dr. Candler stroked the angle of his jaw with his fingers, feeling the stubble of his chin as though speculating as to whether he should shave before going back to bed or whether he should wait until morning.

"Well?" Mason asked.

Slowly Dr. Candler shook his head. "No, Mr. Mason," he said, "I think I've told you all that I can at the moment."

"Do you know where Arlene Duvall is?"

"No. That is, I know she is in her trailer. I don't know *exactly* where her trailer is parked."

"She isn't in the trailer."

Dr. Candler's face showed surprise. "You're certain?"

"Detectives who have been shadowing her are certain."

"You are having detectives shadow her?" Dr. Candler asked sharply.

Mason said, "Let's put it this way. I am having detectives keep an eye on the detectives, presumably police detectives, who are also keeping an eye on her."

"I see," Dr. Candler said.

"Do you know Jordan L. Ballard?"

"Of course. I am the bank's physician. I give all their employees a semi-annual physical checkup. Naturally many of them come to me for treatment.

"I knew Ballard quite well when he was an employee of the bank. I only see him occasionally now."

Mason said, "I'll give you some information about Ballard. You'll get in the morning paper. He was murdered somewhere around ten-thirty last night."

"Murdered?"

"That's right."

"Who murdered him?"

"For reasons which I am not in a position to disclose at the moment police are going to think that Arlene Duvall murdered him."

"The devil!"

"And," Mason went on, "very confidentially, Jordan Ballard, in a conversation with the police some time within the last forty-eight hours, told them that as he had continued to search his recollection he had found a clue as to the number of one of the bills which had been stolen from the Mercantile Security, one of the large-denomination bills. He gave police the number of a thousand-dollar bill that had been stolen."

"How did he happen to remember that at such a late date?" Dr. Candler asked suspiciously.

"Because he remembered the number in connection with the number of a race horse on which he had placed a wager."

"That story sounds very, very fishy to me."

Mason nodded.

"All right," Candler said, "you've smoked me out into the open."

"In what way?"

"I will have to admit that I have had Ballard under consideration for some time."

"As the man who was giving Arlene Duvall money?"

"In a way. But primarily as the man who probably managed to engineer the theft from the Mercantile Security."

"How could he have done it?"

"I don't know," Candler said. "I wish I did. But let's look at the circumstances on a basis of cold reality. Ballard was working in the bank. He was one of the persons who should have been checking the money as it was packed in the carton. He said he deviated from that duty because he was interested in the results of a horse race, the radio report on which just happened to be coming on at that particular time. He hadn't been in the habit of betting on the races. He made this bet because of a tip he had received. He has never stated where he received that tip. The bet was large for a man who was working in a bank on a small salary. After the theft, Ballard left the bank. He went through a period when apparently he was having a hard time keeping body and soul together. Then he got a job. He did everything, in short, that a guilty man would have done in an attempt to throw pursuit off the trail."

"Or that an innocent man would necessarily have done," Mason said.

"Exactly," Dr. Candler said. "But let's look at what happened after that. Suddenly Jordan L. Ballard developed a Midas touch. Everything that he touched turned to gold. He started making investments. He purchased the business where he was working. He started purchasing real estate. He was on the way to becoming a wealthy man."

"There were real estate profits," Mason said.

"Of course. But we are simply looking at the thing from a cold-blooded, realistic standpoint. This penniless, discharged, discredited individual goes through a period of poverty, starts working for wages, and then becomes affluent. He has made investments which account for certain profits, but is *all* of his affluence the result of those profits?"

"That's a question I can't answer," Mason said.

"Nor can anyone else."

"So you suspect him?"

Dr. Candler nodded.

"That was what I wanted to find out," Mason said, and then added, "I have some reason to believe that Arlene Duvall had in her possession the thousand-dollar bill the number of which Ballard had given the police. That, of course, is information which you must treat in the strictest confidence, Doctor, but I had to find out about Ballard before going any further."

"And he has been murdered?"

Mason nodded.

"I think," Dr. Candler said, "he has perhaps come to the logical conclusion of his career. You will understand, Mr. Mason, that while Ballard had an opportunity to assist in perpetrating that theft, while he had an opportunity to cooperate in it so that the theft would have become possible, it wasn't physically possible for him to have actually taken the money. Therefore, he must have had an accomplice."

Mason nodded.

"So," Dr. Candler went on, "Ballard engaged in a course of chicanery which may not have been approved of by his partner in crime. When crooks fall out, Mason, there is apt to be . . . well, there's apt to be a murder."

"Apparently that happened in this instance," Mason said, watching Dr. Candler's face.

"I suppose I should feel sorry," Dr. Candler said, "but actually the information you have given me is the best news I have had for a long time. I think the situation is coming to a head. I think that the police now have *two* crimes to work on. The theft from the Mercantile Security and the murder of Ballard. When they find the murderer of Ballard they will find his accomplice, and in doing that they will have solved the theft of the money."

"And if Arlene Duvall gets in touch with you," Mason asked, "will you notify me at once?"

Dr. Candler again explored the stubble on his chin. "I'll make no promises, Mr. Mason. Where Arlene Duvall is concerned I will do what I think is for her best interests."

"I think under the circumstances," Mason said, "her best interests will be to get in immediate touch with me."

"That is your opinion."

"Exactly."

"I will form mine after I have talked with Arlene — conceding, of course, that she does get in touch with me."

Mason said, "I think it would be much better if she got in touch with me through you."

"Why?"

"Because I have been subpoenaed to appear before the grand jury at ten o'clock in the morning. I have been ordered to bring with me any currency which I may have received from Arlene Duvall and which was in my possession at the time the subpoena was served."

"You'll be questioned by the grand jury?"

Mason nodded.

"As an attorney you are entitled to respect the confidences of your client. They can't examine you as to those matters."

"That's too broad a statement of the rule," Mason said. "The rule actually is that any communication *necessarily* made to me by my client for the purpose of giving me information so that I can advise her as to her legal rights is a privileged communication. There are, however, certain exceptions even to that rule."

"I take it that you will interpret the rule, however, so that it is to the benefit of your client?"

Mason smiled. "I think you can trust me to do that, Doctor."

Dr. Candler got up and shook hands. "As you probably know, Mr. Mason, it was because of my insistence that Arlene Duvall consulted you."

"Yes?"

"Exactly. I felt that things were taking place behind the scenes, events that had some significance. I didn't feel qualified. Someone was trying to use Arlene as a cat's-paw. I felt certain that once you entered the picture things would be brought to a head."

"And you consider the death of Jordan Ballard as one of the results of my employment?"

"You're putting it rather crudely," Dr. Candler said.

"But accurately?"

"Yes. I am not going to lie to you, Mr. Mason. I consider Ballard's death to be one of the results of your employment."

Mason started for the exit door and had his hand resting on the knob when he felt the metal turn under his fingers as someone twisted the knob from the other side of the door.

Mason stepped back and to one side.

Dr. Candler started to say something, then caught himself.

A trimly dressed redheaded woman about thirty-two years old, conscious of her charm and her good figure, stood smiling on the threshold.

"Rose!" Dr. Candler exclaimed with just a trace of irritation in his voice. "What are *you* doing here?"

"I thought I'd run in and see if I could be of help."

Dr. Candler said, "This is Rose Travis, my head office nurse, Mr. Mason. She filters all my night calls."

Mason took the woman's outstretched hand. "Then you're the one I talked with over the phone."

"That's right."

"I'm sorry if I got you up."

"Think nothing of it. I've trained myself so I can waken, answer the phone, then go right back to sleep. I save Dr. Candler a lot of night calls by soothing the patient. Lots of night calls are simply nervous hypochondriacs who get lonely when they can't sleep. I tell them to take two aspirins and a hot bath and that'll hold them until morning."

"Rose is invaluable, Mr. Mason," Dr. Candler supplemented. "I go in a lot for diathermy and sweat baths in light cabinets. Most medical doctors don't go so much for those sweat baths, but I swear by them. Rose has charge of all those treatments. Of course, she has several assistants during the day. I don't see how she stands up to it, but ever since my wife passed away, some five years now, Rose has been handling my night calls. She's been with me for . . . for nearly eleven years."

"Twelve," Rose corrected.

"Has it been twelve? Heavens, so it has!"

"I thought I might be able to help," she said, glancing from Dr. Candler to Mason. "Is anything wrong?"

"Ballard has been murdered," Dr. Candler said.

"What?"

Dr. Candler nodded gravely.

"What time?" Rose Travis asked sharply.

"We don't knew exactly," Dr. Candler said.

Mason opened the door. "Well, I'll be on my way. I have work to do. I'll be seeing you again."

He stepped out into the hallway, then through the reception room and out into the crisp freshness of the night air, leaving behind the close, stale smell of the doctor's office, and two people, a doctor and a nurse, each looking at the other in thoughtful, speculative appraisal.

• 8 •

Della Street was waiting for Perry Mason as he entered the office at nine-thirty.

"I'm subpoenaed to appear before the grand jury," Mason said.

"So I understood," Della Street told him. "There's been a letter that —"

"Forget the mail, Della. Is there anything really important? I'll just have time to get up there. I want to be on time."

"This letter," she said, "you had better see."

"What is it?" Mason asked.

She handed him an envelope bearing a simple typewritten address. The envelope had been slit along the end.

"Well, what is it?" Mason asked impatiently.

"Better look."

Mason held the envelope so as to cup open the cut end. He reached in with his long fingers and scissored out the contents.

"Well, I'll be damned!"

Della Street stood looking at him anxiously. Mason held in his hand a five-hundred-dollar bill and a thousand-dollar bill. A note in pen and ink was attached to the money. The note was in a woman's handwriting and read:

Dear Mr. Mason:

I promised you would have this money

first thing in the morning. I am assured that this mail will reach your office by eight o'clock. I may not be available for a while. Thank you very much.

Arlene Duvall.

Mason studied the postmark on the envelope.

"Postmarked at eighty-thirty last night, Della."

She nodded.

Mason whipped the other envelope from his pocket, the envelope which had contained the fifteen hundred dollars which had been left at Drake's office. He compared the typewriting on the address.

"The same typewriter?" Della asked.

Mason shook his head.

"Well, you're now in the position of having two fifteen-hundred-dollar retainers," Della Street said.

Mason shook his head.

"No?"

"What happened?"

"I got rid of that other money, Della."

"How?"

"Oh, I just can't seem to hang on to money. Besides, Della, we can't tell if that money really came from Arlene Duvall. After all, there was only a note bearing a typewritten signature 'A.' That wouldn't be evidence in a court of law. Suppose she had sent a promissory note in that letter. They would have laughed at me if I had tried to claim that was her signature and that the promissory note had been sent by her with no more evidence than was contained in that letter."

"What are you getting at?"

"The grand jury wants to interrogate me concerning any money I have received from Arlene Duvall. I am quite certain that Mr. Hamilton Burger, the district attorney, will conduct the inquiry in person. I think Mr. Burger is preparing what he would consider a grueling cross-examination, doubtless reveling in the manner in which he is going to make me squirm in front of the grand jury."

"Then you aren't going to tell him anything about that other fifteen hundred dollars?"

"What fifteen hundred dollars?" Mason asked, looking blank.

"Oh, all right," Della Street said. "Have it your own way. Try and come back all in one piece."

"I will," Mason promised.

"Paul Drake told me about what had happened last night. Chief, who *was* that man who was out at Ballard's? The one they saw at the window?"

"Read the afternoon paper," Mason said, and gathering up his brief case, he casually dropped the note and the two large bills into a compartment. He glanced at his watch, smiled and said, "I'll be on my way, Della. I don't want to keep

Hamilton Burger waiting. I want to be there promptly at ten o'clock."

Mason started for the door, thought better of it, turned, said to Della Street, "Della, that envelope Paul gave me last night was delivered by a uniformed messenger. I want Paul to check every messenger service in town and locate the boy who delivered that envelope. I want to find out where he got it and get a description of the person from whom he got it."

Della Street nodded.

"And now," Mason said, "I'll go and let Hamilton Burger give me the works."

"Don't let him get too rough," Della Street warned.

Mason grinned. "This is the district attorney's show, Della. I'm in his back yard now and he can chase me around as much as he wants."

"You mean you don't have any recourse?"

"Oh," Mason said, grinning, "I could always hide behind the Fifth Amendment."

"Don't take it so lightly," she said. "You may have to."

"And don't think that's a joke," Mason told her. "It may be a very conservative, factual statement."

Mason took a taxicab to the Hall of Justice and went at once to the grand jury room.

Newspaper photographers clustered around him, dazzling his eyes with exploding flash bulbs.

"What's this all about, Mr. Mason?" a reporter asked.

"I wish *I* knew," Mason told him. "I've received a subpoena, and as a law-abiding citizen I am obeying the summons. That's virtually all I can tell you."

"Can or will?"

"Can *and* will," Mason said.

An officer tapped Mason on the arm. "You're first," he said.

Mason entered the grand jury room.

Hamilton Burger, who had been addressing the grand jury, stopped as Mason entered. There was a look of smug triumph on Burger's face. Mason noticed curiosity on the faces of the grand jurors, but there was a certain coldness, a lack of warmth that made him realize Hamilton Burger had been outlining a situation which apparently was far more serious than Mason had expected.

Mason was sworn and Hamilton Burger cautioned him as to his constitutional rights.

"You are, of course, an attorney," Burger said. "You are bound by law to answer certain questions which are asked you by the grand jury. You are not required, however, to testify to anything which may incriminate you. You have the right to refuse to answer those questions where you feel the answer may have a tendency to incriminate you."

"Thank you," Mason said coldly.

"Now then," Hamilton Burger went on, "a subpoena duces tecum was issued on you ordering you to produce any currency which might have been paid to you by one Arlene Duvall. Just so that we will have the record straight I am going to ask you, Mr. Mason, if you know Arlene Duvall."

"I do."

"Is she a client of yours?"

"In a way, yes."

"Why do you qualify your answer?"

"Because the employment, if you wish to call it such, was qualified."

"By an exception?"

"An exception."

"And what was that exception?"

"If, in the course of my investigations," Mason said, "I came to the conclusion that she had been guilty of a crime, either as an active participant, or as an accessory before or after the fact, I reserved the right to terminate the relationship of attorney and client, and in fact to use any information I might have gained to assist the law."

"Wasn't that noble of you?" Hamilton Burger sneered.

"I don't think the occasion calls for sarcasm," Mason said. "As matter of fact, it was simple prudence."

"Are you *certain* you made that arrangement with her?"

"Naturally."

"At the time she *first* employed you?"

"Yes."

"Or was that arrangement made in a very recent communication *after* you had been subpoenaed to testify before the grand jury so that you would be in a position to cover your actions with a coat of legal whitewash?"

"I told you when it was," Mason said. "If you want to ask me questions, go ahead. If you've brought me up here to make insinuations about the fact that I was trying to give myself a coat of legal whitewash, I'll walk out. You're a lawyer and you know what's proper in the line of questioning and what isn't. Now stay with proper questions."

"I don't need you to tell me the law," Hamilton Burger flared, his face red.

"You need someone," Mason told him. "Now this isn't getting us anywhere. I'm a busy man and you're a busy man. The members of this body are sacrificing their time in order to perform a public service. Let's go ahead with the hearing."

Hamilton Burger angrily shouted, "All right, let's find out about what Arlene Duvall paid you. She paid you some money, didn't she?"

"No."

"Not a cent?"

"There," Mason said, "we come to a question of fact and of proof. I have credited Arlene Duvall's account with fifteen hundred dollars. I have every reason to believe that that money was received from her but she didn't pay it to me."

"How did you get it then?"

"The fifteen hundred dollars *that I am now referring to*," Mason said, slowing his voice so that he could be absolutely certain that the court reporter who was taking the proceedings in shorthand had an accurate record of what he had said, "came in the mail this morning in an envelope which had been addressed to me on a typewriter. There was a note inside in handwriting and I am assuming that that note was in Arlene Duvall's handwriting since she purported to sign it."

"What was in that envelope?"

"Two pieces of currency. One five-hundred-dollar bill. One one-thousand-dollar bill."

Hamilton Burger showed surprise despite himself. "You mean this young woman sent you two bills, one for one thousand dollars and one for five hundred dollars?"

"That's what I said."

"And where did you think she had secured the money?" Burger asked sarcastically.

"Are you wishing to interrogate me in front of the grand jury concerning my thoughts?" Mason asked.

"Well, where did she *tell* you she got the money?"

"She didn't tell me. As I have told you earlier, I have had no personal contact with her since some time yesterday. I received this letter in the mail this morning."

"What time this morning?"

"Just a few minutes before I came up here.

Which is why I have the money with me. It is the policy of my office to deposit every single dollar that is received in the form of cash in my bank account and withdraw such cash as I need from time to time by check."

Hamilton Burger said, "I am assuming, of course, that a man in your position, carrying on the type of activities that you do, has to take every precaution to see that he can't be convicted of violating the income tax."

Mason yawned.

"Where are those two bills — the five-hundred-dollar bill and the thousand-dollar bill?"

Mason produced them.

Hamilton Burger copied the numbers of the bills on a piece of paper, gave the piece of paper to an attendant who promptly slipped from the room.

Burger said to the grand jurors, "I'll have the numbers on those bills checked in a moment. We'll see if we have any history of them.

"Now then," Hamilton Burger said, turning to Mason, "did you know Jordan L. Ballard during his lifetime?"

"I did."

"When did you see him last?"

"Last night."

"Did you go to Mr. Ballard's place of business, a super service station located at Tenth and Flossman streets?"

"I did."

"And there you met Mr. Ballard?"
"Yes."
"Had you known him before?"
"No."
"Did you get acquainted with him at that time for the first time?"
"Yes."
"Did you offer to drive him home?"
"He asked me if I would give him a lift."
"And you consented?"
"Yes."
"You did drive him to his residence?"
"I did."
"Did he tell you why he wanted you to drive him home?"
"He said his car was laid up for repairs."
"And when you arrived at the bungalow where he lived you saw no car parked in front of it, in the driveway or in the garage, is that right?"
"That's right."
"And you drove your car into the garage, or into the driveway?"
"Into the driveway."
"Why didn't you leave it parked out at the curb?"
"I was going to turn around and go back down the street and Ballard suggested that I swing into the driveway and drive right up to the door."
"By doing that you were able to get closer to the front door than by leaving the car parked at the curb?"

"Very much closer."

"How close?"

"Oh, I would say we were within ten or twelve feet of the front door when I stopped the car."

"By that you mean that the right-hand side of the car was nearer to the front door?"

"That's right."

"When *you* got out *you* had to walk around the car in order to get into the house?"

"Not necessarily. It was easier to slide across the seat and go out the right-hand door."

"Ballard was seated on your right?"

"Naturally — I was driving the car."

"He got out first?"

"Yes."

"And what did you do?"

"Then I slid across the seat and got out on the right-hand side."

"Following Ballard?"

"Naturally. I didn't climb over him."

"There is no occasion to be facetious, Mr. Mason. We simply want to know what happened."

"I am telling you what happened."

"You went into the house with Mr. Ballard?"

"I did."

"Now then," Hamilton Burger said, suddenly pointing his finger at Perry Mason, "you had told your client, Arlene Duvall, that you were going to see Mr. Ballard, hadn't you?"

"I had not."

"Didn't you tell her to meet you at Ballard's house?"

"I did not."

"Didn't you tell her that you were going to try to persuade Mr. Ballard to let you drive him home?"

"I did not."

Hamilton Burger said sneeringly, "After you had entered the house, after Mr. Ballard had taken you into the interior of the house, you took occasion to go to the window and signal someone by partially lowering the roller shade on the window, didn't you?"

"I did not."

"Do you deny that?"

"I deny it."

"You were signaling Arlene Duvall, were you not?"

"I was not."

"You were signaling somebody."

Mason remained silent.

"Do you dare deny that?" Burger asked. "Do you dare deny that you were signaling someone?"

"I deny it."

Burger hesitated a moment, then said, "Mr. Mason, I am going to warn you that we have in our possession evidence indicating that these last answers of yours constitute perjury. So that there can be no misunderstanding I am going to ask you certain questions once more and —"

"You don't need to ask me any more questions about Ballard's house," Mason said. "I have answered those questions. I don't intend to sit here and have you browbeat me. You have asked questions. You say my answers constitute perjury. I say that statement of yours is a mistaken assumption. I was in Ballard's house for only a few minutes."

Burger said grimly, "Some man who raised and lowered the shade on that window was there at the time of Ballard's death. We can prove that."

Mason's face was granite hard. "Go ahead and prove it then."

"Right now," Burger said, "I'm more interested in a charge of perjury. I want to see if I have understood you correctly. You have stated that you didn't signal your client by raising and lowering the window shade, or, rather, by lowering and raising the window shade."

"That's right," Mason said.

"You have said that you didn't signal anyone."

"That's right," Mason said. "You've asked those questions twice and I've answered them twice. Now then, do you have anything else?"

Hamilton Burger said angrily, "I don't need anything else. I've tried to give you a break. I've tried to save your professional career, although I don't know why I should. Now then, I'm going to ask you to sit right there while we bring in two other witnesses."

Hamilton Burger turned to the deputy at the

door and bellowed, "Bring in Horace Mundy."

Mundy, looking very much like a dog who is about to receive a whipping, entered the grand jury room. He gave Mason one brief, flickering glance, then hastily averted his eyes.

"Now then," Hamilton Burger said, "I want to caution Mr. Mason that in a proceeding of this sort he does not have the right to cross-examine. I will concede that Mr. Perry Mason is a very adroit, very able cross-examiner, and if he had an opportunity to do so I feel quite certain that he would try to confuse the issues and confuse the witness. I am going to assure the grand jury that I will make my questions absolutely fair, that I will not try to force an identification. I am, however, not going to permit Mr. Perry Mason to try and bamboozle the witness. Mr. Mundy, do you know the gentleman sitting there, Mr. Perry Mason?"

"I do. Yes, sir."

"Did you see him last night?"

"Yes, sir."

"Where?"

"Well, I saw him several times. Mr. Mason looked me up after I'd made the report to Paul Drake of the Drake Detective Agency."

"You're employed by the Paul Drake Detective Agency?"

"That's right."

"And you were employed by Mr. Mason to shadow — ?"

"I'm sure I can't tell you that. All I know is

that the Drake Detective Agency asked me to do certain things. I am assuming from what was said over the telephone that Mr. Mason was the client."

"All right, all right," Burger said. "Now, last night you were out shadowing Arlene Duvall?"

"Yes, sir."

"And where was she?"

"When we started shadowing her she was in a house trailer. She drove away in a trailer."

"Actually, I take it that she didn't drive away in the house trailer. She drove away in a car that was towing the house trailer."

"Yes, sir. I guess that's the way it was. I'm sorry."

"Not at all," Hamilton Burger said, "and I wouldn't ordinarily make a point of it because I think all of us knew what you meant, but Mr. Mason is now crowded into a corner and we can depend on him to rely on every technicality, to grasp at every straw. Now you saw Arlene Duvall driving her car with a house trailer attached to it. It that right?"

"Yes, sir."

"And where did she go?"

"Out into a secluded part of the unimproved grounds which I believe belong to the Remuda Golf Club. At any rate they were adjacent to the golf course of that club."

"And what did you do?"

"My partner and I took up a position where we could observe what was happening. If she had driven the car back out of that place we would have seen her."

"Then what happened?"

"I thought that it was time to go and telephone Paul Drake and let him know what was happening. Things seemed to have quieted down for the evening. The nearest public telephone that I knew of where I could put through a call at that hour was —"

"What hour was it?"

"Well, I think it was . . . well, it was around . . . well, it was between nine-thirty and ten o'clock. Now please understand me, Mr. Burger, as a methodical detective I always make a note of the time that I telephone the office, and I would have done so in this instance. Therefore, I wasn't paying very much attention to the time at that particular moment. I expected to look at the time and make a note of the time when I put through the call. But it was somewhere between nine-thirty and ten o'clock."

"All right, go ahead. What happened?"

"Well, as I said, the nearest public telephone that I knew of was at a service station on the boulevard at the intersection of the road that turns off to go past the golf club and from which, in turn, there is a private driveway leading to the golf club."

"So what did you do?"

"I felt that I could save myself about . . . oh, between a quarter and a half a mile of walking if I cut across the golf club to the service station."

"And did you do that?"

"Yes, sir."

"The night was dark?"

"Yes, it was dark; that is, there wasn't any moon. There were, however, quite a few stars. In other words, if there was any overcast at all, any smoke or atmospheric impurities, it was not dense enough to keep the stars, at least the brighter stars, from shining through, and it was possible to see your way enough to avoid running into things — that is, after your eyes had become accustomed to the darkness."

"Did you have a flashlight?"

"I carry a little pocket flashlight, one of those that's hardly bigger than a fountain pen."

"And you started walking across the golf course?"

"Yes. First through a brushy path where I used my little hand flashlight, and then I came out on the golf course itself. I then moved over to a fairway and started walking rather rapidly. I didn't use my flashlight then."

"And what happened?"

"Well, I hadn't gone very far before I realized someone was ahead of me, a woman."

"What did you do?"

"I dropped to one knee quickly."

"Why?"

"So that I wouldn't be so apt to be discovered by having my silhouette against the sky and so I could get a better look at her by seeing her silhouette against the sky."

"And did you get a better look at her?"

"Yes."

"Who was it?"

"I didn't recognize her positively enough at *that* time to swear to it, Mr. Burger, but I recognized her so that I became morally convinced of her identity. Later on I saw her clearly."

"Who was the person?"

"Arlene Duvall."

"When did you become certain as to her identity?"

"After I had followed her to the service station."

"She went to the service station?"

"Yes. She was going there to telephone."

"And you followed her?"

"I did."

"Then what did you do?"

"I felt certain she was phoning for a taxicab. I knew that I couldn't get near the phone while she was there and I was afraid a cab would come before I could summon another one. So I went out and stood by the curb at the boulevard and tried to flag down passing motorists."

"Did you do so?"

"I did, finally."

"Whom did you flag down?"

"A gentleman by the name of Fraser."

"Do you have his other names?"

"Yes, sir."

"What are they?"

"James Wingate Fraser."

"And you had some conversation with this individual?"

"Yes, I asked him if he would follow a car for me, and I pointed out Miss Duvall who was at the telephone and told him that was the girl I wanted shadowed. I showed him my credentials as a private detective."

"Did you tell him you were a private detective?"

"Well, I told him I was a detective and flashed my credentials at him. I didn't misrepresent the situation any way. I simply told him I was a detective."

"Let's be fair," Hamilton Burger said virtuously. "You were willing to let him assume that you were a police detective, were you not?"

"He could assume anything he wanted. I told him I was a detective. That's all I said."

"And you asked him if he would follow a car for you in case one showed up to pick up Miss Duvall?"

"Words to that effect."

"And offered to pay him?"

"Yes, sir."

"And then what happened?"

"A taxicab showed up. Arlene Duvall got in the taxicab. It was evidently one she had ordered by telephone."

"Did you get the number of that cab?"

"I did. Yes, sir. That was part of my report."

"What was the number of that cab?"

"245."

"And then what happened?"

"Then Mr. Fraser, following my instructions, followed the cab."

"Now tell us generally what happened. Which way did the cab go? What did Miss Duvall do?"

"After we had followed the cab for a while it went to a residence which I have since ascertained was that of Jordan L. Ballard. It first went to his place of business at Tenth and Flossman streets. Then it was driven to the bungalow."

"What happened there?"

"A car was parked in the driveway. I assumed that it was Mr. Ballard's car. The taxicab stopped. Miss Duvall ran up on the front steps, apparently started to ring the doorbell and then, hearing voices, turned around, came back, paid off the taxicab, and then walked around past the side of the house."

"And what did you do?"

"As soon as the cab had stopped, I had Mr. Fraser drive his car up about half a block, turn it so it was facing the house and then I got out and walked down the street so I could keep an eye on Miss Duvall, keeping in the shadows as much as possible."

"What did you see?"

"I saw someone inside the house pull aside the hanging drapes at the window facing the side street, stand there, vaguely silhouetted in light that was seeping through the parted drapes, and lower the roller curtain shade for a moment, then raise it again."

"Do you know now who that person was?"

"I . . . I can't make an absolutely *positive* identification but I *think* it was Perry Mason."

"Then what happened?"

"Then, after a while, Mr. Mason, that is, whoever was in the house, went out, got in the car and drove away. At that time Arlene Duvall pulled a box up against a kitchen window, tied her skirts up around her waist, and scrambled in through the window."

"Then what happened?"

"She was in there for several minutes."

"How long?"

"Oh, probably five minutes."

"And then?"

"Then she came out."

"She was walking?"

"Rapidly, almost running."

"And what did you do?"

"I went back to Mr. Fraser's car. We followed her for a while and then we lost her."

"How?"

"She pretended that she was going up the front steps of a house, but instead she detoured around to the back and simply disappeared. It's an old dodge but . . . well, somehow I didn't think she was going to pull anything like that, and it caught me unprepared. I may say I am not particularly proud of my detective work for the entire evening."

"Now you say you think the person you saw signaling from the house was Perry Mason?"

"Well, I . . . I think so now. Yes, sir."

"Did Mr. Mason ask you questions trying to find out if you had recognized him?"

"Well, he came to me and asked me to describe the person I had seen at the window doing the signaling, and . . . well, I had to tell him that the man looked exactly like Mr. Mason, that he was Mason's double as to build and size and . . . but at *that* time the significance of it didn't occur to me."

"When did it occur to you?"

"When you had me in your office and . . . and after I had talked with Mr. Fraser. Well, then I began to put everything together."

"I think that's all for the moment," Hamilton Burger said. "I want to call James Wingate Fraser."

Fraser entered the room, was sworn and told his story confirming everything that Mundy had said, except as to the time element.

Fraser thought that the time he first saw Mundy was between nine and nine-thirty.

"How do you fix the time?" Burger asked.

"It's just an estimate, I had been looking over some property. When I returned I ran into this detective and I think this signaling out at Ballard's house took place right around ten o'clock."

"Do you recognize the man who did the signaling?"

"Yes, sir. That man was Perry Mason."

"When did you first know who it was?"

"Well, we were having a little party out at my house and Mr. Mason showed up —"

"When was that?"

"Last night."

"At what time?"

"Oh, around . . . well, it was pretty late. At that time I wasn't at all conscious of the hour. I was with friends."

"And what did Mr. Mason want? What did he say?"

"Well, mainly what he wanted to know was whether I had been able to recognize the man I saw there at the window. I told him it was a man of about his build and . . . and then after he left someone at the party said something about Mr. Mason being mighty anxious to find out whether I could recognize that person in case I saw him again and . . . well, then somebody said, 'Maybe he's worried because he wanted to find out whether he's in the clear.' And everybody laughed, but all of a sudden I quit laughing. I just realized . . . well, it struck me all at once that it might have been Mr. Mason there at the window."

"Now you saw this man at the window and again when he left the house?"

"Yes, sir. That's when I got my best view, when he was leaving the house."

"And when he was getting in the automobile and driving away?"

"Yes, sir."

"Who was that person?"

"I am now satisfied that person was Perry Mason."

"When you say Perry Mason you're referring to the witness who is now seated just to your left?"

"That's right."

"Put your hand on his shoulder."

Fraser walked over to Mason and put his hand on the lawyer's shoulder.

"That's all," Hamilton Burger said.

The district attorney arose, faced the grand jury, then looked at Mason and said suddenly, "We don't need you any longer, Mr. Mason. You're excused."

"Thank you," Mason said. "If you want to be absolutely fair to the grand jury you might point out that I asked both of these witnesses if they could identify the man they had seen. Mundy told me that he didn't think he could. Fraser said that he might if he saw him again. But at that time Fraser was looking right at me."

"You don't need to argue the case," Hamilton said. "The grand jury will draw its own conclusions, particularly its conclusions as to why you were so anxious to hurry out to see these witnesses and, at a time when they thought you would be the last man in the world to have done such a thing, trapped them into stating that they couldn't make a positive identification."

"Don't worry about my motives," Mason said. "Just concentrate on your own for a while. I merely want to point out certain things that are in evidence, and, while I don't have the right to cross-examine witnesses here, if this grand jury does take any action, remember that I'll then have the right to cross-examine those witnesses and that cross-examination will be in public."

"Never mind trying to argue the case," Hamilton Burger shouted. "You're excused. Now get out."

"Thank you," Mason said, and walked out of the room.

A swarm of reporters surrounded Mason.

"What's going on in there?" they asked. "What's this about you being mixed up in the Ballard murder?"

"I believe," Mason said, "a witness before the grand jury is not supposed to discuss his testimony."

"Were you a witness?"

"Yes."

"Then why did you remain in there while two other witnesses were called? Were they called for the purpose of identifying you?"

"You'll have to ask the district attorney or some of the grand jurors about these matters," Mason said, smiling affably. "I have no comment."

"Suppose you were identified?"

"Suppose I was."

"Is Burger trying to get the grand jury to indict you for something?"

"I'm afraid I'm not much good at reading the mind of the district attorney," Mason said. "And now if you gentlemen will excuse me, I'm —"

"Oh no you don't. Come on now. Kick through. Were you out at Ballard's house last night?"

"I was."

"When he was murdered?"

"No. He was alive and well when I left."

"What time was that?"

"I didn't look at my watch."

"Is it true you were the last man to see Jordan Ballard alive?"

"The murderer saw him alive," Mason said.

"Is it true the grand jury is going to indict you for perjury?"

Mason smiled. "If you'll look up the law," he said, "you'll find that fortunetelling by predicting the future is subject to various statutory regulations."

"What happened in the jury room?" another asked.

"No comment," Mason said. "Why don't you ask Hamilton Burger? Doubtless he'll be only too glad to give you the information."

Mason left the courthouse, took a taxi back to his office.

"What happened?" Della Street asked.

Mason said, "Hamilton Burger is getting ready to have me indicted for perjury."

"Did you refuse to answer his questions?"

"Fortunately," Mason said, "Hamilton Burger phrased his questions in such a way that I wasn't confronted with the necessity of determining whether I would have to refuse to answer.

"He wanted to know if I had lowered and raised a curtain at Ballard's house for the purpose of signaling Arlene Duvall. I told him I hadn't and he challenged me to deny that I had signaled *someone* by means of lowering and raising the curtain. That gave me an opportunity to tell him that I hadn't. I was afraid that if he kept on talking he might stumble onto the correct question to have asked, which was simply whether I had appeared at the window and lowered and raised the curtain. So I got angry. Our friend Hamilton Burger doesn't think clearly when he's angry."

"You mean he never asked you any question about what you'd done except in connection with signaling someone?"

"That's right," Mason said, grinning.

"How wonderful! What do we do now?"

"We find out if Drake has had any luck with his messenger service."

"He hasn't. He's covered every messenger service in town."

"Then there's only one other thing to do,"

Mason said, "and that's to cover the theatrical costuming companies. Someone rented the costume of a messenger boy."

"He's already working on that," Della Street said. "That idea occurred to him as soon as he found no messenger service had — Here he is now."

Paul Drake's code knock sounded on the outer door of Mason's private office.

Della Street opened the door.

"Want to kick me?" Paul asked Mason.

"Why?"

"That messenger boy," Drake said. "Of all the damn saps! I should be kicked into the middle of next week!"

"Go on," Mason said. "Tell me about it."

"In the first place," Drake said, "that wasn't a regular messenger service. That was a theatrical costume."

"How could you have detected that?"

"The thing was phony," Drake said. "Apparently there wasn't any badge with a number on it. The cap had a little brass plate with some sort of a name etched on it. My receptionist assumed that it was the name of a messenger service. And that isn't the worst that happened."

"What's the worst?"

"That messenger boy may have been Howard Prim, the guy who was mixed up in stealing that trailer the first time."

"You're certain?" Mason asked.

"No, that's the hell of it," Drake said. "I'm

not certain, and I can't give you evidence that you can use to prove it."

"Go ahead," Mason said. "Tell me what you have."

"Well, of course, Perry, I had a lot of people out last night, a lot of things were going on, all at once. My receptionist at night runs the switchboard and she was jumping around frantically. This messenger came in and said, 'I have an envelope to leave for Mr. Mason in care of Paul Drake.'

"The receptionist didn't think a thing about it. She looked at the address on the envelope and the messenger walked out without asking her to sign a receipt or anything.

"The switchboard was going a mile a minute with calls pouring in, and I was putting through —"

"Never mind all of that," Mason said. "I know you were busy. I know you can't guarantee mathematical results in a job of this kind, just tell me what happened."

"Well, we tailed Prim, or Sackett, all right for a while, and then my men evidently tipped their hand. Anyhow Sackett gave them the slip. He went into an office building and they never did see him go out."

"What's that got to do with the costume?"

"That's just the point," Drake said. "When I started checking the costuming agencies I found one had rented a messenger uniform to a fellow just before closing hour yesterday. He rented both the messenger uniform and the robes of a priest. That costuming agency was in the building where Sackett gave my man the slip. Well, you can see what happened. My man didn't dare to get too close to the building. He was waiting for Prim, or Sackett, to come out. Sackett came out all right but he must have gone into a rest room, put on the robes, and that enabled him to emerge from the office building as a priest carrying a package. The package must have contained the messenger boy uniform. My man wasn't close enough to get a good look at his face. He hadn't expected a switch like that."

"So you think it was Sackett who delivered the envelope to you last night?"

"It may have been, although the descriptions don't match. Sackett is rather chunky. This boy was slender and sort of — Hell's bells, Perry, that messenger boy could have been a girl dressed up in the uniform. I was busy at the time and this kid delivered the message to my night receptionist and telephone operator. She didn't even bother to take a good look — but it *could* have been a girl from her description."

"And where did Sackett go from the place where he rented the costume?"

"We don't know, Perry. That's what makes me mad. It's one of those things. It happened and that's all you can say about it."

"When did your man pick Sackett up again?"

"About six o'clock this morning. He showed

up at 3921 Mitner Avenue, the place that he rents under the name of Sackett. He never let on that he had any idea I had men planted on the job watching for him to come home. He parked his jeep and went up to his apartment, without even looking back over his shoulder. It makes me so damn mad —"

"Never mind that," Mason said. "We have to take things as they come. Incidentally, your man Mundy identified me in front of the grand jury as the man he saw out at Ballard's house last night."

"The hell he did!"

Mason nodded.

"Well, that isn't what he told me."

"What about a written report?" Mason asked. "Did he make a written report?"

"No, he didn't. He . . . say, come to think of it, he must have been tipped off not to. He's supposed to have turned in a written report."

"Did he tell you he was subpoenaed before the grand jury?"

Drake shook his head.

"Well, that's that," Mason said.

"Of course," Drake went on hastily, "you can't hold that against him too much, Perry. If the police picked him up and the D.A. told him what not to do, you can't blame him for not violating the D.A.'s instructions. After all, he's a detective and he has to make a living in this town."

"I'm wondering if the district attorney told

him what *to* do," Mason said. "On the identification, I mean."

"Mundy isn't the type," Drake said. "Mundy is conservative — a good, steady, dependable man. If he tells you anything you can rely on it. The only trouble with him is that he's just a little bit timid. He isn't a fighter. He backs out if the going gets rough. He's a good observer and a good routine operative, but . . . well, he won't fight."

"In other words, he wouldn't have put up a struggle against the district attorney?"

"He wouldn't have sworn to anything he didn't believe."

"But he wouldn't fight with the D.A.?"

"No. You couldn't ask him to. Anyhow you had a right to go out there. No one is really going to suspect you of murder. Your visit becomes important only as it serves to fix the *time* element. Did Arlene Duvall go into the place as soon as you left?"

"That's what Mundy says."

"If Mundy says it, it's pretty apt to be true. What can you do about it, Perry?"

"Nothing. If Burger calls me as a witness and asks the proper questions I'll have to crucify my own client."

"Then what will she do?"

"Do the only thing she can do to save her own neck. She'll swear he was dead when *I* left the house."

"*Then* what will Hamilton Burger do?"

"It's hard to tell. He may have the grand jury indict us both. He's mad. Oh well, skip that for a minute, Paul. What about Arlene Duvall? What's happened there?"

"There's hell to pay over her, Perry. The police detectives found they were shadowing an empty trailer. They went in and searched the place this morning."

"The deuce they did! Have a warrant?"

"I don't think so. It gradually occurred to them that their quarry must have given them the slip during the night. They kept working in a little closer on the trailer. Then they had a conference; then one of them went and telephoned. My men moved up to see what was going on."

"And what happened?"

"They went to the trailer and knocked on the door two or three times. When they got no answer they tried the door. The door was open. They went in."

"How long were they in there?"

"They're in there now," Drake said. "They must be taking the place to pieces."

"All right, Paul. Concentrate on this fellow Sackett. Don't lose him again."

"What's your position?" Drake asked. "What about this testimony of Mundy's? How bad is it going to hurt you?"

"I think," Mason said, "that Hamilton Burger is asking the grand jury to indict me for perjury right now."

"Are they going to do it?"

Mason shrugged his shoulders.

"And what'll you do if they do, Perry?"

"I'll put up bond," Mason said.

"And then what?"

"I don't know."

"You're not being very communicative."

"Right at the moment," Mason said, "I haven't anything to communicate. Put more men on Sackett, Paul. He's important. He's damned important. I don't want him to give you the slip again."

"Do you want him to know that he's being tailed?"

"Not if you can avoid it. That's why I want you to put on enough men to do a good job."

"Okay. Anything else?"

"Found out anything more about Ballard's murder?"

"That's about all there is to find out. Someone cracked him over the head, apparently striking him from behind with a blackjack or something of that sort. When he keeled over they stabbed him three times with a carving knife."

"Where did the carving knife come from?"

"It was his knife. Whoever did the job took it from a magnetic knife rack over the drainboard."

"That's adding insult to injury — making a man furnish the weapon for his own death," Mason said. "However, it would indicate there wasn't any premeditation, that it was one of those affairs that come up on the spur of the moment."

"Who did it, Perry?"

"Hell's bells," Mason said, "according to the police reasoning, and there doesn't seem to be any hole in that that I can uncover as yet, only two persons could have done it — Arlene Duvall or Perry Mason. And I know damned well *I* didn't."

"How do they reason?"

"Arlene Duvall evidently got out there while I was talking with Ballard. She didn't want to go in while I was there. She waited out in the back yard until I'd left. Then she climbed in the back window, was in there five minutes, ran out through the front of the house and ditched your shadows. Dammit, Paul, your shadows don't seem to have been doing anything last night except letting subjects slip one over on them."

"It happens that way," Drake said resignedly. "You know the game as well as I do, Perry. We've had it happen before, and we'll doubtless have it happen again. It's just the fortunes of war. But how do they know Ballard was dead when Arlene Duvall left the house?"

"That seems to be my only hope at the moment, Paul. If she has sense enough to say nothing we may be able to confuse the witnesses on the time element. There's already a discrepancy. Something sure gave Arlene a terrific shock when she was in there. A lot is going to depend on what happens next."

"In what way?"

"Sooner or later they'll pick her up. If she says Ballard was alive and kicking when she left the house, she'll have to explain why she climbed through the kitchen window, also why she went running out of the house leaving the front door half-open. But if she should say that he was dead when she entered the house and that scared her and she ran away — well, then I'd be in the line of fire. And we have to take one very nasty possibility into consideration."

"What's that?"

"That Arlene Duvall hit him over the head in an argument and then, in a frenzy of rage, grabbed a carving knife off the rack and plunged it into his body, and when the going gets tough she'll try to save her neck by pushing the murder off on to me."

"You say a frenzy of rage."

"That's right."

"Then that wouldn't be first-degree murder."

Mason said, "Before we get done it may be that that's where we're going to have to make our fight — as to whether it was first-degree or second-degree murder, depending on the presence or absence of premeditation."

"But what could have been the motive? Why would she have gone into this frenzy of rage?"

"Because," Mason said, "she suddenly found out that Jordan L. Ballard was the one who had manipulated that theft of the Mercantile Security and blamed it on her father. However, I'm not going to cross a whole series of bridges before we even come to the stream. We'll wait until —"

The telephone rang. Mason nodded to Della Street, who picked up the instrument, said, "It's for you, Paul."

Paul put the receiver to his ear, said, "Yes. Hello," then listened for a moment, said, "The deuce!" then turned to Perry Mason.

"Okay, Perry," he said, "the fat's in the fire."

"The police have picked up Arlene Duvall. She admits having gone out to Ballard's house. She won't tell why she went out there. She admits climbing in the kitchen window because after she peeked through the kitchen window she saw him lying on the floor. She says that he was dead when she entered the place."

Mason looked at his watch. "That means," he said, "we're fighting against time."

"How long do we have?"

Mason shrugged his shoulders.

"Burger may not do anything until after he's secured an indictment. He may have a complaint filed and proceed by preliminary hearing. Get out a writ of habeas corpus, Della. File a writ on behalf of Arlene Duvall and we'll make Burger either fish or cut bait."

"Which do you think he'll do?" Drake asked.

"If he's smart," Mason said, "he'll do both."

"What do you mean?"

"He'll bypass the grand jury and have a complaint for murder filed against Arlene Duvall. Then he'll have a preliminary examination and call me as a witness on behalf of the prosecution.

"That will force me into the open and force Arlene Duvall to either take a murder rap or else try to pin it on me. In either event he'll have all the cards in his hands."

Drake contemplated that situation and shook his head. "This is once I wouldn't want to be standing in your shoes, Perry."

Mason grinned. "They *are* beginning to pinch a little."

"How much time do you have, Perry? How much of a headstart?"

"Not very much. We've got to prove what *did* happen, Paul. Either Arlene Duvall killed him or someone else did. Of course, someone else might have been concealed in the house when Ballard and I entered. That's one thing we'll have to investigate carefully, Paul."

"Do you think someone who was concealed in there killed him, then waited until after Arlene ran out before leaving, Perry?"

"Either that or Arlene did it."

"You can have my opinion on that very fast, Perry," Paul Drake said. "This is one case where your client did the job. Of course, we don't know the provocation — it may even been justifiable — but she won't stay put, Perry. She'll walk out on you."

"What do you mean?"

"You know what I mean. She'll pin it on you, get some other lawyer to represent her and in the long run she, her lawyer and Hamilton Burger will all be trying to achieve the same goal — proving you guilty of murder."

"Well," Mason told him, "we have a little time before that happens."

"How much?" Drake asked.

Mason sighed. "Not a hell of a lot," he admitted.

• 9 •

Early editions of the afternoon newspapers made quite a feature of the story. Big headlines proclaimed: PROMINENT ATTORNEY FACES PERJURY CHARGE.

Apparently someone from the district attorney's office had talked to the press, not only in detail but loquaciously.

From reading the account in the paper Mason learned that the grand jury had seriously entertained the district attorney's suggestion that the "prominent attorney" be indicted for perjury, but had decided in the interest of justice to postpone any action until after the trial of Arlene Duvall for the murder of Jordan L. Ballard.

The district attorney, grimly determined to see that nothing stood in the way of the perjury prosecution, had filed a complaint charging Arlene Duvall with first-degree murder when it became known that Perry Mason was preparing an application for a writ of habeas corpus.

Hamilton Burger, the district attorney, pledged himself in the press that the "full facilities of his office" would be utilized to see that Arlene Duvall had a prompt trial, and that he in turn expected the grand jury to "do its duty."

Hamilton Burger had released other information to the press. Not only had Arlene Duvall admitted that Ballard was dead when she had entered the house through the kitchen window, but that it was because she saw his body lying on the floor that she had entered through the window.

Laboratory technicians had found blood on Arlene Duvall's shoe. It had been determined that it was human blood of the type AB, a rare type of blood found in only three to five percent of people. It was the type of blood of Jordan Ballard.

Newspapers went on to hint that there was a new and most incriminating piece of evidence that the police had unearthed, but which they were at the present time holding as a "closely guarded secret."

There was, of course, a rehash of the history of the mysterious theft of nearly four hundred thousand dollars in cash from the Mercantile Security Bank, and the statement was made that shortly before his death Jordan L. Ballard, who had been employed by the bank and had at one time been a suspect in the case, had recalled the number of at least one of the thousand-dollar bills that had been stolen, and had communicated that information to the police.

The old story was again brought up about the package of bills amounting to five thousand dollars that had figured in an extortion case and that the FBI had the numbers of those bills. Those numbers were the most closely guarded secret in the entire case. It was rumored that even Hamilton Burger had tried in vain to get a copy of this list of numbers. The FBI had said they would check any suspicious bills but that no one was to be entrusted with the list itself. In that way, they hoped eventually to trap the thief into incriminating himself by spending some of the listed bills.

The papers quoted Hamilton Burger as stating that in his opinion there was absolutely no doubt that the murder of Jordan Ballard was "closely tied in" with the theft of money from the Mercantile Security.

Newspaper accounts went on to state that on the authority of a person who declined to permit his name to be mentioned, but who was in a position to know, Perry Mason had admitted before the grand jury that he had received from Arlene Duvall by way of a retainer two bills, one in an amount of a thousand dollars, the other in an amount of five hundred dollars.

The numbers of those bills had been taken by the district attorney and "every effort" would be made to connect them with the money stolen from the Mercantile Security Bank.

Police made much of the fact that for the past eighteen months Arlene Duvall had been living a life of leisure, spending money right and left with carefree abandon, money which she certainly had not earned and the possession of which she "could not explain."

Her father in the meantime was living the routine life of a felon in San Quentin, and was quite apt to spend a great many more years in that institution.

"Well," Della Street said as Mason finished reading, "that certainly makes it a smear, doesn't it?"

Mason nodded.

"They do everything except state out and out that you are mixed in with Arlene Duvall, accepting retainers out of stolen funds, and that you conspired to try and silence Ballard so that he couldn't testify against your client in court."

"Of course," Mason said, "it's their inning now. They're at the bat."

"Are you going down to the jail and talk with Arlene Duvall?"

"Not right away," Mason said.

"You can, can't you, now that she's been booked and formally charged? You're entitled to talk with her and —"

"Sure," Mason said. "They're so anxious to have me see her that they've left word I can see her at any hour of the day or night."

"Why not do it?" Della Street asked, puzzled.

"Because," Mason told her, "the police will have that room bugged with microphones all over the place."

"Well, you can be careful what you say," Della Street said.

"But will Arlene be careful?" Mason asked.

"What's to prevent her from blurting out some statement that would put both of our heads in the noose?"

"I never thought of that," Della Street admitted.

"Well, you can bet Hamilton Burger's thought of it," Mason told her.

The unlisted telephone on Perry Mason's desk exploded into noise.

Since only Paul Drake and Della Street had the number of that telephone and it was used only in matters of emergency, Mason grabbed for the instrument, said, "Yes, Paul. What is it?"

Paul Drake's voice, harsh with excitement, came over the wire. "We've got a break, Perry."

"What?"

"You know the secret evidence that the newspapers hinted the police had, evidence which was devastatingly deadly and all that sort of stuff?"

"What about it, Paul?"

"They found a whole cache of money in Arlene Duvall's trailer."

"How much?"

"I don't know, but something over twenty-five thousand dollars, I understand."

"Where?"

"One of the panels could be removed. Ordinally there's a glass-wool lining between that inner panel and the outer shell of the trailer, but this one had been very cunningly devised.

The insulation wasn't glass-wool. It was a whole lot of currency."

"Anything else?" Mason asked.

"Lots else. You remember the five thousand dollars in bills that the authorities had the numbers for — well, they found over a thousand dollars of this money in that cache."

"I guess that does it," Mason said, and then added after a moment, "What do you mean, *we* got a break, Paul?"

Drake said, "I don't know whether you're going to approve of this or not, Perry. Remember that I told you that this man Mundy was a pretty conservative type of fellow. Well, the man that I've got shadowing Thomas Sackett, alias Howard Prim, is just the opposite. He's plenty daring. After Sackett had parked his jeep last night this man went over the thing with a brush and developed enough latent fingerprints so he was able to get a fairly good fingerprint record of Sackett. He got one perfect set of thumb and fingerprints from the windshield where Sackett had taken hold of it to raise it. He got other prints from various parts of the machine."

"What did he find?"

"Sackett has a criminal record a mile and a half long. He's an expert forger and he's done some stick-up work. The guy's dangerous."

"When did you get this information?" Mason asked.

"I knew about the fingerprints early this

morning when my man made his report, but we didn't have the record until just a few minutes ago. It took a little while to get the prints classified and find out about the record."

Mason said, "I think we're going to have to shake this fellow Sackett down and find out what makes him tick. Where is he now, Paul? Is your man keeping him under surveillance?"

"Right now he's down at Laguna Beach. He drove by Newport Beach and picked up a beautiful little redheaded babe who looks swell in a tight-fitting elastic bathing suit. They've been in swimming. They're lying around on the sand and lollygagging."

"Where are your men?"

"One of them is watching the couple, the other one is keeping an eye on the jeep so that just in case Sackett should try another disappearing act we'll have two strings to our bow."

Mason said, "Okay, Paul. You and I are going down to Laguna Beach. We're going to interview Sackett. I don't think he's going to like the interview."

"Of course," Drake said, "we'll have a hard time *proving* that he stole the trailer but —"

"But we'll sure give him an uncomfortable half-hour," Mason said.

"He's an old-timer at the game, Perry. He isn't going to be stampeded. He isn't going to be worried too much about being charged with the theft of a trailer. He's been charged with about everything in the Penal Code. What's more, the guy is dangerous."

"We aren't going to charge him with the theft of the trailer," Mason said. "We may be going to accuse him of the murder of Jordan L. Ballard and see how he takes to that. How soon can you go, Paul?"

"Right away . . . if you want it that way, Perry, but you're playing with dynamite."

"I'm coming down to pick you up," Mason said. "Be ready to go."

• 10 •

Drake's operative was waiting for them at the appointed place in front of the Laguna Beach Hotel.

"Do you know Phil Rice?" Drake asked Perry Mason, indicating the waiting operative.

Mason shook hands.

"I've seen you quite a few times, Mr. Mason," Rice said. "It's a real pleasure."

"Where are they?" Drake asked. "Still there?"

"Apparently so. That's the jeep over there in the parking lot."

"They came down in that?"

"Uh-huh."

"Have you got the girl tabbed?"

"We checked the mailbox on the Newport Beach apartment where he picked her up. It's in the name of Helen Rucker."

"Class?"

"I'll say."

"Are they going steady?"

"They know each other pretty well."

"What are they doing?"

"Just lying around in the sand, doing a little necking and a little swimming. It's beginning to get late. They'll be going out to dress any minute now."

"Let's go," Drake said. "Where's your partner?"

"Out there keeping an eye on them."

"Okay, we'll give it a whirl."

It had been warm farther inland. Now there was just a faint fringe of fog lying off the coast, with occasional wispy streamers drifting in a couple of hundred feet above the beach, dissolving in the late afternoon sunlight.

Rice led the way down on the beach, threaded his way through several couples, then paused to signal a man with a camera who was standing by the water looking around as though trying to find something he could photograph.

"That your other operative?" Mason asked.

Drake nodded.

"Well, there they are," Rice said, pointing to a couple that were now sitting up on the beach looking out toward the waves.

"Looks like they're getting ready to dress and start for home," Drake said. "What'll we do, Perry?"

"Go up and give it to him cold turkey," Mason said. "We may just as well."

Drake said, "This guy is tough and fast, and — Oh-oh, Perry, I think he's spotted us."

Sackett sat suddenly more erect, looked at the three men, then glanced toward the man with the camera. He said something to his companion. She glanced up with quick alarm.

"Okay," Mason said, "here we go."

The three men walked through the sand, approached Sackett and the girl.

Sackett jumped hurriedly to his feet, extended his hand to the girl. She came up with a lithe, smooth motion, dusting the sand from her elastic bathing suit.

Sackett said something in her ear, then leaned toward her. They embraced and Sackett's hand circled around the back of her bathing suit. Then suddenly they separated and Sackett turned to face the three men.

"Hello," Mason said. "Which do you prefer to be called by, Sackett or Prim?"

"What is this? A pinch?"

"Not yet."

"Well, what is it?"

"We just want to talk with you."

"You go get your clothes on, honey. I'll meet you at the car," Sackett said to the girl.

"How soon?" she asked.

"Shortly after you get your clothes on," Sackett said, swaggering slightly. "These people aren't going to hold me up. They're not even official."

"You seem to know all about us," Mason said.

"Well, why not? You're Perry Mason, the lawyer."

"You should know Paul Drake," Mason said. "You arranged to have a message delivered at his office last night."

"You're nuts."

"Oh no, I'm not," Mason said. "You had quite a day yesterday, didn't you, Prim?"

"Sackett."

"All right, Sackett."

"Go get your clothes on, honey," he said to the young woman. "Please, honey. *Don't stick around here!*" There was something significant in the way he said that and in the glance which accompanied it.

She said to Mason, "I think you're horrid, pestering him this way," turned and walked back toward the dressing rooms.

"All right," Sackett said, "make it fast. I'm going to join her as soon as she gets dressed. We're going places."

"You're going to talk awhile," Mason said.

"Who says so?"

"I do."

"You've got lots more guesses coming."

"You have quite a record," Mason said. "It's an interesting record."

"All right, so what? I'm not wanted for anything."

"That's what you think."

"Name one."

"Stealing a house trailer for one."

The man's face stiffened. His eyes, shrewd, calculating and thoughtful, searched Mason's granite-hard face.

"You're bluffing."

"A fellow by the name of Jim Hartsel down at the Ideal Trade-In Trailer Mart would like to make an identification," Mason said. "He's anxious to get the trailer thieves who louse things up for the legitimate dealer. Also we have casts of the tires of your jeep and a few fingerprints from the inside of the house trailer."

Sackett thought that over. "What do you want?" he asked.

"We want to know who gave you the envelope that was delivered to Paul Drake's office last night."

"I don't know anything about any envelope. I don't know Paul Drake. I know you. And I know you're in a hell of a bind yourself. It's going to get worse. Don't try passing the buck to me. It won't work."

Mason said, "The man who rented the theatrical costume to you can identify you."

"All right. I rented costumes. So what?"

"Where did you get the envelope that was given to Paul Drake?"

"Arlene Duvall gave it to me, if you want to get tough about it."

"That's a lie," Mason said.

"Try and prove it's a lie. Start pressing me and I'll go to the D.A. with that information and he'll welcome me with open arms. You can't prosecute me on that trailer charge. The D.A. will give me immunity if I turn State's evidence. Crowd me and you know what you're getting into. Now then, I've put my cards on the table. Put up or shut up."

"I'm putting up," Mason said. "You used that delivery boy uniform to get into the house of Jordan L. Ballard last night, then you hit him over the head and —"

The expression of genuine, astounded surprise on Sackett's face was almost ludicrous.

"What the hell are you talking about?"

"Talking about a murder," Mason said, "and with the evidence I can produce and your criminal record to wave in front of the jury if you get on the witness stand, you can figure what your chances are. Start talking to your friend the district attorney about immunity on that one."

"Now look," Sackett said, "I don't know what your game is but you aren't going to pull any kind of frame-up like that on me. I can go to the police right now and tell them you're trying to blackmail me."

"Blackmail you for what?" Mason asked.

"Information."

"And what have I promised?"

"Immunity from —"

"From what?" Mason asked. "What immunity? I'm not promising you immunity. I'm promising you that you're going to be prosecuted."

"Well, you're intimating I could buy my way out."

"You couldn't buy your way out with all the gold in the United States mint," Mason said. "You're hooked."

He nodded to Paul Drake, said, "Look over here a minute, Paul."

Drake moved over to join him.

Sackett said, "I'm going to go dress and get my clothes on. If you want to get tough about it I'll see a lawyer. You can talk with him."

"Just a moment," Rice said. "You aren't going anywhere yet, buddy."

"Who says so?" Sackett asked, squaring away.

"I do," Rice announced easily, "and while you've got the build for it I don't think you're any good at it. You look to me like you're a sucker for a left hook. I could hang one on your jaw before you could even draw that right hand back. And don't make any mistake, buddy, you're the type that has to draw back in order to hit. I've been in the ring against enough of you muscle-bound truck horses to know what I'm talking about. Now then, you want to start something and get a free demonstration?"

Sackett hesitated, scowling, glancing at Mason and Paul Drake.

Mason said to Drake, "He's a veteran. He's going to be tough. He won't tell us anything worth while, and if he tells us anything at all it'll be a lie. I'm going to pretend to go telephone, but I'll go out to the jeep and wait for the girl. I think he put something down the back of her bathing suit when he gave her that last embrace."

"What?" Drake asked.

"I don't know. But did you notice the muscles on his right shoulder? They were moving back and forth as though he had been pushing something down the back of her bathing suit with his hand. Whatever it was, it was something so important he didn't dare to leave it anywhere. It's something he's keeping with him. I'm going to take a chance. Now who's your man over there with the camera?"

"Harvey Niles."

"Is he a good man?"

"One of the best."

"What about the camera? Does he know how to use it, or is that a blind?"

"No, he's an expert photographer. He can do wonders with that little 35 mm. camera he packs around with him. I bet he's got a whole stack of pictures of this couple from the time they got in the jeep until they got out on the sand."

"All right," Mason said. "I'm going around and work on the girl. You tell Rice to get over to Harvey Niles and tell him to pick me up at the jeep and follow me around in case I need him."

Sackett said, "All right you two. If you want anything out of me, make your proposition."

"All I want out of you," Mason said, "is to have you here when the police arrive."

"You're bluffing. You wouldn't call the police."

Mason said meaningly to Paul Drake, "Hold him right there, Paul. I'll go and phone the cops. Make a citizen's arrest if you have to."

"What charge?"

"The murder of Jordan L. Ballard. No, wait a

minute, let's let the police pick him up on that murder. You can make a citizen's arrest on the theft of the trailer. We've got a dead open-and-shut case on that. Jim Hartsel at the trailer mart will be tickled to death to make an identification."

Mason strode off toward the bathhouse.

Sackett watched him with puzzled eyes. "I don't know a damn thing about Ballard," Mason heard him say to Paul Drake.

Drake said, "Save it for the cops, Sackett," and lit a cigarette.

Mason detoured past the dressing rooms, went around to the parking place and stood by the jeep.

A few moments later he saw Harvey Niles, with the camera around his neck, take up a station at the entrance to the parking place.

Mason signaled the detective, and the detective nodded.

A few moments later the girl who had been with Sackett came hurrying out of the bathhouse.

Mason walked over toward her, timing his strides so as to intercept her near the entrance to the parking lot.

"Just a moment, Miss Rucker," Mason said.

She jumped apprehensively at the sound of her name, clutched at her purse, tried to crowd on past him.

"Take it easy, Miss Rucker," Mason said. "All you need to do is to give us the thing that Sackett put down the back of your bathing suit when he gave you that last fond embrace."

"I . . . I don't know what you're talking about."

Mason said impatiently, "Don't try that line. You're a nice girl. I don't want to have to take you in as an accessory. Give me the paper and then we'll be square."

"What do you mean, square?"

Mason said, "I mean that then you can go. I'm making a deal with Sackett."

"He hasn't said so."

Mason smiled. "Then why would he have told us about what he gave you?"

She thought that over for a moment, then opened her purse and handed Mason a folded sheet of paper.

Mason unfolded the paper, spread it out. There was a long list of numbers on it, a series of numbers arranged in orderly rows. There was no other writing.

Mason glanced at Paul Drake's operative with the camera. The man nodded, hurriedly unscrewed the lens, adjusted a sleeve in the camera, then put the camera to his eye.

Mason held up the list so that the light struck full on the paper.

Niles clicked the shutter on the camera, turned a knob, then gave an involuntary expression of disgust.

"What's the matter?" Mason asked.

The operative shrugged his shoulders, said, "I've got to put in a fresh roll of film. That was the last."

Helen Rucker was looking at Mason suspiciously.

"I think," she said, "I'd rather have Mr. Sackett tell me about the deal than to have you tell me."

Mason give a quick signal to the operative indicating that he was to hurry. He still held the paper in his hand, ignoring Helen Rucker's extended hand.

"What do *you* know about the murder of Jordan Ballard?" he asked.

"The murder of Jordan Ballard?"

Mason nodded.

"Why, nothing."

"Sackett was in on it," Mason said. "Why weren't you in on it?"

"I . . . I don't know what you mean."

"And about the trailer theft?"

"I haven't the faintest idea what you're talking about, and I resent the manner in which you're making these accusations."

"You look like a good kid," Mason said.

"Thank you," she retorted with elaborate sarcasm. "I've heard flattery before. Lots of people use it to get what they want. Just what is it *you* want, Mr. Mason?"

"The truth."

"I've heard all of the old approaches," she said. "I have beautiful eyes. My hair has soft luster. My skin is creamy. People rave over my legs. I have just the right curves in just the right places. I'm alert, intelligent and good company.

I've heard those things until I'm sick and tired to death of them. Now then, if you want to hand out a new line, go ahead."

Mason laughed and said, "I can't think of anything to add to all that."

"So few of them can," she observed with biting sarcasm. The photographer, who had been frantically manipulating the films in the camera, nodded to Mason.

Mason held up the list of figures. The photographer put the camera to his eye, move back and forth getting just the right focus. He clicked the shutter, wound the knob, clicked the shutter again.

"I don't like this," Helen Rucker said.

"What don't you like about it?" Mason asked, moving the list slightly.

Niles took two more shots.

Suddenly the girl's arm snaked over Mason's shoulder. Her hand snatched the paper from his grasp.

"I don't like the idea of you telling me about what Tom Sackett said I was to do about that list. I prefer to have him tell me himself. We'll go and see him. If he says it's all right, you can have it, and if . . . here he comes now."

Sackett, fully dressed, followed by Drake and Phil Rice, emerged from the dressing rooms, crossed the street and barged over to the parking lot.

"Well, well, well," Sackett said sarcastically. "Look who's here."

"Tom," Helen Rucker said, "did you say it was all right for Mr. Mason to have that paper?"

Sackett's face darkened with rage. "What paper?"

"The one —" She bit her lip and caught herself.

"I don't know anything about any paper," Sackett said, "and as far as these guys are concerned, they're running a cheap bluff. All this stuff about the murder of Ballard is just a pipe dream. I was with Helen here all last night, wasn't I, Helen?"

She looked at him for a moment, caught her breath, then nodded.

"Now that," Mason said, "is a new angle. The gentleman of the old school cheerfully stands trial on a murder he didn't commit rather than compromise the good name of a girl. You are using this girl's reputation as a pawn to protect your slimy skin from a murder you *did* commit."

"You make me sick," Sackett said.

"I may make you sicker before I'm done. Where did you have this delightful little all-night party? Where was it?"

"In her apartment," Sackett said.

"In a motel," she answered instantly.

"Which motel? Where?" Mason asked her.

"I . . . I don't have to tell you."

"Where was it?" Mason asked Sackett. "In her apartment or in a motel?"

"It was in her apartment. Now go roll your hoop."

She glanced at him pleadingly. "Tell them the truth, Tom. Not in my apartment."

"In your apartment," Sackett said, "and *you* may just as well tell them the truth, Helen. No one's going to forfeit your lease."

Mason laughed and said, "You're rather slow in your signals, Sackett. She evidently had someone else visiting her for a while last night so she tried to give you a cue you weren't smart enough to pick up."

"Mother's with me, Tom," she said. "She came yesterday."

Mason laughed.

Sackett said, "You guys go peddle your papers. I'm not talking with you any more and neither is Helen. Come on, Helen."

He took her arm.

Rice said to Mason, "You want them stopped?"

"Try and stop me," Sackett said, spinning on his heel.

"I'd love to," Rice said. "You want them stopped, Mr. Mason?"

Mason sized up the situation, slowly shook his head. "Let them go. We can do better that way."

Rice heaved a sigh of genuine regret. "I could tie him up so he'd look like a pretzel, Mr. Mason."

"Let him go," Mason said.

Sackett and Helen Rucker walked toward the jeep.

"Well," Drake said, "we didn't get very far with that one."

"Yes we did," Mason said, "provided Niles' photographs are any good."

"The last picture on that exposed roll probably wasn't any good," Niles said. "Sometimes the last picture isn't just what you want. But I'll stake my life those other pictures are good — the ones that are on the roll that's in the camera now."

"Will they be clear enough to show all those figures?" Mason asked.

"What was it?" Drake wanted to know.

"Some sort of a code message," Mason said, "a whole series of figures on a piece of paper."

"Can we enlarge those photographs and use them, Harvey?" Drake asked Niles.

"You bet you can use them. This sleeve increases the bellows extension so a sheet of paper that size just fills a 35 mm. film. Of course you couldn't read them on the film itself without a magnifying glass, but this lens cuts sharp as a tack and the focus is exceedingly critical. I can blow those things up to an eleven by fourteen and you can read everything on there."

"What sort of a code would it be?" Drake asked Mason.

"I don't know," Mason said. "It probably is some kind of a code message. I bluffed Helen

Rucker into letting me have it and then she began to get suspicious. It was a cheap trick running a bluff like that, but I felt we simply had to know what he had handed her. I thought it might be a piece of paper, but those numbers . . . wait a minute, I wonder . . ."

"Wonder what?" Drake asked as Mason's voice trailed away into silence.

"A string of numbers," Mason said. "Now I'm just wondering if it was a code message after all."

"If it wasn't a code message, what was it?"

Mason said, "Do you suppose there's any chance it could be —"

"Could be what?" Drake asked.

"That list of numbers?"

"What list of numbers?"

"On the five thousand dollars in bills."

Drake shook his head. "Not a chance in the world! That secret is the most closely guarded secret in the whole police business."

"I know," Mason said, "but somehow the more I think of it, the more I have an idea those things could be the numbers on bills rather than a code. How long is it going to take you to get those films developed, Niles?"

"It shouldn't take too long. If you want them developed as negatives I could send them in and have them within twenty-four hours. That's about the best service you can expect from regular channels."

"Let me have your camera," Drake said. "I

have a client who does photographic work. He'll run through that roll of film and make the enlargements. We'll have it all finished this evening."

Niles handed him the camera. "You know how to take the films out? You have to wind them through and then —"

"We'll find out," Mason said. "I prefer to have these films taken out in a darkroom. We don't want to have anything happen to them. Come on, Paul, let's go."

Sackett's jeep came roaring out of the parking lot. Drake jumped to one side.

"I bet he'd like to run us down," he said.

"What about shadowing him?" Rice asked. "Shall we take him on?"

"What about it?" Drake asked Mason. "It's money thrown away now. He knows that we're tailing him and he won't give us a single lead."

"At least until I tell you to stop — we'll give him something to think about."

Drake nodded to his two operatives. They ran to their car.

"Well, that's that," Drake said as the two operatives drove out of the parking lot.

Mason said, "Let's go get those pictures developed, Paul."

Mason and Drake climbed into the detective's car. "Let's go through Santa Ana and have a talk with Dr. Candler," Mason said. "Let's see what he knows about Sackett and see if he has any ideas about that list of numbers on the paper. It'll only take a few minutes longer to stop by his office."

Drake nodded. "Want to phone?"

"Probably we'd better. It's late. Just put through a station-to-station call and say we'll be in."

Drake slid the car to a stop in front of a phone booth at a service station, returned to the car in about three minutes and said, "It's all fixed. As soon as I mentioned your name they put me through to the doctor himself. He says to come right on in. He'll be waiting for us."

As they were once more driving toward Santa Ana, Drake turned to Perry Mason. "Look, Perry, it's none of my business but just who *were* you trying to signal with that curtain business in Ballard's house?"

"No one."

"Oh, all right, if you want to be like that," Drake said. "I just thought it might help you."

"Suppose," Mason said, "I was hiding something in the curtain, Paul?"

"Hiding something?"

"Suppose I found myself in the possession of some documents that were so hot I didn't dare to keep them in my possession. So I might have lowered the curtain, slipped the documents in between the shade and the roller and then raised the shade again, thereby effectively concealing them from any casual search. Everyone has thought I was signaling and —"

"Look," Drake told him, "if you're leveling

with me, Perry, those documents, whatever they were, are now in the hands of Sergeant Holcomb of the Homicide Squad."

"How come?" Mason asked.

Drake said, "Holcomb went out there with a partner. He spotted his partner out on the sidewalk. He walked through the drapes with the light on, pulled the roller shade down and then raised it so that he could have a test under comparable conditions, first to see whether or not his partner could see the signal, second, to see whether there was light enough to recognize anyone."

"And what did they find out?"

"Hell, you know the answer," Drake said. "They wouldn't go to all that trouble just to come back and say, 'We're sorry but there wasn't enough light to see a signal or enough light to recognize a person's outstanding characteristics.' "

"And Holcomb didn't report finding anything?"

"Not a thing."

"Sometimes an officer doesn't feel that he has to report anything, Paul."

"Meaning money?"

"Meaning only a general observation, Paul."

"Of course," Drake mused, "if it had been money . . . well, you know my opinion of Holcomb."

Mason remained silent.

"That would be a break for you," Paul Drake

went on. "It would take that hot money out of the case, but you couldn't count on a damn thing. Holcomb would have it in his power to double cross you at any minute."

Again Mason said nothing.

"And remember," Drake warned, "you may have got by in front of the grand jury by outsmarting Hamilton Burger. He may not have asked just the right question, but sooner or later you're going to be in court on this one, and when you do Hamilton Burger is going to ask the right question."

"How do you know?"

"Because he'll ask them *all*," Drake said.

Drake looked at Mason speculatively, then shrugged his shoulders and drove the car in silence.

• 11 •

Dr. Candler's office was open. There were two or three late patients still in the waiting room. There was about these people that air of bedraggled impatience characteristic of the sick who have been waiting their turn for a long period of time.

The redheaded nurse, whom Mason had met the night before, greeted them with effusive warmth, said, "Step right this way, please, gentlemen."

The waiting patients looked up with expressions of irritation mixed with a helpless acceptance of conditions, as they saw Perry Mason and Paul Drake ushered through the entrance room and into a door leading to the doctor's private office and the treatment rooms.

The nurse escorted Mason and Paul Drake into a small room containing an operating table and two chairs arranged side by side against the north wall.

"Just sit here for a few minutes," she said in a low voice. "The doctor has been terribly busy today and he's just cleaning up with a couple of patients who are in there. He'll see you, however, before he sees anyone else."

Mason and Drake thanked her and seated themselves while the nurse hurried out of the door to reassure the late patients in the outer office that it would only be a few minutes.

Mason and Drake sat for some five minutes waiting.

Drake said, "I wonder if it's all right to smoke a cigarette in here."

"I don't see why not," Mason said.

Drake placed the camera on a small table by his chair and took out his cigarettes.

Both men lit up.

Drake said, "Do you take this Dr. Candler at face value, Perry?"

Mason said, "I don't take anybody at face value. I —" The door of the little operating room opened explosively. "Oh, I'm so sorry," the nurse said, "but Dr. Candler has run into an emergency operation. Can you wait or — ?"

"How long will it be?" Mason asked.

"It's probably going to be twenty minutes. Everything is in an uproar and —"

"Never mind," Mason said. "We won't wait. We were just driving through. I wanted to tell him about some developments and — Will you tell him that he can always reach me through the Drake Detective Agency in case he learns anything? I suppose he knows —"

"He told me to tell you that he's terribly sorry and that he doesn't know a thing," she said.

"Very well," Mason told her. "We'll be on our way. Thanks a lot."

She flashed him a smile that was more than cordial. "I'm sorry I can't see you out," she said. "I've got to help with the patient."

She hurried down the corridor to a private office.

Dr. Candler thrust his head out. "I'm sorry," he called.

"Quite all right," Mason said.

Mason and Drake let themselves out of the building.

"Some dish," Drake said.

"Magnetic personality all right," Mason said.

"I bet she's a great help with the patients," Drake went on. "She could keep a sick man waiting for two hours and he'd still be happy and cheerful."

"Feeling sick?" Mason asked.

"I might consider it," Drake said. "Come to think of it I've been having a little digestive trouble. I think I'll come back and let Dr. Candler look me over."

They drove back to Los Angeles.

"What about dinner?" Drake asked.

"We're going to get these films developed first," Mason said. "Let's go to your office and see if there's anything new. I'd like to know what Sackett, or Prim, did after we left."

"Well, we can find out," Drake said. "How about Della? Do you suppose she's waiting?"

"She's probably gone home," Mason said. "If she hasn't she'll be expecting dinner."

They rode up in the elevator.

"Go down to your office and see if Della's there," Drake said. "I'll check the reports on

Sackett and see what happened."

Mason walked down the corridor. A light was on in his private office. He unlocked the door and found Della Street busily pounding away at a typewriter.

"What's the idea?" he asked.

She looked up with a smile. "I was catching up on a few letters that I didn't want to trust the stenographers to handle. They're things you should have dictated but didn't. They're on your desk all ready for you to sign, and here's another one."

Her nimble fingers flew over the keyboard with the last closing paragraph, then she ratcheted the papers out of the typewriter, separated the letter from the carbon paper copy and put it on Mason's desk.

"I presume," Mason said, grinning, "that you *now* want dinner."

"I'm always hungry," she said, "but what I want mainly is information. What happened with Prim, or Sackett?"

"He's quite a character," Mason said. "He has something on his mind and I don't know what it is."

"What do you mean?"

"When I accused him of Ballard's murder he really went into a panic and tried to give us a synthetic alibi about having spent the night with the girl he was with there at the beach."

"What kind of a girl?"

"Helen Rucker — a nice kid. Apparently in

love with Sackett and terribly afraid of him."

"*Had* he spent the night with her?"

"Not that night," Mason said. "Perhaps some other night. She took it casually, but it happened that her mother was visiting at the apartment with her last night."

"So what did he do about fixing up his alibi?"

"Didn't do anything," Mason said. "We've got some pictures that puzzle me."

"What are they?"

"Photographic copies of a document that Sackett had which he didn't want us to see. When he saw the three of us bearing down on him he was afraid we might be officers and he slipped this thing inside the girl's bathing suit."

Della Street raised her eyebrows.

"It was a thin folded paper," Mason said, "and that's all there was room for inside the bathing suit — except Helen. She and the bathing suit were made for each other."

"So what do we do now?"

"So now," Mason said, "we go up to a client of Paul's who has a photographic studio and get him to run these films through so we can let them dry and then study the contents of the paper."

"What was it?"

"Just a bunch of numbers."

"A code?"

"Could have been. It could have been something else."

"And then we eat?"

"Then we eat," Mason promised.

Della Street closed her typewriter desk, went to the closet and put on her hat and coat.

They walked down the corridor to pick up Paul Drake.

"Any news?" Mason asked.

"Sackett and his girl friend seem to be having quite a fight," Drake said. "They knew, of course, they were being tailed, but they put on the exhibition just the same. They certainly were jawing at each other. He was mad all the way through and she was giving him a piece of her mind."

"Perhaps over that fake alibi?" Mason asked.

"Could be. My men could see them in the jeep but of course couldn't tell what they were talking about."

"What happened?"

"They drove toward Newport, but at the north end of Laguna Beach Sackett went into a phone booth at a service station and telephoned."

"Any chance of finding out the number?" Mason asked.

"No chance," Drake said. "It was a manual telephone."

"But couldn't we check on the records of the phone and perhaps get the telephone company — ?"

Drake said, "Telephone companies won't cooperate with us on that, and what's more, if it was a local call they couldn't help a bit."

"Was it a local call?"

"My man isn't certain. Couldn't see clearly enough, but he thinks Sackett only dropped one coin. Right after he telephoned," Drake went on, "the guy went into the men's room and evidently burned a piece of paper and flushed it down the toilet."

"What!" Mason exclaimed.

"That's right. When they drove away from the service station they were on the main highway. They were driving a jeep and Rice figured he could catch up with them without any trouble. He'd seen Sackett leave the telephone booth and go into the rest room so he went in there just to look around. He could smell paper smoke in there and when he looked in the toilet there were several very small pieces of charred paper floating in the water."

"Enough to do any good?" Mason asked. "Were they — ?"

"Gosh no, Perry. They weren't as big as a pinhead — just little fine pieces of soot."

"Now that's something," Mason said. "What did they do after that, Paul?"

"Rice looked around and saw that there was no evidence that he could pick up so he and Niles put on speed and overtook the jeep about two or three miles north of town. They tagged along behind."

"Sackett know they were there?"

"Oh, sure."

"Where did he go?"

"Went to Newport Beach and drove directly to Helen Rucker's apartment. Sackett went upstairs with her and was there for probably half an hour or so. Then he got back in his jeep and headed for Los Angeles. He's presumably on the road now. My men haven't reported since then. They telephoned a report while he was in the Rucker apartment and said they would follow him when he came out. Then as he came out and got in the car one of the men phoned in a flash report."

"They're going to keep on his tail?"

"That's right. But it won't do any good."

"It may cramp his style a little bit," Mason said. "Now I'm really anxious to see what's on those pictures."

"Well," Drake said, "we'll go to my photographic friend and see what we can find out. I've phoned him and he's waiting with everything in readiness to rush those films through."

Mason said, "I don't see why Sackett would want to destroy that document *after* we had the photographic copies."

"He may have been afraid you were going to slap a subpoena on him or really arrest him."

"One thing's certain," Mason said, "that document is a lot more important than we had anticipated. I'm looking forward to an opportunity to study it. Let's go."

Drake piloted Mason and Della Street to the commercial studio. His friend, anxious to get home, was waiting for them. He listened to

Drake's story about the camera.

"Are you familiar with that make of camera?" Drake asked.

"Sure. Do you know what kind of films are in it?"

"Plus X," Drake said. "That's what Niles told me he was using. You have to develop them in total darkness and —"

"Yes, yes, I know," the photographer interposed. "I'll use the tank."

He looked at the camera. "Only four films taken?"

"That's all," Mason said. "They're all the same thing — copies of a document. We're going to want some big enlargements."

"How big?"

"Just as big as you can get them."

"Well, after a certain point you don't gain anything. You begin to get grain in the film. However, we'll see what we can do. What was on the document that was photographed?"

"Just a bunch of figures."

"Typewritten, printed, pen and ink?"

"Pen and ink."

"Neat figures?"

"Just as neat as could be. They might have been made by an architect."

"That's fine," the photographer said. "I can enlarge those up to eleven by fourteen and you can see the figures just as clear as you could on the original provided the guy had the camera focused right."

"He had it focused right," Drake said. "You can count on that."

"Even so he would have had to have been around three feet away and —"

"He used an extension sleeve on the lens," Drake broke in.

"Oh, well," the photographer announced, relief in his voice, "it's a cinch then."

"How about coming in the darkroom with you?" Mason asked.

The man grinned and shook his head. "It wouldn't do any good and it might do some harm. I have to work in total darkness. You couldn't see a thing. You'd just be standing there, and every so often, no matter what I tell them, some guy in a darkroom gets nervous and wants to smoke. He puts a cigarette in his mouth and lights a match before he thinks. Then he tries to shake the thing out. He's fogged every bit of film in the place. You folks stay out here."

The photographer disappeared through the door into the darkroom.

"Well," Drake said, "we have to wait a few minutes."

He walked around the walls of the studio, studying the various gag photographs and cheesecake that had been pasted up on the walls.

After a moment Mason joined him.

"Apparently," Della Street said archly, "this is a stag studio."

"So it would seem," Mason announced.

"These joints are all the same," Drake said. "Every time you get in a commercial studio they're always pulling gag shots and cheese-cake. Look at this one, Perry. Ain't this a darb?"

Della Street glanced up and said, "Don't let your lustful lechery interfere with the realization that I'm hungry."

"Say," Drake said, "if you wanted to eat fast we could go eat while the pictures are being developed."

"How long will it take?" Mason asked.

"When they use a fine-grain developer I think it takes about eighteen minutes for the developer, then it takes about fifteen minutes for the hypo. Then they have to wash the films. Gosh, we can probably have forty-five minutes —"

The photographer emerged from the dark-room. "How's everything?" Drake asked.

"Cooking in the soup," the photographer announced.

"How long will it be?"

"Sixteen more minutes in the developer. I'm using a fine-grain developer at a controlled temperature. Then there's a stop bath, a hypo and a wash. I can use a chemical to take the hypo out and we can dry them pretty fast."

"How soon can we take a look at the film and make sure the pictures are all right?" Mason asked.

"After they've been in the hypo for about five

minutes we can pull them out long enough to take a look."

"That'll be about twenty-five minutes?"

"Right around there — say twenty-two or twenty-three minutes."

"Let's go have a cocktail," Mason said, "then we'll come back, take a look at the film, and go out for dinner. You can have some enlargements made by the time we get back."

"Okay. You want those enlargements on glossy?"

"Will that show the most detail?"

"That's right."

"That's what we want," Mason said.

"Okay, I'll be on the job."

"Sorry you can't have a drink with us," Mason said.

"Well, that's the way things run. However, a job is a job and there's only one way to handle it."

The photographer smiled at Della Street. "I'm sorry about the leg art all over the walls. We don't usually have women in here, and the customers get a bang out of cheesecake. Also the fellows who work here like to pull interesting prints and tack them up."

"Don't mind me," Della Street said. "Just so all these pinups don't get the men's minds off of food. I'm starving."

"All right. Inside of twenty-five minutes," the photographer promised, "I can let you take a look at the films. They'll be wet but the cloudiness will be off the backs so you can tell what you have. That's a darned good camera you have there and if that fellow knows to handle it you should have some sharp pictures."

"He knows how to handle it," Drake said. "Come on, let's go."

Drake led the way to the elevator, pressed the button, said, "These elevators in studio buildings are always slow as cold molasses. I've waited here before for pictures so I know generally what happens. There's a darned good cocktail place down here and we can get some canapés there. They do a pretty fair job."

"Me for the canapés," Della Street said.

They went to the cocktail lounge, and Mason and Della Street ordered a double Bacardi. Drake had a dry Martini. The waiter brought canapés and Della Street said, "I know I'm supposed simply to toy with these things but I'm going to run up a bill on you right now, Perry Mason. I'm ravenous."

A newsboy came in. "Late paper?" he asked.

Mason took one look at the headlines and took out a dollar. "Leave three of them," he said.

He passed the newspapers around.

The headlines read: STOLEN BILLS RECOVERED IN GIRL'S TRAILER.

There were photographs of Arlene Duvall, of her trailer, and a list of numbers.

"Oh-oh!" Drake said. "Those are the numbers of the bills that they were keeping such a closely guarded secret."

"There's no need of being secretive about those now," Mason said, "because those are the bills that have been found. They haven't published the numbers of the ones that weren't found."

Della Street became so engrossed in reading the newspaper that she forgot about the canapés. The waiter brought their cocktails.

Mason reluctantly put down the paper, picked up his glass.

"Well," he said, "here's confusion to our enemies."

"Right at the present time," Drake said, "the confusion seems to be all one way. What do you think of those numbers, Perry?"

Mason said, "I'm wearing the dial off my wrist watch looking at it, waiting for the twenty-five-minute period to be up. I'm willing to bet you, Paul, that that list of numbers that Sackett had was the list of the stolen bills in that five-thousand-dollar extortion package."

"But how the devil could he have secured that?" Drake said. "I tell you, Perry, it's absolutely out of the question. Only the head guy in this branch of the FBI has that, and —"

Mason said, "I'm just willing to make you a fifty-dollar bet right now that those figures on that paper are a list of the numbers. I'll bet that when we check the numbers on the list with the numbers on the bills listed in the newspapers we'll find every number listed."

Drake was silent.

"Want to bet?" Mason asked.

"Not fifty bucks," Drake said. "I'll bet you ten. I don't make money the way you rich lawyers do."

"Okay, it's a ten-dollar bet," Mason said.

They finished their cocktails, cleaned up the canapés.

"More?" Mason asked Della Street.

She glanced at her watch. "We won't have time. Let's go back up, even if we have to wait a few minutes."

They went back to the photographic studio.

The photographer looked at his watch, said, "You people are about four minutes early."

"We'll wait," Mason said. "It has become damned important to find out just what those numbers are." He indicated the evening paper and said, "We think that some of the numbers that are on these bills may appear on the paper that was photographed."

"Well, what's so important about it then?" the photographer asked. "If it's published in the newspaper you can get the numbers there and —"

"That isn't it," Mason said. "We want to get the complete list. It may be of considerable value as evidence."

"Well," the photographer said, "we can . . . oh, we can take a look now, I guess."

He led them through a U-shaped, zigzag entrance into a darkroom. The acrid smell of acetic acid was in the air. A red safe light glowed at one end of the room.

"That's for the enlarging paper," he explained. "I'm all set up ready to make those enlargements as soon as we can get the films dried. I have the paper under cover. We can turn on the lights now."

He switched on white lights, walked over to a covered tank, took off a stainless steel cover, reached down and pulled up a metallic clip.

"What the devil!" he exclaimed.

"What's the matter?" Mason asked.

"These films are all light-struck."

"What?"

"Every damn one of them," the photographer said. "Take a look. They're just as black as your hat."

Mason looked at Drake, an expression of complete exasperation on his face. "Well," he said, "I guess your friend Niles didn't know as much about photography as he thought he did. He must have left the back loose on the camera or . . . of course he was trying to do a hurry-up reloading job and —"

The photographer said, "Wait a minute. This isn't due to a light leak. A light leak in the camera would have ruined some of the films but not all of them. And the same would have been true if . . . I can't understand this. The whole strip of films is just uniformly black. It's a defective film."

"You run onto those very often?" Mason asked.

"Not a defective film," the photographer said. "Sometimes when you send them in for development you get a courteous note back that the films were ruined in their processing and that by way of restitution the company is making a replacement of a fresh film."

"How reassuring," Mason said sarcastically. "Dammit, of all the films . . . Paul, that means the most important piece of evidence in the whole case has slipped through our fingers."

Mason paused to look accusingly at the photographer. "Now," he said, "you'll pardon me for being suspicious but *you* didn't get nervous about smoking and light a match, did you?"

The photographer said angrily, "Look, Mr. Mason, I've been in this business for twenty-two years. I've developed enough films to stretch from here to the moon. We don't make mistakes in this studio."

"I'm sorry," Mason said. "I just flared up. I just can't understand it, that's all."

"I can't understand it myself," the photographer said. "There's something completely cockeyed."

"It can't have been in your solutions? Someone couldn't have tampered with them?"

"I don't think so," the photographer said, "but, believe me, I'm going to run some films through there myself in order to find out. I'm certainly going to test every solution here in the studio. *I* don't want to be left with the responsibility of this thing."

"Well," Mason said, "it isn't a question of fixing responsibility now. That doesn't do us any good. We're licked! Now I can go back and really enjoy another double Bacardi."

They trooped dejectedly out of the studio.

"Well," Mason said, as they waited for the elevator. "You two had better go get something to eat. I guess I'll go and call on my client, Arlene Duvall. It's a good time to talk with her. She can't add any devastation to the day's wreckage."

"And she may contribute something helpful," Drake said, striving to be cheerful.

"She *may,*" Mason observed dryly.

• 12 •

Mason looked across the meshed screen in the visiting room at Arlene Duvall, said, "I suppose the police have got bugs scattered around here so you'll have to watch your tongue. How much have you told the police?"

"I have told them everything."

Mason said, "Move down here four or five chairs at this end of the screen."

Mason got up and moved and Arlene Duvall moved along on the other side.

A matron hurried forward. "Here," she said. "You aren't allowed to change your position."

"She's changed it now," Mason said.

"She's not allowed to. She'll have to go back."

Mason said, "I'm an attorney. I have a right to confer with my client. The communication is privileged. I don't want it monitored."

"What do you mean, monitored?"

Mason said, "There's a hidden microphone down at that other place."

"What makes you think so?"

"I know it," Mason said. "I have a microphone detector. The law gives me the right to confer privately with my client. I demand to confer with her privately. If the police monitor the conversation that's not a private conference. Now do you want to take the responsibility of denying an attorney an opportunity to confer with his client?"

"You're conferring with her now."

"That's right," Mason said. "I am."

"Then you can move back to that other position."

Mason shook his head and said, "I'm here and she's here. Now do you want to take the responsibility of removing her forcibly before I've had a chance to say anything?"

The matron hesitated a moment, then shrugged her shoulders and said, "All right, go ahead. Remember that I told her to move back. I've done my duty."

She walked away out of earshot.

"Now then," Mason said, "I want the lowdown. I want all of it. I want to know what I'm up against."

"I'm afraid things look pretty hopeless for me, Mr. Mason."

"What makes you think so?"

"It's just one of those horrible chains of coincidences. The whole thing is like a nightmare."

"Well, don't lose your head and don't lose your nerve," Mason told her. "Tell me what happened."

"I went out there to see Mr. Ballard."

"At that hour of the night?"

"Yes."

"Why did you go to see him then?"

"Because I'd discovered a loose panel in my trailer with a whole cache of bills behind it."

"Did you count the money?"
"Yes."
"How much was in there?"
"Twenty-six thousand five hundred and twenty-five dollars."
"In bills of varying denominations?"
"That's right."
"Were there any thousand-dollar bills?"
"One."
"Any five-hundred-dollar bills?"
"Several."
"Hundred-dollar bills?"
"A lot of them."
"What about the others?"
"Tens and twenties."
"Now you're trying to tell me you didn't know they were there?"
"Mr. Mason, I swear to you that I didn't have any idea they were there."
Mason said, "What did you have concealed in the trailer? When we found it there at the Ideal Trade-In Trailer Mart you left your purse purposely so you could get back and find something. Now what was it you were looking for?"
"My diary."
"And where was that?"
"Where no one would ever think to look for it."
"Where?"
"I don't want to tell you the hiding place."
"Why?"
"Because it's still there."

"They'll find it."

"No they won't."

"Where is it?"

She sighed and said, "There's a closet and the wheels come up inside the closet, that is, there's a housing for the wheels on the inside of the closet. It's all enclosed."

"Go ahead."

"There's wood on top, but after I bought it I felt sure they would have something other than wood on the bottom. I knew there would have to be metal of some sort because the wheels would be throwing up mud and in the course of time the wood would rot out unless it was protected."

Mason nodded.

"So," she said, "I took out the screws and I found that underneath the wood there was a metal housing which went over the wheel. There was just room in the side of this metal housing between there and the wood for the leather-backed book that I used as my diary. I slipped it down between the wood and the metal."

"What did you put in your diary?"

"Everything."

"Such as what?"

"Where I was getting my money and how much. I was keeping an account of every dollar I received."

"Where were you getting it?"

"From Mr. Ballard."

"The devil you were!"

She nodded.

"And why was he giving *you* money?"

"He said that he thought he had finally found out how the theft had been engineered and who was back of it. He said he wanted to use me to bait a trap to catch the real thief."

"Did he tell you who he thought the real thief was?"

She shook her head.

"Or how the crime had been engineered?"

Again she shook her head, but suddenly averted her eyes.

"Did it ever occur to you that Jordan L. Ballard could have been the one who was back of the whole thing?"

"I don't think he was."

"Why not?"

"He was too nice to me."

"Perhaps his conscience was hurting."

"No, Mr. Mason. I'm satisfied he was on the up and up. He had made a lot of money out of real estate speculation and things. He had a very shrewd financial mind, and this thing was hanging over him all of the time. He wanted to smoke the man out in the open who was responsible."

"Man or men?" Mason asked.

"He said man."

Mason thought it over, then said slowly, "It almost had to be at least a two-man job."

"All I know is what he said."

"All right. Tell me what happened."

She said, "Shortly after I talked with you at the country club I phoned Mr. Ballard that I was going to need money for you. He gave me a whole scad of money at that time. He said I'd need lots of expense money. Then he gave me a one-thousand-dollar bill and a five-hundred-dollar bill and told me to send them to you in the mail."

"Didn't you think that was a foolish thing to do, sending two large-denomination bills in the form of cash that way?"

"I certainly did."

"And did you tell Mr. Ballard that?"

"Yes."

"What did he say to that?"

"He simply smiled and said we were now getting on the home stretch, that it wouldn't be long before we could close in on the man we were after, and then he promised me that my father would be liberated and my good name would be cleared if I'd do *just* as he instructed me."

"What else?"

"There was a fifteen percent reward offered for the money and five thousand dollars offered for information that would lead to the conviction of the man or men who perpetrated the crime. He said that he didn't need any more money, that Dad and I could have it all, that Dad could use the reward to get another start."

"Had you been telling your dad any of this?"

"Not in letters. They're censored."

"But you told him orally."

"Yes."

"All right," Mason said, "you got fifteen hundred dollars for the retainer from Ballard. Now then, you sent it to me?"

"Why yes, of course. Didn't you get it?"

"That depends," Mason said. "*How* did you send it?"

Her eyes were dark with apprehension. "Mr. Mason, you *must* have received it. I wanted to send you fifteen hundred by registered mail or give it to you personally. But Mr. Ballard said there were reasons why I should send it to you by plain mail. He was laying a trap for someone. At least that's the impression I received."

"That's fine," Mason said. "Now did you send me any other money?"

"Any *other* money?"

"That's right."

She shook her head.

"Don't lie to me," Mason warned. "If you lie to me now you're going to spend your life in prison. You didn't send me any other money, not another fifteen hundred dollars?"

"Another fifteen . . . hundred . . . dollars!"

Mason nodded.

"Good heavens, no! Where would I get that money to send you?"

"I thought you might have taken it from the cache that you found concealed in the trailer."

"I didn't touch a piece of that money except just to look at it, count it and then put it back, and then I wanted to get in touch with Mr. Ballard. I had to tell him."

"Did you know you were being shadowed?"

"Of course."

"And how did you get out?"

"There's a little storage space under the double bed in those Heliar trailers. There's a little door that opens to the outside so you can put things in this storage space from the outside. It's on the opposite side of the trailer, away from the trailer door. The doors on all house trailers open on the right-hand side, but this loading door to the storage space was on the left-hand side."

Mason nodded.

"I knew I was being watched," she said, "but there was nothing stored under the bed. When they had stolen the trailer in the afternoon they had cleaned out everything portable."

"So you went out through that hatch?"

"That's right. I crawled under the bed and worked the hatch door open, then I slid out on my stomach, crawled out to the ground, closed the door and tiptoed off into the darkness, keeping the trailer between me and the men who were watching the door of the trailer."

"And then what?"

"I crossed the golf course, went to the service station, got a taxicab and went to Mr. Ballard's. You were in there with him."

Mason's eyes narrowed. "How do you know?"

"I could hear your voices?"
"Could you hear my voice?"
"Two men were talking."
"Could you hear *my* voice?"
"They said there was no question that you were in there, so I assumed that —"
"Did you tell the police you heard my voice?"
"But it *must* have been —"
"Did you tell police you heard my voice?"
"Yes."
"Go on," Mason said. "What did you do?"
She said, "I knew that Mr. Ballard wouldn't like it if I showed up while someone else was with him, so I went around to the back to wait until you had left. I climbed up on a box so I could look in the kitchen, and just as I did so I heard the sound of a car starting up out in front so I presumed you had left. I got up on the box to tap on the kitchen window and attract his attention to see if the coast was clear and then I could see Mr. Ballard lying on the floor."
"Now here's where I want you to be very careful," Mason said. "How long an interval was it from the time you heard me drive off in the car until you climbed up to look in the kitchen window?"
"I heard the sound of your motor starting and I climbed up right then."
"Go on," Mason said. "What happened?"
"Mr. Ballard was lying there on the floor, terribly still. There was a pool of red oozing out

from under the body and then I saw this big carving knife stuck in his body."

"How much time," Mason asked, "was there between the time I must have left and the time that you got up to the kitchen window?"

"I don't think over . . . perhaps . . . well, that's what the police have been asking me."

"What did you tell them?"

"I *told* them perhaps a minute or a minute and a half."

"You think it might have been longer than that?"

"No, I don't think it was that long."

"Why did you tell them perhaps a minute or a minute and a half if you didn't think it was that long?"

"Because you're my lawyer, you're working for me and I . . . well, I couldn't let you down."

"How long do you think it was?" Mason asked.

"Not over thirty seconds. If he saw you to the front door he wouldn't have had time to any more than get back to the kitchen."

"He saw me to the front door," Mason said, "that is, right up to the corridor leading to the front door. I let myself out."

"Well then there was justly barely time for him to have got back to the kitchen because . . . unless of course, you did something after you got out — fooled around or something. I couldn't hear your voice after I got around to the back of the place. I heard your car motor start."

"All right," Mason said. "We'll cross that bridge later. Now did you tell the police about Ballard being the one who gave you money?"

"Not yet."

"You intend to?"

"I'm going to have to, Mr. Mason. I'm in a jam. The district attorney thinks that I killed him but he's offering me a trade."

"What sort of a trade?"

"He says that if I will testify that you arranged to meet me out there and that you signaled me by lowering and raising the roller shade, he'll let me plead guilty to manslaughter and he'll see I get out in a very short time. He says that he knows you lowered and raised the shade as a signal to me, and that if I'll tell him the truth on that he'll make it very, very easy on me."

"What did you tell him?" Mason asked.

"I told him I'd have to think that over."

"And what did he say?"

"He said I'd have to make up my mind one way or another and do it fast."

Mason said grimly, "He wanted you to make up your mind before you talked with me, didn't he?"

"Well, he said I should. He said otherwise you'd talk me out of it."

"The reason he wants you to do that," Mason said, "is that the minute you make that statement he can then have me found guilty of perjury. I can be disbarred as an attorney. I can be sent to the penitentiary for committing perjury."

"I see," she said, her slate-gray eyes thoughtful.

"That hadn't occurred to you before?" Mason asked.

"I knew the district attorney was very, very anxious to get me to say that you signaled me. He's offering me almost everything."

"He wouldn't keep his promise," Mason said, "that is, he might keep his promise on letting you plead to manslaughter, but once you got up to prison he wouldn't lift a finger to try and help you."

"No, I suppose not, but there's quite a difference between manslaughter and —" Suddenly her eyes clouded with tears and she started to cry.

"And what?" Mason asked.

"And first-degree murder," she sobbed. "The idea of being strapped into that cold metal chair and hearing the cyanide pellets dropped into the pot of acid and then sitting there and . . . choking to death."

Mason said harshly, "Forget it. They've been working on your nerves, trying to undermine your resistance."

She nodded, wiped away the tears, but her mouth still quivered at the corners.

"Where did you go after you found Ballard was dead?" he asked.

"I tried to get in touch with Dr. Candler."

"Were you able to do it?"

"No. I tried to call him long-distance. I used an assumed name of course."

"You didn't get him?"

"No, he was out of town and not expected back until after midnight."

"With whom did you talk?"

"That nurse of his."

"Rose Travis?"

"Yes."

"Do you like her?"

"I hate the ground she walks on, and she hates me."

"Did she know who was calling?"

"No. I disguised my voice and told her it was a patient, that Dr. Candler had told me to call him in case of certain developments, and . . . so I told her I had to talk with him."

"Where did you call — at his office or at his residence?"

"He just has an apartment. He has an arrangement with his nurse by which she takes night calls and filters out the ones that are unnecessary. You can't call him in his apartment."

"He didn't even give you his unlisted apartment number?"

"No. He wanted to but he said he couldn't."

"Why?"

"He said that was one number that no one knew except his nurse, that he had to have it that way in order to run his business."

"So you haven't been in touch with Dr. Candler?"

"No."

"Where did the police pick you up?"

"At the apartment of a friend. I went there to wait until I could see Dr. Candler."

"You trust Dr. Candler?"

"Absolutely. I'd trust him with my life."

"But you didn't tell him about Ballard giving you the money?"

"He knew someone was giving me the money. I just wouldn't tell him who, that was all."

"Why? Didn't you trust him?"

"I'd promised, Mr. Mason. I'd promised solemnly on my word of honor that I wouldn't tell anyone about the money. But I knew Dr. Candler was annoyed and . . . well perhaps . . . not suspicious, but dreadfully annoyed. And I couldn't help thinking what he would think if anything should happen to me and he never knew where the money was coming from.

"And then there was Dad. Suppose someone should kill me, or suppose I should die suddenly. Then everyone would think that Dad had been giving me the money for the trailer and all that.

"So I kept this diary with the whole story in it, and I told Dr. Candler that if anything should happen to me I'd left this diary and where to find it."

Mason's eyes narrowed as he thought that

over. "You told him where to find the diary?"

"Of course. I had to tell someone. If I should die I didn't want the diary to just stay there and rot and never be found."

"All right," Mason said. "They're going to bring you on for a preliminary hearing. They're going to let you think they have you dead-to-rights on a first-degree murder case. If you betray me by swearing to something that is false you can get out of it on a manslaughter rap."

"And otherwise?"

"Otherwise I don't know," Mason said. "If your story is true I'm going to try to get you out of it. If it isn't true I reserve the right to throw you overboard. I told you that when I started and I'm telling you that again — that's as far as the money angle is concerned. As far as the murder case is concerned, once I start representing you I'll carry it all the way through."

Her eyes were calculating. "Just how good are my chances, Mr. Mason?"

"Right now they're not very good."

"Twenty-five chances out of a hundred?" she asked.

"Not right now," Mason said.

"Ten chances out of a hundred?"

"Make it five," Mason told her.

She said, "You seem to be trying to force me to do what they want me to."

"I want to find out," Mason said. "I want to find out how you play ball."

Suddenly she started to cry. "I p-p-play it for k-k-keeps and on the square," she sobbed.

"Well, don't let me influence you," Mason said. "Do whatever you think is for your best interests."

He got up, nodded to the matron that the interview was over, and walked out.

Mason left the jail, got in his car and drove to his apartment.

The phone was ringing as he unlocked the door. Since this unlisted number was known only to Della Street and Paul Drake, Mason hurried to the receiver and lifted it up.

"Hello," he said.

Paul Drake's voice was excited. "Well, my lad, don't give up the ship just yet."

"What do you mean?" Mason asked.

"Maybe it isn't such an unlucky day after all."

"The hell it isn't," Mason told him. "Everything I've touched has gone sour. I'm just waiting for tomorrow."

"Have an interview with your client?"

"How is she?"

"Lousy. She's told the police everything she shouldn't have told them and they're in a position to crucify her if they try her on a first-degree murder charge."

"What's going to stop them?" Drake asked. "Why do you say *if* they try her on a first-degree murder charge?"

"Because," Mason said, "the D.A. has offered

to make a trade with her. He'll give her a manslaughter charge if she'll swear that I raised and lowered the curtain out at Ballard's house as a signal to her."

"Where would that put you?"

"In prison for perjury. But I'd go down fighting and I'd raise a lot of hell while I was doing it."

"How?"

"I'd force her to admit that they'd promised to reduce the charge against her if she'd testify to what they wanted. I'd make it appear that Hamilton Burger was so anxious to get me he was willing to condone first-degree murder in order to have me convicted and disbarred."

"Could you prove that?"

Mason said. "I'd put Burger on the stand. I'd give him hell. He'd either have to admit what he'd done or start lying."

"Provided, of course, she's telling the truth," Drake said.

"Figure it out for yourself. They have a perfect first-degree murder case against her, and if they reduce it to manslaughter that's all the corroboration of her story that *I* need."

"Well, here's the good news," Drake said. "You win your ten dollars."

"What ten dollars?"

"The ten-dollar bet you made on that list being a list of the numbers of the bills in that five-thousand-dollar package, that —"

Mason interrupted him, his voice sharp with

excitement. "What the hell are you talking about, Paul?"

"About that list."

"How do you know?"

"Because," Drake said, "when Harvey Niles telephoned in I told him about what had happened to the films. I asked him how it could have happened and he swore that my photographer friend had botched the thing up either deliberately or accidentally, and the way it was done he thinks it was deliberate. He thinks someone must have known we were going to him and bought him off."

"Do *you* think so?" Mason asked.

"I don't know what to think, but the point is that Harvey Niles remembered that he had one picture on that other roll of film. You remember he'd snapped the last picture on a roll of film on the document you were holding in your hand, and then had changed films and given you the camera with the new roll in it. So he went to his own darkroom and developed that other roll and he has a perfect picture there. In fact he has thirty-six perfect pictures. They're sharp as a knife and clear as crystal. He has pictures of Thomas Sackett, or Howard Prim, whichever you want to call him, and Helen Rucker on the beach. He has pictures of them necking, and you remember when we were walking toward them Sackett evidently thought we were officers and started embracing the girl. That's when you thought he put something down the back of her bathing suit. Well, you sure were right. Niles got a picture of that and it's so sharp you can enlarge it and even see something white in Sackett's hand where he's shoving it down along the back of the girl's swimming suit — and there wasn't much back to it, just a V-shaped cut from the shoulders down to the hips."

"And he was putting something in the back of that swimming suit?"

"That's right."

"And you've checked the numbers on the film?"

"I sure have. That document came out as clear as could be and every number that was listed in the newspaper as being a number on one of the stolen bills is on that list."

"Then the list must be genuine," Mason said.

"That's right."

"Then how the devil did Sackett get it?"

"That," Drake said, "is the question. You could turn the police force completely upside down by letting them know that Sackett had that list."

Mason thought for a moment, then said, "I'll tell you what you do, Paul. Have Niles make half a dozen eleven by fourteen prints of that film. Then put the film in an envelope and put it somewhere in a safe-deposit box. Keep those prints where no one will know where they are. Keep them in a place that's absolutely safe."

"Just how do you plan to use them?" Drake asked.

"As to that I'm damned if I know," Mason said, "but it's the only hole card I have."

"Well, it had better be an ace in order to be high hand," Drake told him.

• 13 •

District Attorney Hamilton Burger was in the courtroom personally taking charge of the preliminary hearing of the People of the State of California against Arlene Duvall. He made no secret as to why he was there.

Addressing the Court, but turning so he was facing the section where a group of interested newspaper reporters had gathered, Hamilton Burger said, "May it please the Court, as will presently develop from the testimony, this is not a usual case. This is a case where the People are prosecuting the defendant for murder, but inextricably mingled with the People's case, with the commission of the crime itself, is the conduct of the attorney who is representing the defendant.

"It is a matter of record that this attorney has already been summoned before the grand jury and has there answered certain questions. I will not at this time go so far as to state that those questions were answered falsely, but I will state that we expect the evidence in this case to show that a condition exists which will be significant not only in the case at bar but in interpreting the answers given by the attorney before the grand jury.

"I will also state that before this case is concluded the People expect to call Mr. Perry

Mason to the stand as a witness for the prosecution. We know that he will be a hostile witness. We know that if he answers questions truthfully it may be necessary for us to proceed against him as an accessory. We therefore wish to be certain that counsel understands the situation well in advance. He is, of course, as an expert criminal attorney, well versed in his constitutional rights. However, so there can be no misunderstanding we wish to inform him that he does not have to answer any questions which may tend to incriminate him; that he is, if he desires, entitled to the advice of counsel at all times; that we are not going to ask him as to any confidential communications taking place between his client and himself, but we are going to ask him as to certain facts concerning his conduct.

"It is with great regret that I make such charges against a member of the bar. However, I feel that the bar has nothing to gain by condoning unethical or illegal conduct upon the part of one of its members."

Hamilton Burger sat down.

Judge Cody glanced at Perry Mason. "The Court is, of course, advised that there is more to this case than is usually the case in a preliminary hearing. The Court assumes that the district attorney's statement was made in all good faith and that it was and will be supported by evidence. In the event it is not so supported the Court will be heard further in the matter. In view of the fact that these statements are made publicly I feel that the attorney for the defense should be given an opportunity to reply at this time. Mr. Mason, do you care to reply to the district attorney's statement?"

Mason got to his feet. "All that I want to say, Your Honor, is that if the district attorney proceeds on that theory he should have witnesses to present the evidence, and if he puts witnesses on the stand who try to testify to any such theory at a time when I have an opportunity to cross-examine them I'll rip their testimony to pieces."

Mason resumed his seat.

"I accept that challenge," Hamilton Burger shouted. "Call Marvin Kinney to the stand."

Marvin Kinney came forward and testified that he was forty-seven years of age, gave his residence, announced that his occupation was that of a process server, and then turned to face Hamilton Burger's questions.

"On the evening of Wednesday, the tenth of the present month, were you given papers to serve on one Jordan L. Ballard?"

"I was given such papers. Yes sir."

"And what time did you receive those papers?"

"At approximately nine o'clock in the evening. Between nine and ten."

"What instructions were given you at that time?"

Mason said, "I don't think the defendant in

this case is to be bound by any statements made outside of her presence."

"Well, this relates to the time element," Hamilton Burger said. "It enables him to fix a time in his own mind."

"In that case I'll cross-examine him about it," Mason said, "if I want to. If the district attorney is going to use the case against Arlene Duvall as a stalking horse to try and get me indicted for perjury, I want him to conform to the strict rules of evidence. He knows all this is inadmissible."

"I was merely trying to get the picture clearly in focus," Hamilton Burger said apologetically to the Court.

"It is certainly hearsay as far as the defendant is concerned," Judge Cody snapped. "The objection is sustained. I feel that counsel for the defense is entirely correct in stating that under the circumstances as disclosed in this case the strict rules of evidence should be followed."

"There's no justification for stating that I am using this case against Arlene Duvall as a stalking horse to make a perjury case against Perry Mason," Hamilton Burger said. "I resent that."

Mason said, "You referred to a lot of things that you expected to prove. Now I'll state that *I* expect to prove *that is a fact*."

"To prove that I am using this case as a stalking horse to try and get you on a perjury charge?" Hamilton Burger shouted. "That's absurd!"

"That's *exactly* what I'm going to prove," Mason said. "Otherwise why did you personally tell the defendant that you would let her plead guilty to manslaughter if she'd testify to facts that would enable you to proceed against me in a perjury charge?"

"I only wanted her to tell the truth," Hamilton Burger snapped.

"Then why hold out a bribe? Why offer to let her plead guilty to manslaughter?"

"Because — You can't prove that I made any such offer."

"Are you denying it?" Mason asked.

Judge Cody banged his gavel. "I have let this discussion between counsel proceed," he said, "because I felt that in view of the charges made against Perry Mason by the district attorney, Mr. Mason should have an opportunity to set forth his side of the case. I think that has now been done and I think the matter has gone far enough. I'm going to ask counsel to refrain from all further personalities."

Judge Cody looked from one to the other and said, "I mean that. I want counsel to refrain from all personalities. You will address your remarks to the Court and we will conduct this hearing according to the strict rules of evidence. Now then, Mr. District Attorney, the objection to your question calling for hearsay evidence was sustained. The witness Kinney is on the stand. Ask another question."

"Where did you go after you received this

document to serve on Ballard?"

"I went to Tenth and Flossman streets where Ballard conducted a super service station which is open all night. I thought I might catch him there."

"Did you catch him there?"

"He had left a little earlier."

"Move to strike out the answer as not being responsive to the question, as being a conclusion of the witness," Mason said, "and predicated on hearsay evidence."

"Motion granted," Judge Cody snapped.

"Oh surely, Your Honor," Hamilton Burger said, "that's a routine matter. He arrived there just after Ballard had left. He's entitled to testify to that."

"How does anyone know Ballard had *just* left?" Mason asked.

Judge Cody looked at Hamilton Burger. "I think counsel's question is sufficient to show the impropriety of your question. He could only know that because of what someone told him. The objection is sustained. We're going to conduct this hearing according to the *strict* rules of evidence."

"Very well," Hamilton Burger snapped. He turned to the witness, "Where did you go after you left Tenth and Flossman?"

"I went to the residence of Jordan L. Ballard."

"What time did you leave Tenth and Flossman?"

"About ten-fifteen."

"What time did you get to Ballard's residence?"

"I can't tell you the exact time. I stopped to fill up with gas, and had a cheeseburger. I guess it was around ten-forty, something like that."

"Now then, tell us what happened when you arrived at Ballard's residence, what you saw, what you did, what you found."

"I parked my car. I went up the steps to the front porch. There were lights on inside the house. I started to ring the bell, then I saw that the door was standing partially open. I called out, 'Mr. Ballard.' There was no answer. I called again. 'Mr. Ballard.' When there was still no answer I pressed my thumb against the bell button. I could hear the bell ringing inside of the house. I called, 'Is anybody home?'

"When I received no answer after that, I entered the house. I walked through to the kitchen and found the body of Mr. Ballard lying on the floor."

"What else did you find?"

"I found a cigarette on an ash tray on the drainboard."

"Did you notice anything unusual about that cigarette?"

"Yes, sir."

"What?"

"Smoke was spiraling up from it."

"Now let's get that straight. Do I understand that you want the Court to understand that cigarette was still burning?"

"Yes, sir. That's exactly what I wish the court to understand. That's my testimony. The cigarette was still burning."

"You're certain of that?"

"Yes, sir."

"Did you notice anything else about that cigarette?"

"There was about half or three-quarters of an inch of ash on the cigarette."

"Anything else about it?"

"There was lipstick on it. I saw three tumblers on the drainboard of the sink. I saw a bowl of ice. I saw a couple of spoons. I saw a bottle of Scotch, a bottle of bourbon and a bottle of Seven-Up."

"Now let's come to the body on the floor. What did you notice there?"

"The body was lying face down. There was a pool of blood oozing out from under the chest. A knife had been plunged into the back just a little to the left of center."

"The body was lying face down?"

"Yes, sir."

"Whose body was that?"

"The body of Jordan L. Ballard."

"What did you do?"

"I went to the telephone and notified the police."

"Cross-examine," Hamilton Burger snapped at Mason.

"That cigarette was still burning when you

first saw it?" Mason asked.

"Yes, sir."

"Did you know Jordan L. Ballard in his lifetime?"

"No, sir."

"Then how did you know the body was that of Jordan Ballard?"

"I learned that afterwards."

"How?"

"Why . . . the police told me."

"Then you don't know of your own knowledge that the body was that of Jordan Ballard?"

"Only what the police told me."

"Yet you testify to it as a fact."

"Well, naturally."

"In other words, when the police tell you something is true you accept it as a fact, do you not?"

"Something like that, yes."

"Now did the police tell you about any of these other facts that you have testified to so positively?"

"No, sir."

"Those were things you saw with your own eyes?"

"Yes, sir."

"The cigarette was still burning in the ash tray in the kitchen?"

"Yes, sir."

"How much of it was unconsumed?"

"There was about an inch and a half of it left."

"And what did you do? Did you put it out?"

"No, sir. I didn't touch anything. I let it burn."

"And did it continue to burn?"

"It went out shortly afterward."

"How do you know?"

"Because when I went out to the kitchen with the police after they arrived the cigarette was out and it . . . well, it hadn't burned any more."

"How was it lying?"

"There was a grooved handle on the ash tray. The cigarette had been placed on that grooved handle, not on the little curved receptacles around the edge of the ash tray which were made for placing cigarettes. Therefore the ash hadn't dropped off. There was half or three-quarters of an inch of ash on it."

"Intact?"

"Yes, sir. Still retaining its round form."

"Wasn't it that ash which led you to believe the cigarette was still burning?"

"No, sir. It was still burning."

"Did you see smoke coming up from it?"

"Yes, sir, I did."

"Did you see the glowing end of the cigarette?"

"Yes sir."

"How was it glowing?"

"Well, it was a dull red, just the way any cigarette would glow."

"Did you go into the living room?"

"Yes, sir."

"Why did you go in there?"

"To locate a telephone so I could call the police."

"Did you notice anything in the living room that impressed you as being unusual?"

"No, sir."

"Lights were on in the living room?"

"Yes, sir."

"Lights were on in the kitchen?"

"Yes, sir."

"What kind of lights in the living room?"

"Floor lamps."

"How many of them?"

"I couldn't say for certain. Two, or perhaps three."

"What kind of lights in the kitchen?"

"A big, brilliant, incandescent in the ceiling. It was surrounded by a white reflector."

"A big bulb?"

"Yes, sir. A very big bulb."

"It flooded the kitchen with light?"

"Yes, sir."

"Then you couldn't have seen the *glow* from a burning cigarette, could you? You could only see the smoke eddying upward."

"I . . . I . . . I . . . er . . . I thought I remembered —"

"Did you or didn't you see a glow?"

"I . . . well, now, I stop to think about that big, bright light being on, I guess I . . . well, I *think* I saw the glow."

"Because you saw the smoke eddying up you

thought there must have been a glow and therefore thought you must have seen it. Is that right?"

The witness looked helplessly at Hamilton Burger. "I think I saw a glow."

"Notwithstanding the bright light being on?"

"I know I saw smoke spiraling upward and there must have been a glow."

"Did you or did you not see the red glowing end?"

"I saw it."

"Are you willing to swear that with that bright light on in the ceiling you could see the glowing end of a cigarette?"

"My eyes were accustomed to the darkness. I'd come in from outside."

"Then the ceiling light would have so dazzled you that you couldn't have seen a thing."

"I distinctly saw the smoke eddying upward from the end of the cigarette."

"Did you see the glowing end?"

"Yes."

"What color was it?"

"A dull red."

"You could see it in that light?"

"I saw it."

"You'll swear to that?"

"I am swearing to it."

"When you first saw that cigarette and saw that it was still burning did you appreciate its importance?"

"Well . . . no, not right then."

"When did you first appreciate its importance?"

"After the police arrived."

"And the police told you to remember that you had seen that cigarette while it was still burning?"

"Yes, sir."

"The police told you to remember you had seen the smoke coming up?"

"Well, I told them about the smoke."

"I understand," Mason said, "but they told you to *remember* about having seen the smoke."

"Yes, sir."

"Now did you tell them about the glow?"

"I . . . I think I did. I'm not certain."

"But they told you to remember about the glow?"

"Well, not in so many words."

"Well, what did they say?"

The witness blurted, "They said I was to remember about that cigarette being burning when I entered the room and that under no circumstances was I to let any smart lawyer confuse me on cross-examination."

"So, on account of that admonition," Mason said, "you are determined not to become confused and to stay with the statement you made to the police?"

"Well, I . . . yes, sir."

Arlene Duvall leaned toward Perry Mason. "It was my cigarette," she said in a whisper. "I had trouble lighting it, my hand was shaking so, and —"

Perry Mason pushed her back. "Skip it," he said.

He faced the witness. "That's all," he said.

Hamilton Burger hesitated as to whether to ask another question on redirect, then made a little shrugging gesture with his shoulders and said, "That's all. We'll call Sidney Dayton to the stand."

Sidney Dayton, a tall, loose-jointed individual, in his late thirties, walked to the stand with a certain air of belligerency about him and held up his hand to be sworn.

It speedily developed from the preliminary questions that Dayton was an employee of the police department, that he was employed in a capacity described as a "police expert technician."

"What does that include?" Hamilton Burger asked.

"Technical matters, ballistics, toxicology, fingerprints and matters of that kind."

"How long have you studied fingerprints?"

"I had a training of something over two years."

"Now then, were you called on to go to the house of Jordan L. Ballard on the evening of Wednesday, the tenth of this month?"

"Yes, sir."

"What did you do with reference to searching for fingerprints?"

"I found three glasses. I dusted them for fingerprints."

"Did you identify those glasses in any way?"

"Yes, sir. A photograph was taken of the glasses in place on the side of the sink. I then marked those glasses for identification numbers one, two, and three."

"Calling your attention to glass number two, did you find fingerprints on that glass?"

"I did. Yes, sir."

"Do you know whose fingerprints those were?"

"Yes, sir"

"Whose?"

"The fingerprints of Mr. Perry Mason."

"You are referring now to Mr. Perry Mason, the attorney at law who is sitting here in court?"

"Yes, sir."

"How did you determine whose fingerprints they were?"

"By developing the latent prints, photographing them and comparing them with a set of fingerprints of Perry Mason, a set that we had had in our files from another case."

"Did you examine a cigarette that was on an ash tray, the end of a cigarette that had been burning on the grooved handle of a portable ash tray?"

"I did. Yes, sir."

"What did you find on that cigarette?"

"There was lipstick on it."

"What did you find out about that lipstick?"

"By a spectroscopic analysis and by matching for tint and chemical composition, I came to the conclusion that the lipstick on that cigarette was the same as the lipstick found in the purse of the defendant in this case."

"You mean Arlene Duvall, the person sitting there beside Perry Mason?"

"Yes, sir."

"Cross-examine," Hamilton Burger snapped at Perry Mason.

Mason said, "Mr. Dayton, when you described your occupation you gave it as that of a police expert technician. Is that correct?"

"Yes, sir."

"That is your occupation?"

"Yes, sir."

"What is an expert technician?"

"Well, I have studied extensively in certain fields of science that are frequently called upon in the science of criminology."

"That is what you meant by an expert technician?"

"Yes, sir."

"Now what is a *police* expert technician?"

"Well, that means that . . . well, it all means the same thing."

"What means the same thing?"

"An expert technician."

"An expert technician is the same as a police expert technician?"

"Well, I am in the employ of the police department."

"Oh, the police employ you as an expert witness, do they?"

"Yes, sir . . . I mean no, sir. I am an expert investigator, not an expert witness."

"You are testifying now as an expert witness are you not?"

"Yes, sir."

"Then what did you mean by saying you were an expert technician but not an expert witness?"

"I am employed as a technician but not as a witness."

"You draw a monthly salary?"

"Yes."

"And are being paid for your time while you are on the stand as an expert witness?"

"Well, I'm paid for being a technician."

"Then you won't accept any pay for being a witness?"

"I can't divide my salary."

"So you are being paid?"

"Of course — as part of my employment."

"And you are *now* employed by the police?"

"Yes."

"And are an expert witness?"

"Yes."

"Then you are now being employed as an expert witness?"

"I guess so. Have it your own way."

"When you described yourself as a police expert technician that means your testimony is always called by the police. Isn't that so?"

"No, sir."

"Who else calls you?"

"Well, I . . . I could be called by either party."

"How many times have you been on the witness stand?"

"Oh, I don't know. I couldn't begin to tell you."

"Dozens of times?"

"Hundreds of times?"

"Probably."

"Have you ever been called by the defense as a defense witness?"

"I have not been directly subpoenaed by the defense. No, sir."

"So that you have always testified for the police, for the prosecution?"

"Yes, sir. That's my business."

"That was what I was trying to bring out," Mason said. "Now you found my fingerprints on glass number two?"

"That's right."

"Did you find fingerprints on glass number three?"

"Yes, sir."

"Whose prints were those?"

"The prints of Mr. Ballard."

"Now did you make any attempt to analyze the contents of the various glasses?"

"The glasses were empty."

"Entirely empty?"

"Well, yes and no."

"What do you mean by yes and no?"

"Well, there had been some ice left in glass number three, and there was a very faint odor of whisky."

"Did you determine whether it was Scotch or bourbon?"

"It was Scotch."

"How did you tell?"

"By the odor."

"Now in glass number two what did you find?"

"Nothing. The glass was empty."

"Now let's come to glass number one. What did you find in that?"

"I found some ice."

"And what else?"

"A small amount of liquid."

"What kind of liquid?"

"I don't know."

"You didn't analyze it?"

"No, sir."

"Could it have been bourbon and Seven-Up?"

"It could have been."

"Did you find any fingerprints on that glass?"

"Yes, sir."

"Whose fingerprints?"

"I found some of Mr. Ballard's and some of another person. Those fingerprints have not as yet been identified. Of course, Mr. Mason, I don't know *when* those prints were put on the glass."

"Certainly not. You are intimating, I take it, that they may have been put on the glass some time before the visit to Mr. Ballard's house which you infer that I made?"

"Exactly."

"And by the same sign," Mason said, "you

don't know when the fingerprints on the glass number two were made. In other words, *my* fingerprints may have been made a long time prior to the prints on the other two glasses."

"I . . . I infer —"

"I think that's the trouble with your testimony. You're inferring," Mason said. "I'm asking you now what you know. You don't know when those prints were made, do you?"

"No, sir."

"None of them?"

"No, sir."

"Now then, you found ice cubes in a bowl?"

"Yes, sir."

"Did you find any ice cubes in the sink?"

"I don't remember any ice cubes in the sink."

"What about the photograph of those glasses? You referred to a photograph. Do you have that photograph?"

Hamilton Burger said, "I expect to introduce a series of photographs later on."

"This witness has testified concerning a photograph," Mason said. "I want to look at it."

"I have a copy, with the glasses numbered on the copy," the witness said.

"All right, let's look at the copy."

The witness nodded to Hamilton Burger, who opened a brief case, took out a photograph and carried it to the witness stand.

"Is that the photograph?" Mason asked.

"That's it. Yes, sir."

Mason got up and walked over to the witness, stood looking at the photograph.

"This photograph is taken from a height," he said, "looking down on the sink."

"Yes, sir."

"Why did you use this photograph?"

"Because that shows everything on the sink. The other photographs show the glasses but something might have been concealed behind the glasses. In this way you can see everything."

"Did you look for fingerprints on the Seven-Up bottle?"

"Yes, sir."

"Find any?"

"Mr. Ballard's."

"Anyone else's?"

"No, sir."

"What about the whisky bottles?"

"The same."

"Now then," Mason said, "I call your attention to this photograph. You will notice in the sink two little spots of light. Aren't those the reflections of light from two small pieces of ice, perhaps as big as the end of your thumb?"

"I . . . that *could* be the case. Yes, sir."

"Were you there when this photograph was taken?"

"Yes, sir."

"And you directed that the photograph be taken from this position so that it could show the glasses with the numbers that you had placed beside the glasses?"

"Yes, sir."

"These little squares of numbered pasteboard bearing the numbers one, two and three, which you have placed by these glasses, were placed there by you just before the photograph was taken?"

"Yes, sir."

"And yet you didn't notice ice in the sink?"

"No, sir."

"You noticed that there was ice in glass number one, and in glass number three?"

"Yes, sir."

"But no ice in glass number two, the glass on which you found my fingerprints?"

"That is correct."

"Then," Mason said, "isn't it a fair inference that I had been at Ballard's house and had a drink with him, that he had then taken my glass to the kitchen, had tossed out the remnants of the ice cubes that were in my glass in the sink, that another person had called on him who had asked for bourbon and Seven-Up that he had mixed that bourbon and Seven-Up and that this person was in the kitchen with him when he was killed? Doesn't the fact that there were ice cubes in glass number one and in glass number three indicate that Ballard had had a drink with this individual subsequent to the time I had left the place?"

"Oh, Your Honor, I object," Hamilton Burger said. "That's getting into the realm of conjecture. That's arguing with the witness about the *effect* of evidence."

"I think the objection is probably well taken," Judge Cody ruled.

Mason smiled. "I'm not asking the question to establish a fact, Your Honor."

"Then for what purpose, may I ask?" Judge Cody snapped.

"To show bias on the part of the witness," Mason said. "The inference is perfectly obvious. The facts are there. Here is an expert witness who was very careful to get the facts that the police wanted as far as their case against me is concerned, but he overlooked the perfectly obvious fact of the two small pieces of ice in the sink which apparently could only have been placed there when Ballard emptied my glass into the sink after my departure. The extreme reluctance on the part of this witness to admit that fact indicates his bias."

"Well," Judge Cody said, smiling, "you've made your point now. However, I'm going to sustain the objection."

Mason turned to the witness. "Now you say that it was Miss Duvall's cigarette because of a spectroscopic analysis of the lipstick?"

"Yes, sir."

"How many different lipsticks by the same manufacturer have you examined to see whether there was a variation in the spectroscopic analysis?"

"By the same manufacturer?"

"That's right."

"Why . . . I didn't make *that* test. I tested the

lipstick on the cigarette and the lipstick that was found in her purse."

"Isn't it reasonable to suppose that the same manufacturer would follow the same general physical chemical composition with every lipstick that was made by that manufacturer?"

"Well, of course, the color differs."

"But the chemical base of the lipstick would ordinarily be the same?"

"I'm not prepared to answer that question."

"Exactly," Mason said. "You have assumed that the lipstick on the cigarette was that of Arlene Duvall, therefore you haven't tested any other lipstick, either those of the same manufacturer or of other manufacturers, for the purpose of determining how much similarity there is in the spectroscopic analysis."

"No, sir."

"A spectroscopic analysis is not a quantitative analysis. It simply gives you certain elements that are in the substance tested."

"Yes, sir."

"You found my fingerprints on glass number two?"

"Yes, sir."

"Didn't you also find Ballard's fingerprints on that glass?"

"Yes, sir. Some of them."

"And didn't you find that in virtually every instance Ballard's fingerprints were superimposed upon mine on that glass, showing that he had handled it last?"

"There were some instances where his fingerprints were superimposed, yes. But that doesn't mean anything."

"Why doesn't it mean anything?"

"Because Ballard would have handed you the glass."

"In which event my fingerprints would have been superimposed on Ballard's. Isn't that right?"

"Well . . . I suppose so."

"Yet you found Ballard's fingerprints were superimposed on mine?"

"Yes, sir, some of them."

"And that could only have been caused by Ballard having taken the glass from me, or picking it up after I had left it, taking it to the kitchen and dumping the ice cubes in it in the sink?"

"I can't permit myself to speculate on matters of that sort," Dayton said virtuously. "I only testify to facts as I found them."

"Now did you find any of Ballard's fingerprints on glass number one?"

"Yes, sir."

"And you found the fingerprints of some unidentified person on that glass?"

"Yes, sir."

"And did you find any instance, referring now specifically to glass number one, where Ballard's fingerprints were superimposed upon those of the unidentified person whose prints appeared on that glass?"

"I . . . I can't remember. I was interested in fingerprints, not in the sequence."

"I think that's all," Mason said.

"Just a question or two on redirect," Hamilton Burger said suavely. "Your investigations show that Perry Mason was there at that house within a relatively short period of time prior to the murder. Is that correct?"

"Yes, sir."

"And that Arlene Duvall smoked a cigarette in that house almost immediately prior to the murder. Is that correct?"

"Just a moment," Mason said. "That's objected to as calling for a conclusion of the witness as to facts which are not in evidence and which can't be in evidence. He doesn't know that Arlene Duvall smoked that cigarette. He doesn't know that she placed the cigarette there. He doesn't know what time it was placed there."

"Oh, all right, all right," Hamilton Burger said. "I'm not going to quibble over these points. I'll let the entire matter drop. I think the Court understands the situation."

"And *I* think the Court understands the situation," Mason said. "You aren't going to quibble about them because if you quibble you'll find your erroneous conclusions are crucified on a cross of facts."

"That will do," Judge Cody said. "I want no personalities. Are there any further questions, Mr. Burger?"

"None," Hamilton Burger said. "I'm quite content to let the testimony of this witness speak for itself."

"Any further recross-examination?" Judge Cody asked.

Mason smiled. "None, Your Honor. I am quite willing to let the attempt of the witness to speak for the facts speak for his bias."

Judge Cody smiled briefly. "Very well. Call your next witness," he said to Hamilton Burger.

"Call Horace Mundy," Hamilton Burger said.

Mundy, with obvious reluctance, took the witness stand, gave his name, address, age and occupation.

"You are employed by the Drake Detective Agency?"

"Yes, sir."

"And were on Wednesday, the tenth of this month?"

"Yes, sir."

"And Mr. Perry Mason had, in turn, employed the Drake Detective Agency to shadow Arlene Duvall, the defendant in this case?"

"I don't know."

"You know, however, that you were instructed by the Drake Detective Agency to shadow Arlene Duvall?"

"I don't know what you mean by shadow," Mundy said.

Hamilton Burger's face flushed. "You're a detective. How long have you been a detective?"

"For twenty years."

"And you don't know what the word shadow means?"

"I beg your pardon, sir," Mundy said. "That wasn't what I said. I said that I didn't know what *you* meant by the word shadow."

"Well, I mean it in its ordinary usage," Hamilton Burger shouted.

"Then I don't think I was employed to shadow Arlene Duvall in that way. I believe I was employed to keep her in sight for the purpose of protecting her."

"All right, all right, have it your own way," Hamilton Burger said. "The point is that you were keeping her under surveillance."

"I was keeping her in sight. That is, I was trying to keep an eye on her house trailer and her car. The trailer had been stolen earlier in the day and —"

"All right, all right," Hamilton Burger interrupted impatiently. "I understand you're a hostile witness. You're here because you've been subpoenaed. Now I am going to ask you if it isn't a fact that you saw Arlene Duvall at the residence of Jordan L. Ballard on the evening of Wednesday, the tenth?"

"Yes, sir."

"And what did you see her do?"

"I saw her drive up in a taxicab. I saw her leave the taxicab and go to the front door. She stopped for a few moments, then went back to the taxicab and paid off the cab. Then she walked around the house."

"And while she was walking around the house did you see Perry Mason signal her?"

"No, sir."

"Now just a moment," Hamilton Burger said, shaking a finger at the witness. "I have a tape-recorded statement from you. I understand you're an unwilling witness, but I'm going to —"

"Just a moment," Mason interrupted. "I object to counsel browbeating his own witness. I object to counsel cross-examining his own witness. And I object to counsel threatening any witness in order to secure favorable testimony."

"Your Honor," Hamilton Burger said, "the district attorney's office is laboring under great handicaps here. We have to prove a certain element of our case by calling on the opposition. This witness is hostile."

"He has given no evidence of hostility as yet," Judge Cody said. "He has attempted to be accurate. I believe he has answered the question that he didn't see Perry Mason signaling the defendant. Go on with your next question."

"Didn't you specifically state in my office that as the defendant walked by the window you saw Perry Mason raising and lowering the window shade?"

"Not in so many words I didn't make that statement. I did state that at or about the time Arlene Duvall was walking around the corner toward the back of the house I saw a man of about the build and size of Perry Mason step through the drapes and lower and then raise the window shade."

"And that was when Arlene Duvall was walking past the house?"

"Now as to that point I'm not entirely certain. It was at *about* that time."

"And didn't you tell me that you had now come to the conclusion the man was Perry Mason?"

"I said it looked very much like Perry Mason, but I think I always told you, Mr. Burger, that I couldn't see his face."

"And after Arlene Duvall went to the back of the house, what did you see her do?"

"After the person, whoever it was, left the house, I saw Arlene Duvall drag a box up to the back kitchen window. I saw her climb on the box. Then I saw her raise the window and climb in through the window."

"Then what?"

"Then after a few minutes she left the house."

"How long?"

"About five minutes."

"And how long was it after Perry Mason left the house before she entered the house?"

"She entered almost as soon as the person, whoever he was, left by the front door."

"How did she leave?"

"She left through the front door."

"What was her manner?"

"She was . . . well, she was walking very rapidly."

"Running?"

"You might almost call it a run, it was such a fast walk that it was virtually a run."

"There can be no question as to the identity of Arlene Duvall?"

"No, sir."

"Cross-examine," Hamilton Burger said, and then added to the Court, "I am assuming, of course, that this witness, within reason, will testify to any words that Mr. Mason puts in his mouth. I am, therefore, suggesting, if the Court please, that while the rule of law permits leading questions on cross-examination, the Court should bear in mind that a peculiar situation exists in this case. I would like to have the witness give his testimony rather than repeat words placed in his mouth by counsel for the defense."

"You can make specific objections when specific questions are asked," the judge said, his tone a rebuke. "Leading questions are permitted on cross-examination."

Mason smiled at the Court. "No questions, Your Honor."

"Call James Wingate Fraser," Hamilton Burger said.

Fraser testified to his encounter with Mundy, to having driven the detective while following the taxicab. He himself had not seen Arlene Duvall climb in the window at the back of the house. He had seen her walking around the house. He had glimpsed a man at the window, whom he couldn't identify, lowering and raising a shade "just at about the same time that Arlene Duvall walked past the house."

Fraser went on to testify, however, that he had "had a good look" at the man who had emerged from the house, entered the car and driven away, and that man was "to the best of my judgment Perry Mason."

"Cross-examine," Hamilton Burger said.

"When did you *first* know that the man you had seen leaving the house was Perry Mason?" Mason asked on cross-examination.

"As soon as I saw you."

"When did you first know that I was that man?"

"When you left the house."

"I called on you later that evening?"

"Yes, sir."

"And asked you if you could describe this man?"

"Yes, sir."

"And you described the man?"

"Yes, sir."

"I asked you if you could recognize him?"

"Yes, sir."

"You told me that you could if you saw him again, or that you thought you could?"

"Yes, sir."

"And at that time you didn't say that I was that man?"

"No, sir."

"Why?"

"Because I . . . the idea hadn't occurred to me at that time."

"When did the idea occur to you?"

"Right after you left."

"And how did that happen?"

"One of the guests at the party said, 'The way you described the man it might have been Perry Mason himself.' "

"And what did you say?"

"At that time I laughed."

"You didn't think that I was the person?"

"Well, I did, but it hadn't registered with me."

"When did it register with you?"

"Right after that when we got to talking, and later on, when I was talking with the police."

"After you talked with the police and they told you that I was the man and that my fingerprints had been found on one of the glasses in the house, then you suddenly realized that I must have been the man? Is that it?"

"Well, that's not a very nice way to put it."

"How would *you* put it?"

"Well, after I got to thinking the matter over I came to the conclusion that you were the man."

"You were 'thinking it over' in the presence of the police?"

"Well, yes, if you want to put it that way."

"Now you thought it over when I asked you that evening in the presence of a group of witnesses at your house if you could identify the man, didn't you?"

"Well, I suppose so, but my mind was pretty much preoccupied with other things."

"You thought it over when one of the persons at the party suggested that I might have been the man, didn't you?"

"Well, there again I was thinking about other things."

"You didn't know what you were saying?"

"Oh, I knew what I was saying, but I hadn't really given the matter mature consideration."

"You gave it mature consideration after the police told you I had been at the house?"

"Well, there again I think you're expressing the thing rather unfairly."

"Suppose you express it fairly then."

"I wasn't really positive until after I talked with the police."

"It had been suggested to you?"

"Well, yes."

"But you weren't really certain until after you talked with the police?"

"Yes . . . but I'd thought before that you looked like the man. I mean he looked like you. I told you that."

"That's all," Mason said.

Hamilton Burger, with the air of a magician bringing a startling trick to an astounding conclusion, said, "Now, Your Honor, I have under subpoena Dr. Holman B. Candler of Santa Ana. I will ask the bailiff to bring Dr. Candler from the witness room."

Mason turned to Arlene Duvall.

"What is he going to testify to?" he asked.

She shook her head. "They must have served a subpoena on him at the last minute," she said. "He surely would have let us know if —"

"Are you sure he would?"

"Of course."

"You have great confidence in him?"

"I'd stake my life on him."

"That may be exactly what you're doing," Mason said.

A deputy entered the courtroom, his hand placed lightly on Dr. Candler's elbow.

"Dr. Candler," he announced.

"Come forward and be sworn, Doctor," Burger said.

Dr. Candler flashed Arlene a reassuring glance, then advanced to the witness stand, held up his right hand, was sworn and answered the preliminary questions.

Dr. Candler turned to face the district attorney. "I think it is only fair to tell you," he said, "that I know absolutely nothing about this case."

"*You* may *think* you know nothing, Doctor," Hamilton Burger said with an air of triumphant good nature, "but *I* think you do. You knew Colton P. Duvall while he was employed at the Mercantile Security?"

"I did."

"You were his personal physician?"

"Yes, sir."

"Also the bank's physician?"

"Yes, sir."

"You knew Arlene Duvall?"

"I have known Arlene Duvall since she was a little girl."

"For how long?"

"Oh, for the last twelve years anyway."

"How old was she when you first knew her?"

"Somewhere around twelve or thirteen."

"Now then, you have remained friendly with Arlene Duvall during the time her father has been incarcerated?"

"I have."

"And been in constant communication with her father?"

"Yes, sir."

"You had or were instrumental in having a petition circulated asking that Colton P. Duvall be released on parole?"

"Yes, sir."

"Did you circulate that yourself?"

"I secured some signatures myself and my office nurse, Mrs. Travis, secured some signatures."

"Who was that?"

"Mrs. Travis. Rose Rucker Travis, if you wish the full name."

"She secured some of the signatures?"

"Yes, sir."

"But she did so while she was in your employ, while you were paying her and while she was acting under your instructions?"

"Yes, sir."

"And you have communicated from time to time with Arlene Duvall during the past eighteen months?"

"Many times."

"In person, by correspondence and on the telephone?"

"Certainly I have," Dr. Candler said. "I am a busy man. If you called me here simply to —"

"Now just a moment, Doctor. Keep your temper. I ask you if you're familiar with the handwriting of Arlene Duvall?"

"I am."

"And I am going to ask you, Doctor, to remember that you are under oath. I am now showing you what purports to be a diary in the handwriting of Arlene Duvall. I am going to ask you to look at that diary carefully and tell us if that is in the handwriting of Arlene Duvall."

And Hamilton Burger triumphantly advanced toward the witness holding a book in front of him.

Behind him Mason heard Arlene Duvall's gasp of dismay. "Oh, no . . . no, oh no!" she said in a choked whisper. "They mustn't, they can't. You *must* stop them!"

From the witness stand Dr. Candler said in his close-clipped, methodically professional voice, "Yes, that is in the handwriting of Arlene Duvall."

"All of it?" Hamilton Burger asked.

"Well, I haven't examined each page."

"Examine each page, please," Burger said.

"Don't stop to read it, just look at the handwriting to see if it is her handwriting."

Dr. Candler turned page after page of the diary. From time to time he nodded his head. When he had finished he said, "Yes, that is all in her handwriting, or so it would seem."

Mason's client leaned forward to whisper to him. "I planted a dummy diary to throw searchers off the track, but the police have evidently found the real diary hidden in the wheel housing. You mustn't let Dr. Candler read this. There are some things in there that will turn him into an enemy."

"Now then," Hamilton Burger said, "I am going to direct your attention specifically to entries marked the seventh, eighth and ninth of this month, and ask you to look at those entries carefully, Doctor. I would like to have you read those entries so that you can notice the handwriting of each and every word. I want to know whether every word in that is in the handwriting of the defendant, Arlene Duvall."

"Stop him," Arlene said in a hoarse whisper to Mason.

"That question is objected to as already asked and answered," Mason said. "The doctor has already testified that all of the diary seems to be in the handwriting of the defendant."

Dr. Candler, on the stand, seemed entirely oblivious. He was reading the diary.

"And," Mason said, getting to his feet and approaching the witness stand, "since the document has now been shown to the witness I am entitled to look at it myself."

Mason stood by the doctor's side. Dr. Candler, however, didn't even look up. He was busily engaged in reading.

"If you please let me have it, Doctor," Mason said.

"Just a moment, just a moment," Dr. Candler said. "Don't interrupt me."

Mason glanced up at the Court. "I would like to see the document, Your Honor."

Hamilton Burger said, "I feel that it is quite proper for the doctor to read each and every word on these particular pages."

"He has already testified that they were in the handwriting of the defendant," Mason said. "I object to this question and submit that this argument is merely for the purpose of gaining time and trying to keep me from seeing what is in this document. I have the right to take the document and show it to the defendant. I want to see what *she* has to say about it."

"So do I," Hamilton Burger said sneeringly.

Dr. Candler continued to read.

"You may give Mr. Mason the document, Doctor," Judge Cody ruled.

Dr. Candler paid no attention.

The judge rapped his gavel smartly.

"Dr. Candler."

Dr. Candler looked up. "Yes, Your Honor?"

"You may give the purported diary to Mr. Mason."

Dr Candler hesitated, then with visible reluctance, surrendered the diary to Mason.

Mason walked back to the counsel chair and conferred with Arlene Duvall.

"Is this in your handwriting?"

"Oh, my Lord, yes," she said, "and I'm crucified."

"What's wrong with it?"

"Read what Dr. Candler was reading," she said.

Mason read under date of the seventh:

> Have just come from a long talk with Jordan Ballard. He is convinced that he knows what happened and how that theft occurred. He insists that it must have been through the connivance of Dr. Candler. I am terribly shocked and hurt but Mr. Ballard has amassed an imposing array of evidence. Dr. Candler was the official physician for the Mercantile Security. All employees were examined by him periodically. He was the personal physician of Edward B. Marlow, the bank president. It was Dr. Candler's nurse, Rose Travis, who gave Ballard the tip on the horse race and dressed it up with enough factual background so that Ballard bet on the race. Moreover, Dr. Candler, accompanied by his nurse, had been in the bank just about half an hour before the shipment of cash went out. He would have had ample opportunity in passing out of the bank entrance to have

opened one of the filing drawers for canceled checks and scooped out a whole drawer full of canceled checks which he could have put in his empty instrument bag. He was the only one aside from the bank officers permitted to use that door. He was the only one who could have carried the bag in and out of the bank without arousing some suspicion. He . . .

Hamilton Burger said, "I submit, Your Honor, that this is my exhibit. I don't think that counsel and his client are to be permitted at the present time to study my evidence before it is introduced. All they should be allowed to do is to inspect the document and see whether it is in the handwriting of the defendant. They certainly can answer that question very readily."

Mason said, "I don't agree with counsel. I feel that we have a right to read this document before it is introduced in evidence. We may want to object to it. We may not want to object to it. We may stipulate as to the authenticity of the document. We may also find that there have been some passages interpolated which were not in the handwriting of the defendant but were clever forgeries."

"I think that is true," Judge Cody said. "I think that the better practice is for counsel to be permitted to read the entire document before it is offered in evidence."

Hamilton Burger said desperately, "I am not offering it in evidence at the present time. I only want it marked for identification. I merely asked the doctor if that was in the handwriting of the defendant and he said it was. Now then, Your Honor, I would like to have it marked for identification. I think under the circumstances counsel is entitled at this time to a brief inspection. Later on, and before I offer it in evidence, he has the right to read it in order to see if he wishes to admit it without objection or whether he wishes to object to it, and if so on what grounds."

"Very well," Judge Cody ruled. "If you merely wish it marked for identification at this time, counsel can be given an opportunity later to inspect the document."

Hamilton Burger bore down triumphantly on Perry Mason.

As reluctantly as had Dr. Candler, Mason surrendered the diary.

Hamilton Burger said, "That's all for the moment, Doctor. I want to recall you later, but in the meantime I wish to lay a further foundation for the introduction of this diary."

"Just a moment," Mason said, as Dr. Candler started to leave the stand. "I wish to cross-examine."

"But he hasn't testified to anything on which you can cross-examine him as yet," Hamilton Burger said. "He will give that testimony when I seek to introduce this diary and when I recall him on the stand."

"He's testified that the document was in the defendant's handwriting."

"Well, there can't be any question about that," Hamilton Burger said. "Of course it's in her handwriting."

"Don't be too sure," Mason said.

He got to his feet, walked toward the witness stand where a puzzled, white-faced Dr. Candler sat rigidly erect in the witness chair.

"Now, Doctor," he said, "you are familiar with the handwriting of the defendant?"

"I am."

"I show you a photographic copy of a document, Doctor, and ask you if *that* is in the handwriting of the defendant."

Mason whipped from under his arm an enlarged eleven by fourteen photograph of the sheet of figures which had been in the possession of Thomas Sackett.

Dr. Candler looked at the figures and shook his head. His face, which Mason was studying carefully, was absolutely blank.

"Just a moment," Hamilton Burger said. "Now *I* am entitled to see that document, if the Court please."

"Certainly," Mason said, extending him the photograph. "Take a look at it."

Hamilton Burger looked at the photograph. Suddenly his eyes widened in surprise. He turned, hurried toward his seat at the plaintiff's table, whipped out a notebook from the file of papers on the table, opened it and started comparing numbers with the numbers on the photograph. Mason quietly followed him over to the plaintiff's counsel table. As Hamilton Burger turned toward his notebook to verify a figure Mason quietly slipped the photograph off the table and was halfway back to his own table before Burger knew it was missing.

"Here," Burger shouted, "bring that back here! I want to see it."

Mason merely smiled.

"Your Honor, Your Honor," Hamilton Burger shouted. "This is an important development. This document has no right to be in the possession of counsel. This . . . I want to see that document."

"You had a chance to look at it to see if it was in the defendant's handwriting," Mason said.

"But I demand an opportunity to examine it. I insist that —"

Mason said to the perplexed judge on the bench, "I ask, Your Honor, merely to have this marked for identification. Therefore, under the rule promulgated by counsel himself, he has no right to read it himself at this time. He has glanced at it and that is sufficient."

"Your Honor," on Burger pleaded, "that is a document so very confidential that . . . the existence of that document has been one of the most closely guarded secrets in the entire case. That is . . . I demand that that document be produced."

"It was produced," the judge ruled.

"I mean I demand it to be put in as evidence in the case."

"Is that a part of the prosecution's case?" the judge asked, obviously interested.

"It's probably going to be used as a razzle-dazzle, a red herring, something with which to confuse the issues. It —"

"That will do," Judge Cody ruled. "Do you wish to introduce that document in evidence?"

"I . . . I will if I have to. Your Honor, that document apparently contains a list of the numbers of bills which were in that five-thousand-dollar package of extortion money."

Mason smiled at the angry district attorney. "Later on, when I offer it in evidence you will have an opportunity to examine it, Mr. Burger. Now, under the rule of law you yourself promulgated, you were entitled to look at it. You looked."

"But, Your Honor," Burger protested. "Those figures are so confidential that even I haven't been able to secure a copy of the list. And here is counsel for the defense with a copy. It isn't fair."

Mason merely smiled, turned back to the witness.

"Now then, Doctor, I am going to ask you a technical question. You have stated you are a physician and surgeon."

"Yes, sir."

"There is an X-ray machine in your office?"

"Yes, sir."

"Doctor, I am going to ask you to go to the blackboard and make a diagram of your office. I want to know the room in which your X-ray machine is located."

"What does that have to do with any of the questions in this case, Your Honor?" Hamilton Burger protested. "A diagram of his office. That is meaningless."

"You qualified him as a physician and surgeon. You had him testify that's what he was. You also had him testify that he was practicing in Santa Ana. I have a right to test his recollection as to such matters."

Judge Cody glanced at Mason with a puzzled frown. "May I have your assurance that this matter is pertinent and important, Counselor?" he asked.

"You have that assurance, Your Honor. I think it may well be one of the most important factors in the case."

"Very well."

Dr. Candler went to the blackboard and made a rough diagram of his offices.

"Now then," Mason said, "I am going to ask you, Doctor, if two people should be seated here, in chairs against the partition wall of this office, which, as I now understand it, is next to your X-ray room, would it be possible for an X-ray to be turned against the dividing partition in this X-ray room and the current turned on in such a way that it would fog all of the film of any sort that might be in any camera placed upon the little table in the corner of this room, a table directly against the wall in this position as shown in this diagram?"

Dr. Candler's face was completely puzzled. "Well, I don't know . . . wait a minute. Yes, I guess it could. Yes, that X-ray machine would, of course, penetrate the wall. Now I am assuming the camera did not have a lead shield of any sort, that it was only plastic or some form of the light aluminum that is usually used in cameras."

"That is correct."

"Yes," Dr. Candler said, "that would fog the film."

"All of it?"

"Certainly. There is nothing to stop it. The X-ray machine doesn't go through metal as easily as it penetrates flesh or bone, but it certainly would go through any metal that was not shielded by lead."

"So if someone in your office thought I had valuable evidence photographed on a film in a camera and wanted to destroy that photograph, it could be done by using that X-ray machine in that manner?"

"Yes. If anyone wanted to, which is very unlikely."

"Thank you, Dr. Candler," Mason said. "There's just one more question. You stated that the full name of your office nurse was Rose Rucker Travis?"

"That's right."

"Her maiden name was Rucker?"

"Yes, sir."

"She was married to a man by the name of Travis?"

"Yes, sir. I believe so. That was before she went to work for me."

"She has a sister, possibly by the name of Helen Rucker?"

"I believe she has."

"Do you know Howard Prim?"

"No, sir."

"Does the name mean anything to you?"

"No, sir."

"How about Thomas Sackett? Does that name mean anything?"

"Thomas Sackett, I . . . I believe I have treated a patient by that name. Yes, I have treated a patient by that name."

"And do you know a William Emory?"

"Yes, sir, I do."

"Mr. Emory was, I believe, the driver of the armored truck from which the cash shipment disappeared in that historic theft of the Mercantile Security."

"Yes, sir."

"He was a patient of yours?"

"Yes, sir."

"He still is?"

"Yes, sir."

"Thank you, Doctor," Mason said. "That is all."

"Any redirect examination?" Judge Cody asked.

"No, Your Honor."

"Call your next witness."

Hamilton Burger said grimly, "I will call Perry Mason as my next witness."

Perry Mason promptly proceeded to walk forward, hold up his right hand and take the oath.

"Now then," Hamilton Burger said, "I demand to know where you got that document."

"What document?"

"The list of the numbers of the bills of the five-thousand-dollars' extortion money. It was absolutely impossible for you to have obtained that list."

"Then if it was absolutely impossible it's quite apparent that I don't have it."

"But you do have it. That's what those numbers were."

"How do you know?" Mason asked. "Did you check them?"

"I checked the numbers that I have — that list is so secret that the local head of the FBI refused to deliver it even to me."

"Then," Mason said suavely, "permit me, Mr. District Attorney, to present you with a photographic copy of the numbers you were unable to obtain from the FBI. I have had a copy of the photograph made for your exclusive use."

And with something of a flourish Mason left the witness stand, stepped to the counsel table and handed Hamilton Burger an eleven by fourteen photographic enlargement of the numbered list.

"That isn't answering my question," Burger shouted. "Where did you get it?"

Mason smiled and said, "That question, Mr. Burger, I decline to answer on the ground that it calls for a privileged communication; that it is a part of the case which the defense intends to put on and at this time it is incompetent, irrelevant and immaterial. We are trying the defendant, Arlene Duvall, on a murder case and not for the theft of money presumably taken by her father from an armored truck of the Mercantile Security."

And Mason resumed his position on the stand, crossed his long legs, folded his arms and smiled patronizingly at the angry and harassed district attorney.

"Of course," Hamilton Burger said with exasperation, "it was to have been expected that counsel would resort to every technicality in the books to try and protect himself, but I intend to keep hammering away here until I at least get the pertinent facts before this court."

"Keep your questions as to pertinent facts and I won't raise a single objection," Mason said.

"All right," Hamilton Burger said. "I'll ask you again point blank, did you go out to Jordan L. Ballard's house on the night of Wednesday, the tenth?"

"Yes."

"Did you go to the window in the front of the living room?"

"Yes."

"Did you lower and raise the roller shade?"

"Yes. Certainly."

"What!" Burger shouted. "You admit that now?"

"Certainly I admit it."

"You denied it before the grand jury."

"I did nothing of the sort," Mason said. "You asked me if I had lowered and raised the roller shade as a signal to the defendant. I told you I had not. You asked me if I lowered and raised it as a signal to anyone. I told you I did not."

"But you now admit you lowered and raised the roller curtain?"

"Certainly."

"Why didn't you say so before the grand jury?"

"Because you didn't ask me."

"I've asked you now."

"I've told you now."

"Then what possible explanation do you have for lowering and raising that shade if you weren't signaling someone?"

Mason said, "I found that I had in my possession a thousand-dollar bill and a five-hundred-dollar bill; that the thousand-dollar bill had the number 000151."

Burger's jaw sagged open. His eyes seemed about to pop out like marbles. He looked at Mason with an expression of such utter incredulous surprise that some of the spectators, equally startled by Mason's answer, nevertheless began to laugh surreptitiously.

Judge Cody pounded for order.

"Go on, Mr. District Attorney," he said.

"But you appeared before the grand jury and produced two other bills — another five-hundred-dollar bill and a thousand-dollar bill. Where did you get those?"

"Just where I told the grand jury I received them — in a letter purporting to come from Arlene Duvall."

"And where did you get the other money, that which you have just testified to as having been in your possession?"

"In a letter purporting to come from Arlene Duvall."

"You didn't tell us that."

"I wasn't asked that."

"I asked you to produce all money that you had received from Arlene Duvall."

"Certainly. I told you that I didn't *know* I had received any money from Arlene Duvall, that I had received a letter purporting to be in her handwriting containing a thousand-dollar bill and a five-hundred-dollar bill. I then specifically mentioned that the money I was *then* producing was the money I had received in the letter I had just referred to. You didn't bother to ask me if that was all the money I had received which *purported* to come from Arlene Duvall. If you can't interrogate a witness so as to close up loopholes I see no reason for the witness to voluntarily assist you."

"That will do," Judge Cody warned. "I have warned counsel to refrain from personalities."

"If the Court please," Mason said, "this is not a personality between counsel and counsel — it is a personality between witness and counsel. Counsel chose to interrogate me as a witness and I have answered him as a witness."

"Very well, the matter is finished. Go on with the examination," Judge Cody said, but there was the ghost of a smile at the corners of his mouth.

"Why, I never heard anything like this," Hamilton Burger said.

"Doubtless," Mason commented dryly, and there was a quick burst of laughter in court which was again silenced by Judge Cody.

"And where did you get this other five hundred dollars and thousand dollars? How did it come to you?"

"It was delivered to me by Paul Drake, who in turn *said* it had been delivered to him by a messenger."

"And what did you do with the money?"

"I lowered the window shade at Ballard's house while he was in the kitchen, inserted the two bills in the top of the roller, then raised the shade and left it in that position. I slipped back through the drapes, finished my drink with Jordan Ballard, and left."

"Then you want us to understand that

Jordan Ballard was alive when you left?"

"Exactly."

"Then since Arlene Duvall entered immediately after your departure —"

"I beg your pardon," Mason said, "you're overlooking one essential fact."

"What's that?"

"The person having my size and build who was keeping the house under surveillance, the person who saw me lower and raise the curtain and wondered why I had done so, the person who parked his car in the driveway and entered the house immediately after *my* departure, the person whom Jordan Ballard knew well enough to receive in the kitchen, the person who had a bourbon and Seven-Up after Ballard had emptied the ice from my glass, which had contained the Scotch and soda, into the kitchen sink."

"And how do you know there was any such person, Mr. Mason?" Burger demanded sarcastically.

"For the simple reason that when the police officers went out and made the experiment of lowering and raising the curtain they didn't find any money there — unless, of course, it is your contention that the police officers found the two bills, appropriated them and decided to say nothing about them. Otherwise it stands to reason there must have been some other person in the house."

"What other person?" Burger demanded.

"Well," Mason said, "if you are really searching for information I would suggest that you try matching the fingerprints on glass number one which contained the bourbon and Seven-Up with the fingerprints of Bill Emory, who was the driver of the car at the time of the theft, a man who, I understand, is generally my size and build, and then you might take the photograph which I have given you of the numbers of the five thousand dollars in currency of which the police had a list and see if the figures are in the handwriting of Bill Emory. As you have so aptly remarked, the list was one of the most confidential records in the entire FBI office, so confidential that they wouldn't even trust you with a copy. Only one other person could possibly have had the copy and that was the thief who found the five thousand dollars in small currency tied in one bundle and who, learning that the police had the numbers of five thousand dollars in currency, assumed that this was the package of bills and so copied the numbers from the bills so as to make certain that he wouldn't spend any of that money himself, but could plant some in the wallet of Colton Duvall, and in case the time ever became ripe to frame Arlene Duvall by leaving some of those bills in her possession.

"And in the meantime the fallacious reasoning on the part of Jordan Ballard that Dr. Candler must have been mixed up in the case was due to the fact that Ballard failed to take into consideration the fact that Rose Rucker

Travis, Dr. Candler's office nurse, had an equal opportunity to abstract keys or other data from the pockets of patients while they were in the light cabinet taking a sweat bath. In that way she was able to get copies of the keys to the cash compartment in the truck and, since *she* was in the bank with Dr. Candler within an hour of the time the theft was perpetrated, then she had opportunity to take out the canceled checks and have them with her in a substitute package which had been carefully prepared in advance by an expert forger.

"You'll find incidentally that the boy friend of Helen Rucker, Mrs. Travis' sister, is Thomas Sackett, who is also known as Howard Prim, who has a long record of expert forgeries and fraud.

"And now," Mason went on, addressing the district attorney conversationally, "speaking entirely as a witness, if you haven't got enough there to solve the case I'll try and answer any other question you wish to ask."

Hamilton Burger put his hands on the arms of the swivel counsel chair, raised himself to his feet, started to say something to Mason, shook his head as though to clear it, turned to the judge as though to say something, then abruptly sat down again.

Judge Cody came to the district attorney's rescue.

"The Court," he said, "will take a fifteen-minute recess."

• 14 •

Arlene Duvall, Paul Drake, Perry Mason, Della Street and Dr. Candler were seated around the big table in Mason's law library.

"I'm sorry that that diary was discovered by the police," Perry Mason said. "You can see that Ballard was on the right trail but he had the wrong idea."

"Well, I never suspected Rose," Dr. Candler said. "Of course, now it's quite apparent. I was the official bank physician and many of the bank employees consulted me as their private physician. I had long been a believer in diathermy, physical therapy and sweat baths, keeping the pores of the skin open and . . . well, of course, I relied on Rose Travis as my head nurse to take care of the patients and give them their treatments. Naturally it was absurdly easy for her to go through the clothes of the patients and get duplicates of their keys, to have Thomas Sackett forge the seals that were used by the bank employees — when you stop to think of it it's so perfectly obvious that the only wonder is no one ever thought of it before."

Mason said, "Ballard thought it through but only part way through. He became convinced that if Arlene started spending money in the form of cash that it would only be a question of time until someone would steal her trailer and plant the incriminating cash somewhere in the trailer where it could subsequently be found by the police. The only flaw in his reasoning was that he made the mistake so frequently made by professional as well as amateur detectives of making up his mind in advance as to who was guilty and then trying to fit the facts to suit the guilt of that particular person.

"Evidently he had been cultivating Bill Emory in order to get certain information from Emory, and it wasn't until after I had left and Emory had entered the picture that Ballard began to get the idea."

"How do you suppose he got it?" Paul Drake asked.

"Evidently Emory was watching the house. When he saw me drive home with Ballard he kept the place under surveillance. He saw me go to the window and pull down the curtain and then raise it. He thought perhaps I was concealing those bills since he knew that he had delivered them to me."

"How did he deliver them?" Dr. Candler asked.

"Sackett went to the costumers and got a messenger boy uniform. The attendant finally remembered that the uniform he had picked wouldn't have fitted Sackett at all. It was for a much smaller, slim-waisted individual. It was probably a girl. That means that it was either Rose Travis or her sister dressed as a messenger.

"It may be we'll never know *exactly* what happened there at Ballard's house, but Emory undoubtedly drove up right after I had left, parked his car in the driveway and went in to call on Ballard.

"At about that time Arlene's taxi drove up and the detective followed in Fraser's car. Ballard went to the kitchen to mix a drink.

"Emory, who had been watching the place and who had seen me at the window, didn't make the mistake Burger made of thinking I was signaling someone. He suspected I was hiding something.

"So he went to the window, lowered the shade and took out the two bills I had concealed. You can imagine his chagrin when he found that the two bills they had been at such pains to plant in my possession had been concealed *before* the service of the subpoena duces tecum.

"Of course, they had arranged for that subpoena to be served — probably by an anonymous telephone tip to the police or the district attorney.

"Evidently Ballard must have seen Emory taking the money out of the curtain. When Emory returned to the kitchen Ballard asked him questions. Emory saw that Ballard, who had been suspecting Dr. Candler, was finally getting on the right track, so Emory killed him in order to protect himself."

Arlene Duvall said, "And *I* thought the only

reason they wanted to steal my trailer was to search for my diary. It seems they really wanted to plant that money where the police could find it later."

"Once again," Mason said, "the greatest obstacle to any fair and impartial investigation is jumping to conclusions."

"But how did Bill Emory know . . . oh, I see, Ballard must have told him the number he had remembered on the one bill of the thousand-dollar denomination and —"

"Exactly," Mason interrupted. "So he decided that bill should be in my possession. He saw that I got it and then tipped off the district attorney anonymously that it would be a good plan to serve a subpoena duces tecum on me to turn over any money that Arlene Duvall had given me. And he included Ballard in that so that it wouldn't sound like too much of a put-up job."

"Well," Arlene Duvall said with a sigh, "I acted as bait for a year and a half before they finally walked into the trap that Mr. Ballard had set. It's a shame that he couldn't be here to enjoy it. Now I'm going to have to go back to work."

"Don't be too certain," Mason said. "Remember there's a reward for recovery of the money. Your father will be released from prison and that reward will amount to a substantial sum. You'll also have the car and the trailer. You may take another two or three months with your dad. It might not hurt him to have a little sunshine."

"Poor Dad," she said. "He said there was never any sunlight in his cell," and abruptly she began to cry.

Gertie came into the office with a telegram. "It's addressed to Arlene Duvall, care of Perry Mason," she said.

Mason handed the telegram to Arlene.

She wiped the tears from her eyes, tore it open, read it, then smiled through her tears and passed the message to Mason.

The message was sent from San Quentin prison. It said:

> JUST HEARD NEWS OVER RADIO STOP CARRY ON ARLENE AND WE'LL BEGIN LIFE AGAIN TOGETHER STOP YOUR LOVING DAD.

Mason turned to Della Street. "Call the press, Della," he said, "and let them know that I am going to see to it that Arlene Duvall and her father get the reward money offered by the insurance company. That news will be on the radio broadcast this evening. We may as well give her dad something else to cheer him up."